CINCO PUNTOS PRESS ❖ EL PASO, TEXAS

the Amado women

Helloooo   Altadena !

By Désirée Zamorano

FIRST EDITION
10 9 8 7 6 5 4 3 2 1

Library of Congress Cataloging-in-Publication Data

Zamorano, Désirée.
  The Amado women / Désirée Zamorano. — First edition.
    pages cm
  ISBN 978-1-935955-73-3 (paperback); ISBN 978-1-935955-74-0 (e-book)
  1. Hispanic Americans—Fiction. 2. Hispanic American women—Fiction. 3. Sisters—Fiction. 4. Mothers and daughters—Fiction. 5. Hispanic American families—Fiction. 6. Domestic fiction. I. Title.

  PS3626.A6279A36 2014
  813'.6—dc23

2013040576

Book and cover design by Paco Casas of Blue Panda Design Studio

To my mother

Kathe Zamorano

in honor of her ever-present love, generosity and adoration.

February 2001

S ylvia Levine (née Amado) had been brooding for months. She had begun to worry in November, looking through the checking account history, a task which had once afforded her relief and pleasure. Now she couldn't stop obsessing over what she had discovered. Her mother-in-law had passed away over a year ago, and her husband Jack had inherited everything. They had considered the inheritance a dream fund—safety net, parachute, college savings, retirement, security, all rolled into one. Beginning in November, the inheritance was nowhere to be found. Nowhere.

Sylvia had not wanted to risk poisoning their household further during the holidays. She hadn't been eager to confront Jack either. But she had made it her goal to discuss it in January, and now January had slipped away. They were headed towards the heart of February.

She stood at her granite top kitchen counter contemplating a cold cup of coffee. Jack was in the office, working from home this morning. Miriam was at school. Kindergarten had today off so Becky was asleep upstairs. All Sylvia had to do was to knock on Jack's office door, poke her head in and casually ask.

But it was hard to casually ask something that she had been agonizing over for months.

The office door opened. Jack nodded at her and helped himself to another cup of coffee, then headed back to his office.

"Morning." Sylvia managed to sound cheerful and hearty. "What're you working on?"

Jack turned back to face her. Sylvia was always surprised at how young and innocent he still looked, even after ten years of marriage—his hair curly and light brown on top, no signs of gray on the side. He was dressed for casual Friday in light khaki trousers and a pink polo shirt. It brought out the color in his cheeks and deep blue eyes.

"The assholes in New York."

Sylvia nodded. His tone had been neutral, almost friendly. New York was his target of animosity, not her. When would the right time to ask be, if not now? Would she know a better time when it presented itself?

Now. It had to be now. She had to press ahead. "You know, I've been wondering—"

That familiar amused smirk appeared on his face as he approached her and said, "Always dangerous, Syl."

"—about your mother's money. I find it hard to believe that we've gone through it all and I was—"

That was all she was able to say before Jack stopped her with the back of his hand to the side of her face, then with his open palm to the other side of her face. Sylvia's head rang with the force of the blow. She could feel her mouth moving and no sound coming out, tears of pain and rage springing from her eyes—*it had been the wrong time to bring it up, there never was the right time, she shouldn't have brought it up, how could she have been so stupid*—when she felt the air knocked out of her and she collided with the kitchen floor.

He was talking to her but she couldn't make out the words. She couldn't look at him, his face would be ugly and distorted. She tried to scramble away from him, but the sweatpants that covered her knees were slipping on the cold Spanish pavers of the kitchen floor. She felt a blow to her back and then another. She knew she was going to die. How could she have been so stupid to have let this happen?

Then she heard a shriek, a howling. *Oh, dear God, Becky.*

She scrambled to reach her daughter but Jack kicked her back to the floor and kept her there. She heard a thud and Becky cried out. Sylvia pushed and lunged at him until he was practically standing on her while he hit Becky. Then silence and Jack let Becky run weeping to her on the floor.

Sylvia held Becky as she shook, listening to her stuttering breaths, the choke of tears, the silence filled with her own humiliation. *What kind of mother lets this happen? You fucking loser. You let him hurt your daughter.*

Never again. Never again.

The two of them didn't move. Jack walked up the stairs, entered their bedroom, slid open the mirrored closet door, then came back down the stairs and through the kitchen.

"Pull yourself together, would you?" he said, stepping through the side door into the garage. Becky whimpered.

Sylvia waited, motionless, listening for the noise of the electric garage door, Jack's car to pull out in reverse.

"Come on, baby, let me take you upstairs."

Becky clutched Sylvia, brown arms around her neck, the tiny body trembling against her own. *Who was she that she let this happen?*

As Sylvia crossed the kitchen, she saw a broken wooden spoon on the floor. Thank God. Thank God it was only wood.

What kind of a mother prayed like that? Sylvia asked herself. Never, never again.

Sylvia picked up the phone as she carried Becky to her room. She sat in the rocker. She would call her sister Celeste, far away in San Jose. She would find out what had happened to the money, Celeste knew everything about money.

But first she would call her friend Tamara.

She rocked Becky as the phone rang, and Tamara picked up.

"I need you," Sylvia said. "Please bring a camera."

As she waited for her friend, Sylvia stared out of Becky's window. She could see a shimmering strip of yellow sea, forty miles away, glowing with the impossibility of hope.

O f all people, Mercy Amado (nació Fuerte) should know that happiness is a decision. You simply cast aside that which you are tired of looking at, weary of battling, unable to accept and focus on that which remains. She had to have learned something during the span of her lifetime, with its marital therapy, grief counseling, past life-regression, born-again Christianity, flirtation with Buddhism, Judaism, Catholicism and atheism. When did you figure it all out? When did you understand the world? When did God take you by the hand and explain it all to you, elaborating that you were indeed His child—special, gifted, divine—and apologize for the mess along the way?

Mercy dabbed the concealer over her age spots. She streaked the crease of her eyelid with gray, rimmed the edges with black. She placed her iridescent violet contact lenses on before she stretched her lashes with mascara. She used a plum lip liner and a slightly lighter lipstick. She covered that with a shimmering lip gloss. She ran her fingers through her hair, fluffing the layers for fullness. She wasn't sure she liked its recent coloring, it seemed too dark and strident for the frosted tips she had requested. *Well, at least the gray was gone.* A quick peek in the full-length mirror to ensure that the waist of her purple sheath cinched neatly, that the hem hit exactly where it should, five inches above the knee. *Yes, very nice.* She would slip on the silver heels when Nataly arrived to drive her to her birthday celebration. Sixty years seemed so long ago.

It didn't matter: it was her birthday and an afternoon with her three daughters was ahead. She decided to be happy.

She always told her students—encouraged, implored, cajoled them—to do their best. Had she done her best? Had she given her daughters what they had needed? Mercy set her silver heels at the screen door of her modest apartment. Either she hadn't or she had, and it still wasn't good enough.

"You look fabulous," Nataly said, entering the apartment, the screen door slapping shut behind her. "Are we ready to go?" Nataly did a mock rhumba as she danced her way to her mother and squeezed her tight. "Happy birthday, Mama."

Mercy knew it wasn't right, it wasn't fair—for years she had tamped it down as best as she could—but the sight of her baby always gave her unalloyed pleasure. Thirty-two years old, Nataly was still her puppy, young, playful, endearing and joyful. (*Her favorite!* There, she confessed! But no one else had to know, right?) Mercy noticed the embroidering on the hem and seam of the jeans and knew it to be Nataly's own. The sheer black blouse she wore, with a black bustier underneath, were both gifts from Mercy. "Stay young forever," she always wanted to tell her, to hold her tight. *Don't give it up, don't give it away, don't squander it. Hold on to it.*

Which is what Mercy would have done, if only she'd known how.

Nataly leaned over the end table and said. "Why do you still keep this picture of me out? I hate it. I look so—stupid."

Mercy said, "I like it."

Nataly shook her head and sat down heavily. It had recently struck her as odd and unfair even that she lived in a better apartment than her mother. How had that happened? Well, of course she knew the answer to that. But still. She hated her mother's exuberant lifestyle squeezed into a one-bedroom, one-bath in a still-acceptable corner of Santa Ana. Sixty years old! Would this be her own story? Nataly batted the thought swiftly away.

"Do you want your gift now or at the restaurant?"

Mercy made a face. "Why don't you give it to me now, and I can open it again at the restaurant."

Her mother's own logic. Nataly dangled a gift bag in her mother's direction. "No card?" her mother demanded.

"The appropriate response is 'thank you' and you know I'm terrible at cards. I'm good at other things though." Nataly heard a slightly disapproving snort.

Mercy reached into the gift bag and pulled out a wad of pink tissue paper.

"Careful!" Nataly said.

Mercy unwrapped the tissue paper, revealing a photograph of her and her three daughters. The frame was Nataly's artwork, found objects. Among the fabric, tatting and embroidery, Mercy recognized markers of her daughters' and her own life there—coins for Celeste, braided thread for Nataly, chalk for her, plastic brown babies for Sylvia. Within the frame Mercy, (*God, how beautiful I had been once, how old I've gotten, take me out and shoot me*) smiling proudly into the camera, her infant Nataly in her lap, Sylvia and Celeste clutching her side, smiling wildly as if the new baby were their very own.

Those three little girls were now all gone.

Nataly wouldn't have any understanding of that. By thirty-two, Mercy had been married for twelve years, and her daughters were already growing up. Especially Celeste. Mercy stood abruptly and went to the bathroom, to see what she could salvage of her eye makeup.

On the brief flight from San Jose to John Wayne Airport, Celeste Amado entertained herself with a Bloody Mary. Tomato juice to make her feel virtuous, lime and spices to prick her tongue, vodka to make the flight as smooth as possible. She limited herself to one drink per flight.

On the plastic tray bobbing slightly in front of her, Celeste sifted once more through the statements Sylvia had sent her. Columns and columns of figures: automatic deposits, transfers, withdrawals. The statements were all very clear to Celeste. Part of the reason she was so successful was that she had no emotional attachment to money. What she cared about was how people spread the muck around, as Francis Bacon said. Celeste knew she was right about what she had found. What she didn't know was whether Sylvia would hold that information against her.

Sylvia checked the clock on her dash: she was running late to the airport. She was always running late. She had always thought of herself as a punctual person, punctuality being the courtesy of kings and all that, but found herself always late—to the parent teacher conferences, to school registration, mailing off payments. In general, late to the party. She groaned at the traffic on the 5 Freeway heading south (why had she followed Jack's directions? She knew since childhood the 5 was dense with congestion and fumes. And thick with billboards— corporate graffiti, she liked to call them). Sylvia cheered herself with the thought that Celeste's flight would run late—and realized as she drove past the Matterhorn in Anaheim that she'd been listening to Radio Disney all the way down from Pasadena.

Nataly admired the tilt of her mother's heels and the shimmer in her tights before closing the passenger door of her car.

"The Ritz or bust, Ma," she said. She headed towards Laguna Beach, skirting Santa Ana's Main Place, rejecting Costa Mesa's South Coast Plaza, heedless of the lure of Newport Beach's Fashion Island. Nataly despised Orange County's shrines of ostentation and their label fixation. That shit was all Celeste.

"Have you heard from your father?" her mother said.

Nataly glared in her mother's direction and swerved to miss a small truck changing lanes. "No. Not recently. Should I have?"

Her mother shrugged, in that way she had that implied so much was going on she wouldn't know where to start or stop. Nataly ignored the challenge and lobbed back with, "Is Sylvia bringing the girls?"

"Maybe. I don't know. Maybe not. She's stopping to pick up Celeste. Are you two going to be okay?"

There. Lay it right out on the cutting table, pin it down repeatedly, pick up the sheers and rip through the fabric. Nataly felt it was hotter than it had a right to be, this early February afternoon. Up ahead it was blindingly blue, a shimmer of shore appearing sporadically through the marine layer.

"Are we going to be okay?" Nataly echoed.

"It would mean so much if you two could just, you know, be kind to each other. Is that asking so much?"

The traffic stalled. Nataly's Altima shook. She thought of Celeste— Celeste under the tree, blossoms falling around her. Celeste and Michael at their wedding. Skye. By the time of Celeste's graduation from Humboldt State, Nataly felt Celeste had abandoned them, her most of all. Celeste, all brains and money and contempt.

"I am always kind," Nataly said, shifting gears and exiting the crammed freeway, sure of an alternate route.

Sylvia passed the statue of John Wayne twice before spotting the spiky short hair of her sister Celeste, head tilted downwards, tapping on her PDA, a deceptively simple beige coat over her arm (Sylvia knew it was cashmere), the ever-present black Longchamps bag hanging on a shoulder. Sylvia rolled down the car window and called, "Hey, lady, you want a ride!" Celeste looked up, the hint of a wry smile starting.

"I meant to meet you at the gate, I'm so sorry," she said, as Celeste threw a bag in the trunk.

Celeste, peering in the back seat. "Where's the rest of you?"

"Honestly, it just seemed like an endurance event. Jack's busy, of course, but my friend Tamara said to leave them with her and not to worry."

"New car?"

Another sigh from Sylvia, "Yeah, long story, Jack says it's cheaper in the long run."

Celeste left that unchallenged. Jack certainly had an idiosyncratic approach to money. It was too soon to bring all that up. Celeste just wanted some time with Sylvia. She didn't want to talk about the money, about what she'd found, about what she was worried about.

Sylvia frowned. "I'm so happy to see you it hurts. Why do you live so damn far away?" Sylvia shook her head and squeezed her sister's hand. Here was sanity, here was composure. "You up for today?"

"I really feel bad that you made this detour for me. I could've gotten a taxi, a shuttle, something."

"I couldn't let you do that. I would feel like a terrible sister. Really, I'm doing this for me. You staying the night?"

Celeste nodded.

"In that case I'm not going to be able to drive you back here. How you doin'? You gonna be all right? With Nataly, I mean?"

Celeste looked at the clock on the dash. "We've got plenty of time. But whenever we get there, I'm stopping at the bar for a drink first."

Sylvia nodded. "Oui, mon capitaine." Sylvia signaled and looked over her shoulder. Their new van had terrible rear visibility, but Jack liked the size of it, its statement.

"Tea at the Ritz was Nataly's idea?" Celeste said, fussing with the seat belt, flipping down the visor to check her eye makeup, glancing left at Sylvia, wondering if Sylvia would bring up the money or if she would have to. Why was it that whenever she came home, she wanted immediately to be somewhere—anywhere—else?

"Oh, you know, we get to talking with Mom, she says one thing to me, one thing to Nataly, it gets confused mid-translation and here we are, at the far edges of nowhere, convenient to no one. But with a beautiful view. Provided the sun pops out."

During the forty-minute drive, the two women spoke of Sylvia's children, Celeste's business, books, movies, their mother. Neither sister brought up the pages of accounting that Sylvia had faxed Celeste two weeks earlier.

Celeste went directly to the bar.

"Ketel One martini, dry, with a twist."

She watched Sylvia in the wide mirror. Sylvia stood in the lobby, unable to decide whether to wait there for Nataly and their mother or to go with Celeste into the bar.

The bartender shook the ice and alcohol, lips together in concentration. Celeste enjoyed this moment, the anticipation of the drink, the adroit curl of the lemon twist onto the rim of her cocktail glass. She felt the frozen stem between her fingers and tasted a little bit of icy heaven. Not too much vermouth, the vodka softened, not watered down, by the shaking.

Celeste loved the grandeur of luxury hotels, the elaborate flower arrangements, plush furniture, ornate fixtures. It all fostered an illusion of benevolent, impersonal wealth. A challenging pose to maintain.

Sylvia tugged at her shoulder bag. "They're here."

And so they were. They came into the bar to greet her—her mother in lilac and silver. Nataly in black with embroidery up the seam of her pants, bursts of range red and yellow, a sheer black top. Stunning. Gorgeous. Did Nataly know how beautiful she was?

Why had Celeste worried? It was all right. It was fine. They could try again.

"Are you two sisters?" Celeste said, repeating the line that had given her mother so much pleasure since they were tiny girls.

Her mother giggled in response. "Today, maybe we are," she said.

Nataly scowled at Celeste. "You had to order a drink before we got here?" she asked in that familiar tone of judgment, as if she were in any position to judge anyone. All the love Celeste felt an instant earlier curdled and evaporated.

Celeste picked up her martini from the bar, took a sip, and smiled at Nataly. *I could ask you how waiting tables is going or mention the failed exhibition you recently had,* she thought. Instead, she turned to her mother and hugged her close, feeling her mother's breastbone against her chest. "I've missed you," she said.

"Ay, sweetheart, but not enough to move back home."

Celeste stiffened, disentangled herself, picked up her martini and walked with it to the elaborate table set for four.

Nataly inspected the chintz teapot, the silver tea strainer, the black lapsang souchong that the server poured. The server did a deft job of it too, not a drip or a trickle down the teacup or teapot to disturb or distract from the floral pattern. Nataly dissolved a misshapen lump of brownish sugar into her cup with a heavy silverplate teaspoon and sipped. The table, the settings, the people around her, her sisters, her mother, dissolved into amber. Even Celeste. The tea was warm, smoky and sweet. She inhaled the amber and felt herself about to dissolve as well until she heard Celeste talking to their mother about another bill she had gotten in their father's name. "Just send it to me, I'll take care of it." Celeste said.

And she would too. She did everything she said she'd do. People like that, like Celeste, were fierce and frightening. But not to Nataly. She knew Celeste had constructed and surrounded herself in a plaster artifice. It was difficult to look at this Celeste. She wasn't real.

Nataly watched her mother unwrap Celeste's gift: a necklace with a glass pendant. The glass glowed with a light Nataly had not seen before. It swirled green and blue, streaked with gold. It was luminous. Nataly's frame was crude and artless in comparison.

"I saw it in Venice and thought of you," Celeste said.

Nataly set her teacup down noisily. They turned towards her. "Really? Oh, come off it." Celeste looked at Nataly as if not understanding the language. Then she turned back to their mother. Nataly stabbed a scone with a small butter knife, spread the clotted cream thickly over it, added raspberry jam, swallowed without tasting and choked on her mouthful. It was Sylvia who patted her back, pressed a glass of ice water on her and ultimately walked her towards the ladies' lounge where Nataly could clean her sheer blouse of the spray of half eaten food.

"So you're against me too," Nataly said, wiping her shirt with a wash cloth. The wet cloth left white fibers and an unattractive smear of water behind.

"For a baby sister, you sure got the baby role down. Look, nobody's against you. Be a big girl and put on a pretty face. While you can," Sylvia winked at her.

"Don't you see what Celeste's doing?" If Sylvia asked Nataly what she thought Celeste was doing, Nataly wouldn't know how to explain it. It was just a humiliating feeling that Celeste was, was—what? Winning. Celeste was winning and Nataly had lost. But lost what?

"I don't know how many times I have to tell you this," Sylvia said. "I am Switzerland. I'm not going to say a bad thing about Celeste to you, and I'm not going to say a bad thing about you to Celeste."

"I'll bet that news will go over well with her."

Sylvia held Nataly's hands and said. "Nataly, I already have two children. You need to grow up."

"What about Celeste? *She* needs to grow up."

"I'm talking to you."

Mercy looked around the table at her daughters: Celeste with her spiky brown hair and serious eyes. Sylvia, the curvy mama who had given her grandchildren, Nataly, the artist, the minx. Their windowside table was filled with a view of the terrace. The marine layer obscured the beach and the sea beyond. It didn't matter to Mercy. *Where your heart lies, there lies your treasure also.* Her treasure was seated at this table.

"Where would I be without you three? You are my life."

Later, after Nataly escorted their mother home, Sylvia accompanied Celeste to the bar. "A neat trick," Sylvia said, "that both of you could spend an entire hour talking without addressing a kind remark to one another. Remind me to not do that on my 60th."

Celeste turned on her bar stool to face Sylvia. "Miriam and Becky will always talk to each other." She leaned forward, hugging her sister.

"Listen to me," Celeste said into Sylvia's ear, more forcefully than she had intended. "You have to promise me, whatever I say—*whatever I say*—you won't stop talking to me. You won't shut me out of your life. Promise me."

Sylvia pulled back. "It's that bad?"

"I want to know I can tell you the truth, and you won't punish me for it."

"Oh my God, Celeste, what did you find?"

"I don't know where the money is. I don't know what he did with it. And that's not good."

After their drinks, Sylvia drove ninety minutes north to pick up her daughters at Tamara's. Her back and stomach were beginning to ache. She wasn't willing to take more pain meds on top of the glass of wine Celeste had ordered for her, hoping to soften the news. By the time she stepped out of the car, she was aching too much and too stiff to walk without crouching forwards. Tamara opened the door, waiting.

She was tall and elegant and wore a fashionable wrap around her shoulders. She reached out to hug Sylvia.

"You should have let them spend the night. They're upstairs, asleep."

Tamara released her and looked at her carefully. "You look like shit. What did the bastard do this time?"

Sylvia wanted to laugh, but only managed a small snort. "It's what he did last time."

"You want a glass of wine?"

"Tea," Sylvia said, sinking into a soft armchair and waiting as Tamara fussed in the kitchen. "And aspirin," she called out.

Sylvia closed her eyes and thought how blessed she was to have a friend who knew the worst thing about her and loved her anyway. Tamara brought in a tray with a small glass of water, a couple aspirin and a large blue and white mug.

Sylvia held the mug between her hands to warm them. And said, "'The soul's freedom'" and waited.

Tamara scrunched up her face. "Friendship. Anna Akhmatova."

Sylvia smiled. Russian poetry, literature was one of their deep connections, their lawyer husbands a more superficial one. Jack liked to point out that *he* was all mergers and acquisitions, while Tamara's husband was a mere litigator. Perhaps she could close her eyes, stay here with Tamara and never worry about a thing. Tamara would find a way to make it work. Tamara could move easily from wearing her power jewelry and spearheading a capital campaign for their children's school to dancing in a track suit with the banda music at their park. Everything came naturally to Tamara. Sylvia felt as if she had to watch Tamara and the other mothers at their school, the other people at the park, to see how things were done, and then act as if she had everything figured out.

"How am I going to survive while you're in Israel?"

"Passover's months away. Don't worry about it now. What did Celeste say?"

"Not months. A little over one month. Stop trying to make me feel better about it." Sylvia sipped at the tea. Excellent, of course. "She can't figure out what he's done with the money. She thought I was going to hate her for giving me the bad news." She looked at her friend and saw that Tamara was reserving judgment. "Don't you think that's a little ridiculous?"

Tamara raised her eyebrow. "I don't know if that's ridiculous. What did you tell her about Jack?"

Sylvia glanced across at Tamara, "Nothing. All she knows is that the money is missing."

Tamara nodded. "I see she's not the only one afraid of losing a sister."

Sylvia struggled against the lingering pain to sit upright. "You promised," Sylvia said. "You promised, Tamara, and if you can't keep that promise, tell me now."

Tamara kneeled beside the armchair and held Sylvia's hand between hers.

"I will keep it because I love you, but it's not right."

"Nobody ever needs to know. Ever. You don't understand. It would change how they look at me, think of me. Don't, don't, don't let that happen."

"And you need to do what you promised me."

"I know, I know."

Monday morning Celeste flew back to San Jose. Now it was over. Sylvia had taken the news about the money like the woman she was, calm and unruffled. Celeste could imagine her sitting at her immaculate kitchen counter, pouring herself another cup of coffee and planning her next step.

Sylvia and Jack *had* had a lot of money. Most of it was gone, and Celeste couldn't find what Jack had done with it. In Celeste's business, missing money meant addiction: drugs, sex, gambling. That's the part she couldn't tell Sylvia, because she had no proof of what Jack had done with hundreds of thousands of dollars—only that it was missing.

Celeste dug around in her bag. She opened her wallet and peered at that scrap of paper. *Skye Amado Neidorf,* it read. *One brief, almost life, that changed everything. "This I do, in remembrance of you."*

Mercedes Amado arrived at Franklin Elementary in Santa Ana every morning at 6:30 a.m, even though school didn't start until 8. Today she wore a softly woven linen suit, peach colored. She loved dressing up for her students. Most of her thirty-five sixth graders had mothers who were younger than her own daughters. When Mercy made phone calls home, she marveled at *esas madrecitas* who were often busy extricating themselves from boyfriends or in the process of pursuing new loves while leaving their sons and daughters to Mrs. Amado.

Sixty years old. She hardly believed it herself.

Each fall Mercy was happy to adopt those thirty-five sixth graders, inoculate them with her brand of philosophy and education and say good-bye at year's end. Sometimes the infusion took, sometimes it didn't. She had a certain reputation. Problem students were routinely transferred in and somehow became less problematic. Mercy once thought it might be interesting to follow the paths of some of her students and then changed her mind, certain that the results would only depress her. She had to focus on the class at hand, just love them for the time they were given to her.

Why couldn't she transfer that skill to her daughters, giving them all she could for the time they were with her?

Each morning Mercy studied the photos on her desk as she prepared herself for the day. There was Celeste, her first born, graduating from Humboldt State. The cap obscured how short and spiky her hair had been, but you could see the delicate bones of her face and a small smile as she posed. That diploma had cost all of them so much, but most of all, Celeste. You could see the determination, the grimness, underneath the smile, even at twenty-two. Her sense of humor had evaporated with Skye.

There was Nataly, her baby, at her senior year's gallery opening. Nataly's lank brown hair straggled down to her shoulders, her face even paler in the excitement of the evening, those green eyes twinkling at the camera, at her mother.

In one, the brown heads and long braids of her granddaughters, Becky and Miriam, were capped by Mickey Mouse ears, marking the spring she had taken them to Disneyland. Miriam smiled behind Becky, her arms wrapped around her younger sister, as if protecting her from life's unpredictability, even here at the Magic Kingdom. Becky smiled, her two front teeth missing, looking so much like Nataly at that age it always momentarily confused Mercy. "Whose little girl are you?" Mercy often asked her.

Mercy had looked forever for a photograph where Sylvia was the center of attention, not her children, where she wasn't reaching protectively towards her husband. She settled for one in high school, where Sylvia's full, frothy curls hit past her shoulders. *As gorgeous as Cher in* Moonstruck, Mercy thought.

At the far end of her desk was a picture of Celeste and Michael the weekend she visited them in Trinidad. The fog had been heavy that summer afternoon, so you really couldn't see the craggy rocks behind them, but you got a sense of the damp air, the coast. Michael and Celeste were smiling like fools, young beautiful fools in love, Michael's cool eyes twinkling into the camera, Celeste eight months and three weeks pregnant, breathlessly waiting, waiting, waiting.

And she's still waiting, thought Mercy each time she saw the photograph. Celeste would die, or kill her, if she ever found this photo, which was why Mercy kept it safely on her school desk. Mercy continued to love Michael, because he had loved Celeste.

Currently there were no men in Mercy Amado's life. At the end of the day, after organizing her desk for the next morning, then reapplying her lipstick, Mercy walked into her principal's office. "John, I need to talk to you." Mercy approved of her principal, John Wolfert. One, because he was attractive. And two, because he always wore a suit.

"Mercy, if it's about the air conditioning, the district has sworn up and down it will be fixed this weekend."

"No, John. It's about me. I really admire you. You've got to know somebody." John didn't understand.

"Somebody, John, somebody you could fix me up with."

"Oh," he said. "Oh." He swiveled sideways in his chair. "Oh."

"Just wanted to be sure you were thinking about that," she said. Then she went back to her classroom.

Monday night. The minute Jack stepped into the house Miriam sang out, "Dad, Mom let Becky miss school again."

His jaw tightened. He closed the front door, shook his head, kissed Miriam's smug face and walked upstairs without another word. He was going to talk to Becky.

Right then, Sylvia hated Miriam. She hated the cheap door Jack had walked through, the creaking stairs as he trod upwards, the cold granite counter top island where Miriam sat. They had moved to Pasadena for Jack's law practice. Instead of ending up in a rustic Spanish, a sweet bungalow, or an imposing craftsman, Jack insisted on a new home in a gated community. *Gated*, for God's sake. Was it to protect her daughters from the kind of people she herself had grown up alongside or was it to keep all the bad things inside her home from spilling out into the community?

The thin veneer of brand-spanking newness of their home swiftly rubbed off, revealing underneath the cheap materials, the haphazard design and the shoddy construction. Brand-new light fixtures didn't work due to brand-new faulty wiring. The carpet unraveled and the kitchen countertops stained. Jack had wanted a maintenance-free, turnkey house. They had paid a mountain of money for it.

After she put the girls to bed in their rooms, she hid in the office, catching up on her Russian Lit chat group. Jack walked in.

"Why did you let Becky stay home again?"

"Her back was bothering her."

"It's hard enough me getting ready to go on this business trip without you destroying any shred of confidence I may have left in your skill as a mother and a homemaker."

"So don't go," Sylvia said. Her eyes were fixed on the slick monitor with its bold colors. Her chat group always valued her insight into Babel or Gogol or Bukanin.

"What?"

"I told you," Sylvia said, turning around to face him. He wore blue silk boxers. His chest muscles were well-defined and lightly covered with brown hair. She didn't remember the boxers, but he was as fastidious about his dress at night as he was in the day. She had found it rather charming after all the grungy guys she had dated, hung around, then slept with. Jack was different. Jack was crisp and clean and smooth. *Look at him*, she thought. *Even his pajamas sing money*.

"Don't start," Jack said.

"I told you, you want the kids raised a certain way, you stay at home and raise them. No more arguments." Sylvia smiled. She tried to make it as pleasant as possible.

"The problem with that, Sylvia, is that you don't earn a red cent. You haven't worked in eight years. You don't make those decisions."

"I make the decisions that affect my children in this house. And, if you're going to second guess me every day, I'll…" she faltered.

"You'll what?" Just a slight raise of the eyebrows. Sylvia knew that look. "Hmmm? You want to tell me what you'll do?"

At that moment Sylvia hated only one person more than Jack:

herself, for not being able to find a way out of this. Not a way that she could live with.

Jack closed the door behind him. The steps creaked as he made his way upstairs. He was leaving tomorrow for New York, some kind of merger/arbitration/litigation/who the hell gave a shit. Sylvia stopped listening.

After a moment, she actually felt quite calm, almost happy. Jack would be gone for two weeks. That gave her plenty of time to figure out her next step. *Wasn't there a Chekhov story like that?* She tapped in her question.

At the end of the day, Celeste drove to her townhome, started boiling water for the pasta she would make, then opened a bottle of wine. Pinot Noir. Oregon.

Over a bowl of pasta, she opened her laptop and ran through her own accounts online. The mortgage balance was dropping nicely—the savings, the retirement, the mutual funds, the emergency funds, all accruing at the rate she had anticipated, some even higher.

But that's how it should be. No use having a financial planner who can't make her own money grow. Just to spice up the emotional component, Celeste had invested in something she never recommended to her clients unless they had a tolerance for risk as well as the financial capacity to lose money—a high risk investment. This one was a telecom in Ecuador.

When it quadrupled, Celeste sold half. When it next doubled, she sold half again. Now she held on to it just to see how low it could go.

Celeste logged off. No elation, no guilt. Not even a sense of accomplishment. Just another item to cross off her list. The charitable giving that she preached to her clients manifested in her own life through monthly automatic deductions. Her returns were higher than she anticipated, so now she wrote out a number of checks, little bonuses to Save the Children, World Vision, and Doctors Without Borders. Little bonuses to the masses of people living on such a mean scale of pain and desperation that it was almost, but not quite, incomprehensible to Celeste.

Celeste had heard Oprah say, "It's not about writing a check, it's about touching someone else's life."

"No, my dear Oprah," Celeste said out loud, "Now there you're wrong." *It is about writing a check. It's quick, clean, simple and easy. As long as you have the money in the bank to back it up, it's easy to give money, but it's hard to give of yourself.*

Herself, she had conserved for her family. Where had that gotten her?—Nataly cursing at her.

Well, there was no point in thinking about that now. Celeste poured more wine. Nataly, what did she know? How long would everyone let her be a thirty-two-year-old kid? How long would everyone pretend there was actually a future in stitching remnants of material together and labeling it as some kind of lofty art?

During college, Celeste had brought up the topic of socking something away for retirement. Celeste mentioned compound interest. Nataly had looked blankly at her, yawned and changed the subject. Why did that irritate her so much?

Because, *for Christ's sake,* if she had yawned when Nataly was explaining the theory behind her tactile installation pieces, Nataly would have savaged her. Nataly was an artist, after all, something beyond the comprehension of practical-minded Celeste, right? Isn't that exactly what Nataly said?

Celeste occasionally wished she were an artist. The hideous behavior of artists was so often excused because of their occupation. Financial planners, on the other hand, weren't given much leeway in throwing fits and living irresponsibly.

She had brought up the thought of retirement because she could see that, at the rate Nataly was going, she would be impoverished at sixty. Because she could predict that if he wasn't stopped, her father would permanently destroy her mother's credit and all her dreams of security. Because she knew Sylvia was on a sinking ship, with two little girls.

Two little girls. What was that like? What could that have been like?

Nataly had already trampled her heart with all the force and skill of a flamenco dancer. Celeste retreated, exiling herself even further from her family, beyond her own borders. Would Sylvia ever dare to ask Jack about the money? *Cada loca con su tema.* Every crazy has her thing. Celeste's craziness was that every word and every deed reverberated into the future.

She sipped the last of the wine. *That had been a decent bottle of wine,* Celeste thought, glancing up at the clock. Just 9:30. Where had she picked it up, anyway?

Tuesday afternoon. As Nataly ironed the white shirt until the collar and cuffs were crisp, she recalled visiting her father's restaurant when she was eleven, trailing Sylvia and Celeste, a few steps behind their mother. Nataly watched as the waiters inspected her sisters out of the corners of their eyes. Nataly was somehow invisible. So she improvised with a cartwheel. And it would have been just fine, except that her sneaker collided with a tray table full of salads.

Nataly slipped into the black polyester pants she hated—except that they hugged her just right—and headed to work. She supported her artistic ambitions and addictions by working in a swank restaurant in downtown Los Angeles. Rimsky's was proud of its vodka selections and Californian-Continental cuisine. It was occasionally featured in national magazines and catered to a glamorous clientele. She had once waited on Brad Pitt, who had left her a fabulous tip. (But she hadn't wanted his tip, had she really? She wanted her work on his walls. She wanted him to see her as the artist she was, not the server she was forced to play).

Nataly had refined her serving skills as she put herself through Otis, then CalArts. She started out at a coffee shop, then worked at a steak house, where she grew familiar with complicated drinks and menus. She got her current job through her friend Yesenia. Nataly vowed that when she made it, when her stuff was selling, she would have Rimsky's cater the event. She pictured the enormous specialty vodkas encased in blocks of ice, decorated with leaves or flowers or twigs. A few nervous and frighteningly thin young women would circulate with the blinis, crème fraiche and salmon caviar. They would carry trays of vegetable pirozhkis. The guests at her gallery opening would mirror precisely the glamorous clientele she waited on here.

She'd show them. In the meantime, there didn't seem to be a particularly high demand for the intricate, labor-intensive textile work that Nataly loved to create. At Rimsky's, Nataly appreciated the delightful allure of the place, especially during a quiet moment. The bar was sleek, shiny and intoxicating in its promise, the dining area quietly opulent with its floral accents and towering wine glasses. The table linens were crisp, gleaming and luscious to the touch. Everything was there to satisfy the whim of its clients. It was the product of the hidden work of undocumented busboys and immigrant cooks. There was a connection to her textile work, Nataly knew, a connection between invisible labor and exquisite presentation.

Eric, the manager, kept asking her out. She had made the mistake of accepting once during a lonely dry spell and sleeping with him. She had felt absolutely nothing. Pleasant looking fellow, tall, black hair tied back into a short, neat ponytail. He had five different pairs of glasses and was a few years older than her—thirty-four or thirty-five. But completely ordinary. Boring. That was the worst thing Nataly could think to say about anyone or anything. The ordinary life was not worth living. No, worse was trying to pass as ordinary. Look at her sisters, Celeste. Sylvia. Look at her mother. Shit. Look at herself.

But, besides that, Eric would never mix with her friends. He could make the effort, but her friends wouldn't let him in. She had tried one night at Yesenia's, and it was a disaster. A few of the men and women from Otis kept asking him what he did outside of his day job, and he kept insisting managing restaurants was what he wanted to do. Eric had mortified Nataly by revealing to her crowd that his ambition in life was to own a restaurant with an A-list clientele.

Nataly pulled her Altima onto the road. What kind of dream was that? It rankled her.

She knew the restaurant business from years of watching her father manage his C-list clientele. And what was her name? Jeannie? Jolene? Earlene?—that nasal-voiced, beady-eyed waitress bitch who was always calling their house and pretending it was a wrong number. Even now, she burned a hateful smoky orange at the memory of those phone calls.

Nataly could apply for a grant. Lots of paperwork, lots of photographs, lots of networking with the people in charge of nominating, choosing and disbursing. The thought of begging for financial support on paper made her skin crawl, as if she were disrobing in front of them to gawk. She'd rather wait tables. There the contract was clear. Besides, when you were a server, you were an aesthetic object all by yourself.

Nataly arrived at work. She dropped her keys in her bag, tucked her purse safely away, said hello to the busboys. By her reckoning, it had been six months. Maybe another six months, max, and she could strike out living on her art alone. Maybe book that tentative New York showing with Yesenia. October in New York City. What would they wear?

"Vodka gimlet, Belvedere vodka, please," said the natty-looking gentleman. Late 30s, early 40s, hair cropped close but stylish to disguise the fact that his hairline was receding. His rugged face hinted at interesting experiences and immediately appealed to her. For a moment, she wondered how that face would feel alongside her own. For just a moment.

She was thinking how cool and low his voice was when she brought him the drink, misjudged and spilled the whole thing on his lap. This was her job. This was her rent! This was the trip to the New York galleries with Yesenia. Her entire future lay in a glass of spilled ice and alcohol.

The customer shook his head. "I'd like to speak to the manager," he said, dabbing with his cloth napkin.

This only intensified her personal misery. She gave her friend Eric a pleading look, then sent him over to table 12. Nataly hid in the kitchen.

Eric came back, his face impassive. "The client at 12 wants to speak with you."

I will go out with a swagger, Nataly thought. She walked tall and straight and smiled sincerely, apologetically.

"It was all my fault," the gentleman said looking up at her, staring intently into her eyes. "I'm terribly sorry."

"You're very kind," she said, with much less swagger, looking away.

There was something very intense in his face. Something challenging, very masculine and slightly mocking, very attractive. Good grief, now they were conspirators. They had an understanding. This could be the start of something.

Then she noticed the wedding band. And all she could do was to repeat herself, "Very kind. May I take your order?"

It was the end of a bright sparkling March day. Celeste sat at her favorite Italian restaurant in San Jose having a glass of wine with Victor Resnick. "Thank you, Victor, once again, for the referrals. It's been a very lucrative year."

Victor waved his hand and sipped at his wine. "It embarrasses me that you feel you need to bring me here and thank me. You do both me and your clients a service. Who else am I going to send them to?"

He said that with his familiar lopsided grin. When most men his age seemed to be losing their hair, his kept sprouting out into impossibly militant curls. How many times had Celeste thought her life would be so much simpler if only she could conjure the necessary erotic feelings for this man?

The waiter set a platter of antipasti down between them. Victor raised his eyebrows, then helped himself to half of the mozzarella and a slice of the salami. "The clients I have that are the hardest to work with are the ones who don't call you. Half way through the settlement proceedings, they're kicking and screaming at me." He ate the cheese in one bite and shook his head. "These women. You know as well as I do that most of the time they've dug their own grave. What's that phrase? *The suspension of disbelief.* They sure as hell got that down."

Celeste smiled and said, "Is that wife number two or number three that you're talking about?"

"Ms. Amado, you offend me deeply. Wives number two and three signed solid prenups. There were no negotiations, and, if they had read what they had signed, there would have been no surprises."

Celeste smiled at Victor again and shook her head. What a pragmatist. Ah, the pinot bianco was so cool and crisp, Celeste didn't realize she had finished her glass. Victor filled hers, then his.

"What about you?" Victor said, with less dissatisfaction on his face and a hint of keen curiosity. "You and Keith still—."

Celeste shook her head. "You know that I gave him his pink slip. A while back."

Victor finished the last drop of wine, set his glass down with fervor, sat back and waved a finger at her. "This isn't right, Celeste. I see now this meal is founded on false pretenses. You're plotting my seduction."

Celeste laughed. "You are one of the most insightful men I've ever known."

"Hmm. I suppose I was hoping you wouldn't have found that quite so funny."

The waiter deftly removed their empty plates and changed the glassware. He returned with a bottle of red.

As Victor inspected, sipped and savored, Celeste glanced around the restaurant. She recognized a couple in the corner. She'd have to say hello before they left. She turned to Victor and saw him frowning.

"Something wrong with the wine?"

He shook his head. "I don't understand why you're not with someone," he said.

"Why aren't you with someone?"

"Me? Everyone knows I'm merely between wives. You, Celeste, you of all people, should know you're between husbands. But you have to know that in order to realize that."

"Victor, you're very sweet to care."

Victor stared at Celeste. "I mean it," he said, "you're too beautiful and too smart to squander this life, Celeste. You and I both know the world's not just about money."

She said, "I have two little nieces who remind me of that every time I see them. Miriam, I swear, she's so grown up for eight years old. So smart. And Becky, I think she's like my mother and my sister combined." The same silky skin and bony body of Nataly. That same mischievous smile.

Victor shook his head. The sides of his face shook ever so slightly with him. "You see, that's what I mean. You need a man, and you need a kid."

"Jesus, Vic, look, I thought the unwritten agreement here was you speak about your love life, and I talk about business." Celeste watched Victor set his fork down. There was a rupture going on inside of her.

"But come on—"

"Could we change the subject, Vic? Let's not spoil this wonderful meal by talking about me? Really, who the hell cares?" She was not going to trot out that story of Michael. Display Skye, turn her into a wound that time still had yet to heal. She sipped her wine. Maybe that would quell what was going on inside.

"I do, Celeste," Victor said, picking up his fork and looking down at his plate.

"Once again you're the better man, because I don't."

The next morning—what a morning! Celeste had already had two clients. Both of them made her so angry she wanted to shake them.

Client #1: For the past fifteen years, she had been receiving statements from two different brokers and not opened a single envelope. She brought all of the (unopened) statements to Celeste.

Client #2: A young woman named Andrea Paz, clearly anxious, very attractive, very demure. She had a court settlement worth $100,000. Ms. Paz didn't go into the details of the settlement, but for some reason Celeste thought it was related to sexual harassment.

"I'd like to be able to invest $50,000 for my children, for their college," Ms. Paz had said. That had quite literally filled Celeste's day with sunshine, and her business woman's heart with joy. Halfway through the necessary questions, Celeste asked her what she was doing with the other half of the settlement.

"My husband invested it in his brother's boss' business."

Celeste nodded, very slowly. "Did you happen to bring a copy of the paperwork?"

"What paperwork?" Andrea Paz asked, her large innocent eyes making her look fifteen, not twenty-seven. Celeste gritted her teeth and inwardly promised herself to make this money grow for Andrea's sons.

Client #1's statements revealed that one brokerage firm had kept her funds in a money market fund for the past fifteen years, where it had shrunk a bit because of the management fees. That was far better, however, than the other brokerage firm, which had simply churned and churned the money until they had the temerity to be billing her!

What was it about women that made them refuse to look? Okay, maybe once they looked they couldn't see, couldn't recognize the problem or the indicators, couldn't decipher the financial statement. But they had to look first, in order to realize it.

What made them think that the money would take care of itself or that the money, their money, would be better thrust blindly into the hands of a stranger?

Celeste got so angry with these women—these women whose anxieties, neuroses and prayers were layered on to their funds. Money was neutral! Money can't spend or invest itself, she wanted to yell at Client #1.

What the hell does your husband's brother's boss know about investing? she wanted to yell at Client #2. But she couldn't. She knew they had both used all of their emotional reserve to just enter her office. No use scolding a person for that. She knew how to treat women like this, coddle them more gently than she would her two young nieces. Otherwise they would bolt, and who knew what kind of swindler would find them next?

What were these women so terrified of? To Celeste, the unknown was more terrifying.

Celeste sipped her coffee. She knew her own sin had been pride. She was once Celeste Amado, eighteen years old, National Merit Scholar, perfect 1600 on her SATs, invitations to attend nearly every Ivy League School back East and a hundred private colleges throughout the country. Celeste Amado, something bright and shiny, even to herself, an eighteen-year-old Celeste who had left midway through an insipid church service, choking on her tears. She wished she were far away. She wished it was next year.

"Whatever it is," her mother said, following her, putting her cool hand on Celeste's hot cheek, "it's not the end of the world."

That's exactly what it was, the end of the world. The end of her world, at any rate, and of the way she had planned on living it. So many plans, they had made her dizzy with possibility. Dizzy with being eighteen, standing on the very edge of the world and the things that are the most important, the most meaningful.

"We love you," her mother said. This was her mother, with the golden brown eyes and gentle touch Celeste had known all her life. This was the mother who had tied her shoes as Celeste read, who still dabbed a tissue at her face as she headed out the door, who continued to tuck all three daughters in at night. This was her mother—peace, consolation, solace all wrapped into one person.

Her mother stroked her face. "Everything seems impossible when we look at it for the first time. I know you, it will work out, it will be all right."

Celeste felt her mother's cool hand on her face, and the tears stopped. Her mother knew her and loved her. Michael loved her. Her mother was right, it would work out. Somehow. "Mom, I'm pregnant."

At which point her mother, Mercy Amado, began to cry.

There were women who refused to look at the truth. Celeste had borne it, faced the implications of her pregnancy head on. Celeste thought of her sister Sylvia and stilled her interior rant. As she had told Sylvia, she could only find transfers and withdrawals of funds. Legally, those funds were all Jack's, and he could do with them as he pleased because that inheritance had been bequeathed specifically to him. Although—and this is what Celeste did not say—what kind of marriage is it where the husband hoards it all for himself?

Celeste already had a sense about what kind of marriage it was. Early in their marriage Jack had pinned her in a closet, then apologized for thinking she was Sylvia. Sylvia had laughed when Celeste told her —what else could she do? Jack was just a little drunk, a little toasted, Sylvia said.

Since their chat at the bar in Laguna back in February, Sylvia hadn't told Celeste if she had found out or done anything further about the money. Here was another woman, her Sylvia, she was going to have to shake some sense into, very very gently.

Sylvia had graduated from the University of California at Irvine with honors in Comparative Literature. That literature had included Russian, French and ancient Greek. Raised Protestant, she joked to her Catholic friends that she had given up Spanish for Lent—and had forgotten it completely.

Her degree had prepared her for a wide variety of jobs, all of which were unpaid internships. Sylvia knew there were adults in this world whose parents would subsidize their self-actualization for any number of years, but she was not one of those. Without drama or self-pity, she went out to find a job to cover her student loans.

She worked briefly for her father as a hostess in the restaurant he managed. She went home nightly cursing the fact that her parents had never taught her Spanish. With the intensity she had reserved for Anton Chekhov and Stéphane Mallarmé, she pored over vocabulary books and 1001 Spanish verbs. After a few months, even the dishwashers understood her.

But the commute inland was gritty, the pay absurdly low. At this rate she'd still be living with her parents when she retired. And it was getting very odd at home, the phone rang and rang and when Sylvia picked up no one answered—then it was tense between her parents, Nataly was in Pasadena racking up mountains of debt at CalArts. So she shifted gears and followed her mother's example: she applied as a substitute teacher and was quickly hired as a full-time teacher on an emergency credential and placed in a structured English immersion classroom in Anaheim.

This Lincoln Elementary looked a little like the elementary school in Compton Sylvia had attended before her family moved to the city of Orange. The classrooms were filled with blacks, Mexicans—although she was supposed to call them Hispanics—Filipinos, Asians, mixed-race kids, white kids.

She began her teaching career in January in a third-grade classroom that had had five previous substitutes.

If the mysteries of a cash register had perplexed her, its technical complexities were silly putty compared to a class of thirty-five third-graders and their exponential demands.

Sylvia would arrive at seven in the morning and leave at five-thirty in the afternoon. At home, she read wretched compositions filled with illiterate spellings and painfully formed printing. Her red pen flew across pages and pages of worksheets.

Sylvia realized a few things:

She didn't know how to teach spelling.

She didn't know how to teach writing.

She didn't know how to teach math.

She threw away her red pencils. Apparently teaching was a lot more difficult than it looked.

While the students—oh my God, the beautiful students, they all looked like they could be her or her sisters or her uncles or her cousins—chased each other in the classroom, Sylvia pored over her teacher's manual, looking for the correct phrasing.

"Maestra, maestra," the students would say, the parents would say, with their admiring eyes, their needy eyes.

Sylvia knew she was an imposter. An imposter! And what was the point of Victor Hugo or Dostoyevsky or Anna Akhmatova or de Maupassant if she couldn't help a classroom of eight and nine-year-olds, for God's sake?

For the unit on Columbus, she asked her students to tell her about the longest trip they had ever taken. When she was in third grade, the longest trip her family had ever taken was an hour drive to see relatives.

She called on Robert, a slim dark boy with lightly muscled arms who had earlier demonstrated his terror of spiders.

"Two years," he said.

"Two years, Robert? Where were you going?"

"When we walked here from El Salvador."

Pause. Well, Columbus' three month cruise was going to have a hard time following that. Sylvia shared the story in the staff lounge.

"You didn't believe him, did you?" a stridently gray-haired teacher scoffed, dipping her herbal teabag into a mug. "El Salvador's an island, for heaven's sake, he couldn't have walked." Perhaps Sylvia wasn't as underqualified and incompetent as she had feared

Carrot, stick. Carrot, stick. Carrot, stick. Carrot—stickers, praise, candy. Stick—missed recess, detention, standards, late to lunch. But still the children spilled out of their chairs, tripped each other, ran wild through the hallways and onto the playground.

"All right," she said one Wednesday in March. "If we can get through the next two days with you following my directions, we can have a class party."

If they had spilled out of their desks before, now they were bouncing on the table tops. Sylvia raised her voice, "And if we have a party, you can bring treats, music—"

Lena, a little girl Sylvia had seated in the front row, a little girl who never finished her work but who betrayed such powerful neglect that Sylvia rewarded her with candy anyway, said, "Ms. Amado? Ms. Amado? Music? We can bring music?"

"You betcha," Sylvia said.

Lena's eyes became slits as she glowered at Sylvia. *Now what had she done?*

She found out Thursday afternoon when the principal asked Sylvia to come to a meeting after school. Lena sat outside the principal's office, accompanied by a woman so huge she appeared inflated.

The little girl sucked on a piece of candy Sylvia had given her just as school had ended. The principal, Ms. Marroquin—a Latina Sylvia found incredibly beautiful and incredibly intimidating—smiled at the parent, asked her into her office, then looked at Sylvia. "Come in here," she commanded Sylvia.

Sylvia felt two sets of eyes glaring at her.

"Now," the principal said. "Would you please explain to Lena's mother, Mrs. Wilkinson, why you called her daughter a bitch?"

After the meeting Ms. Marroquin said, "You are warned."

In April her toughest kid, Saul, the eleven-year-old in a class of eight and nine-year-olds, listened, rapt, as she read *The Little Match Girl.*

"That's a true story, ain't it, Ms. Amado?" he said, as Sylvia finished.

Sylvia stammered. How did Malamud put it in *The Assistant?* How could she translate that here? It IS the truth, it IS the truth.

"It could be," she said. But in elementary school, you taught them that nonfiction is truth and fiction is pretend. It's pretend.

"It's nonfiction, ain't it, Ms. Amado."

"It's fiction, Saul."

The light in Saul's eyes clicked off.

Days later, weeks later, Malamud's line ran through her head: "I lie to tell the truth." Teaching was the hardest thing she had ever done, and she was terrible at it. This was all confirmed one morning in May. She was leaning over Lena's desk to work on her daily oral language when she heard something so strange and unfamiliar. Thuds, then grunts, then the commotion of kids.

She jolted upright, scanned around, and saw Saul sitting on top of Robert, whacking Robert's face with all his force.

"You monster!" Sylvia shouted. "You monster!" She bumped into children and knocked over desks before yanking Saul off of Robert, dragging him by the arm and leading him to the office. "Line up outside," she told her class, and, to her shock, they did. Two orderly lines, filled with eyes, watching her drag Saul up to Ms. Marroquin's office. "You filthy monster," Sylvia said, over and over again.

The next day Ms. Marroquin, petite and brittle as a bird, tough as industrial cleaner, asked her into her office a second time. She said, "Saul was beating up Robert."

Sylvia nodded.

"You were upset."

"Very."

"You hit Saul."

Sylvia froze. She wasn't even asking her. She was telling her.

"You hit Saul."

"No."

"You were upset. We would all have been upset. Now I have to talk to Saul's parents. And I need the truth. He was being violent, you needed to stop him, you hit him."

"No, I did not. Ask the kids. Thirty kids in there could tell you I didn't."

"Sylvia, stop making this difficult. We have a witness."

"Who? Lena again? Even you must have known she was lying. That whole meeting was a way of getting attention—"

Sylvia was stopped by the look on Ms. Marroquin's face.

"I'm not stupid, Sylvia. Four children who are not Lena saw you hit Saul."

"Oh, Christ," Sylvia said. Her insides flipped over, and she concentrated on holding in the tears that were on the verge of bursting out.

There was to be no last day of school for Sylvia Amado. While her mother was annually showered with plastic flowers, pen and pencil sets, jewelry boxes, perfume, candy, cards and coffee, Sylvia left that day with nothing.

She was mortified. She didn't tell anyone and pretended that she still had a job. She left for work and returned just like before. During the day, she hid in libraries and coffee shops, hoping not to run into anyone. It was a very uncomfortable month. For the very first time in her life, she couldn't escape from the feeling of being an idiot in a classroom.

She had met Jack on the deck of a friend's home in Laguna, overlooking the beach. They watched the waves crash, the sun set, and by the time she'd been fired, had been dating for a year. He was Jewish, God's chosen people, her grandmother insisted. He was clever, entertaining, and she did love him, the attention he gave her and the possibilities he represented. So it was very easy to say yes when Jack asked her to marry him. Yes, she would convert to Judaism. Yes, they could live in Pasadena. Yes, yes, yes.

Tonight Sylvia cleared the table, poured herself another glass of water and sent the girls upstairs to play in their rooms. That day she had gone to buy summer clothes for the girls, and two of her credit cards were declined. Before dinner she had opened a bill from her daughters' school, a kind, gentle letter, telling them that they were far behind in tuition payments, and if there was a significant change in the household income, to set up an appointment to talk to their financial aid office.

When Jack came home, Sylvia said, "Hey, honey, I got this letter today. Is there something I should know?"

He read the letter, crumpled it up. "It's been handled."

"Great," she said. "Is there some way I could help?"

He stared at her. "I am so sick of this," he said. The dining room lighting emphasized the highlights of his hair and made his skin look sallow. *He needs more time outdoors,* Sylvia thought. It had been a warm winter and he still looked as gray as a European. "Look, you think your father's a loser, you have 'issues' with men, and I have to deal with the fall out. And you think what? What's in that simple brain of yours?"

"I'm asking you if I can help," she said, trailing him as he picked up his dinner plate, stalked grimly into the kitchen, set it down on the countertop that had set them back six thousand dollars—six thousand dollars Sylvia had argued over—how could a piece of marble be worth that? Jack made his way to the office off of the kitchen.

"I'm not going to sit here and listen to this. I have work to do," he said. "Somebody's got to pay the bills."

She couldn't help herself and followed him into the office. "Then how was that bill not paid?"

"Go the fuck away." He didn't even turn to face her. God, she hated that contemptuous tone of voice as if he knew everything, and she knew nothing. *I know something!* she wanted to shriek. *Something's not right here!*

And it was eating away at her, eating at her morning and night. She tried to put on the right face for her daughters. They needed her face constant and caring and moral and right, and she needed that face for them, but she was furious with Jack.

"Fuck you, Jack," she said.

He swiveled around and turned to look at her. Now she was afraid. "What did you say?"

"Fuck. You."

"All right." He pulled his belt through the pant loops. He unzipped the pants that had cost $215 at Nordstrom's.

"You win," Sylvia said and walked toward the office door. *Don't show fear*, she thought. *Shit shit shit, you fucking did it again. Can you never fucking learn?* Jack was at the door before her, shutting it tight.

"I am so sick of your whiny shit," he said. "What do you want? Huh? You want me to ask you for permission every time I take a piss? Every time I go to lunch? Or maybe you want to pay the quarterlies? Is that want you want? Take your blouse off."

"Don't," was all Sylvia could say. Jack blocked the office door. On the other side of it was her kitchen, with the floor she had mopped that afternoon. *Don't make me do this, Jack, there's no going back after this, don't kill the little that's left Oh, Christ, the girls, the girls.* She took her blouse off. She wasn't wearing a bra underneath.

"Turn around," he said. She turned.

He was quick behind her, his hands all over her, strong and unyielding. "Don't fucking ask me about my business again. It's my business, and you don't have the fucking brains for it, do you understand?"

He had grabbed her from behind, he was hard against her, his voice was thick. With one hand he cupped her breast. With the other he pulled down her sweatpants, pulled down her underwear.

"Don't," Sylvia said, in almost a whisper. What if the girls saw this? Oh, Christ, she had pushed him over the edge, Christ, just like last time. "Jack, Jack, Jack, don't do this."

"I'm going to fuck you," he said. "Like you fucking deserve."

Sylvia twisted around. "Jack, Jack, Jack, don't do this! For God's sake!" There were tears in her eyes and voice. Jack looked back at her, those green eyes of his cold and empty. Something flickered behind those dead eyes. He stopped.

"Get dressed," he said, his voice still thick, his hands tucking himself back into his pants. "And don't ask me about my business again."

Sylvia stepped out of the office and into her kitchen, closing the door behind her. The fixtures had cost four thousand dollars. Jack had picked them out.

She threw up into the copper kitchen sink.

She ran the garbage disposal, wiped down the sink, rinsed her mouth. Her hands were shaking as she placed the dinner dishes into the dishwasher and washed the pots and pans.

She wiped the counters, swept the kitchen, then mopped the floor again.

She had made an agreement with Tamara. Tomorrow was an appointment and a promise she would keep. Why, why, why had she thought married life would be a refuge?

Nataly's phone rang at two in the morning. Even though she knew who it would be, she answered it, keeping her eye on the TV, half-following the long dead actors on the shimmering grey and white screen. "Hey, Dad," she said. "You call to take me out to breakfast?" It was her own private joke. Every time he offered to take her out, she ended up paying the bill.

"Kinda late for breakfast, isn't it? Or kinda early? I guess you artists are in your own time zone. How's your mother?"

"You can always call her yourself, you know. She's fine." Silence on his end of the phone. *Great.* She tried not to fall into that trap but heard herself ask, "Something wrong?" and heard her father's heavy sigh in response.

"I should have never divorced your mother," he said for the hundredth time. Long ago, Nataly stopped pointing out that her mother had divorced him. It never seemed to make a difference.

"I messed up major," he added. Nataly nodded silently and could picture his watery brown eyes, tinted red with self-pity, the dark brown hair parted on the side, his sideburns neatly trimmed, whatever the fashionable length, thin lips mouthing the words into the speaker. "Eight years, and not a day goes by I don't think about it and regret it."

Nataly wondered if he also regretted Jolene or Earlene or whatever the hell her name had been.

"You and Celeste ever patch things up?"

Jolted, Nataly said, "What do you mean, Dad?"

"You two used to be so tight. Then she goes away, and it's like you're always mad at her. Celeste left us all, baby, not just you, so don't be that way. Don't be like your mother and make it personal. Be like me. There's a lot of me in you."

Shit, thought Nataly. *Just great.*

"Where do you think you got your talent from? You're an artist, a visionary like your old man. Hey, tell your mom for me that I will always love her. Only her. Got that?"

"Sure thing." He hung up.

Nataly moaned, stretched and got up out of her bed. A double espresso couldn't have blasted her into consciousness more than that random phone call from her father. She slipped on a chenille robe and a pair of scruffy slippers and stepped into her work room.

She was currently obsessed with scarlet and purple. In the center of her loom was a small practice piece. She was experimenting with the textures and the colors, a small sketch for the larger piece she was planning. It wasn't right yet.

To Nataly, colors had rich meanings. *Red, that's obvious*, she thought. It's love, passion, lust, sex. Purple more of the same, but layered with obsession, creativity, ambition, anger, jealousy. But combined with red, the two colors became loyalty, fidelity, eternal bliss.

She chose fabrics, ribbons, yarn around those reds and purples— braiding, knotting, cutting, stitching them into a collage that ultimately she would stretch and starch and dry until it appeared to flutter around the shoulders of an invisible mannequin.

She lost herself in the repetitive task and started thinking again about her father. He had started taking her to the restaurant when she was young. Maybe she was just ten or eleven, sitting on a bar stool during the afternoon, sucking Shirley Temples through two squat straws, savoring the sweet, sweet grenadine. At the empty bar, Nataly drew or did her homework or watched the TV. She was there, her father told her, because she was his favorite, and Nataly knew that was true. Later though, she realized, there had been no one at home to watch her so the job had fallen to her dad.

She had liked how attentive one of the waitresses was, always getting her something from the kitchen—a cheese enchilada or a bean burrito. This waitress always asked her about her day, her teacher, her friends. The woman's attention made her feel special, but she also began to notice how that waitress laughed around her father, how she looked at him, how she *touched* him. Did they think she wouldn't notice?

Nataly worked on the tapestry until late morning and then took a nap followed by a shower just before she set out for her shift at Rimsky's.

She found herself looking forward to Thursday nights. For a series of Thursday nights, she waited on Dr. Roeg, the name on his credit card. He usually ordered the sole, always two gimlets before dinner and nothing but water during. She kept her server smile on her face and noticed the insistent gold band. She spoke pleasantly with him about nothing at all and then gave her attention to the rest of the clients in her station.

Dr. Roeg had broad shoulders and manicured nails. He never spoke on his cell phone or tapped on his Blackberry during dinner. He always ate alone.

On a Friday in March, Nataly and Yesenia hunted through the fabrics in the garment district of downtown LA. It had poured the day before. The streets were filled with rubbish and haphazard tents of green trash bags made by the street dwellers. Nataly looked closely at the way the bags were slung around cardboard boxes, how belongings were protected by more boxes, plastic wrap, bungee cords, even tent spikes. These were installation pieces.

Yesenia said, "What are you going to do with the doctor? You've got it bad." Yesenia kept her sleek black hair trimmed like glossy fringe around her pale chubby cheeks, dark eyes, expressive mouth.

Nataly laughed and said, "I'm not going to do anything at all with a married man."

"Self-denial. Good for the soul. Bad for the body, good for the art."

Yesenia had just returned from Manolito's Gallery in New York City. As they passed more tents, Yesenia said, "Do you know, I think the subway is New York's answer to democracy. Crazies and homeless, ethnics and WASPS, city and suburban, wealthy and underclass. Hmmm. Maybe they have something on us after all."

"So the owner's deep into ethnic pieces?" Nataly asked.

"He really likes my stuff." Yesenia looked sideways at Nataly.

"That's terrific," Nataly said, jealousy battling within.

"I told him about you," Yesenia said. A wide red smile spread across her face, her black hair rippled by the wind. "He wants you to send him your portfolio."

"Why?"

"I just told him about what you did."

Nataly paused, thought, then said, "Yesenia, can you imagine? Both of us doing a show in New York?"

Yesenia said, "*Las dos, chica.* That's what they'll be calling us five years from now. It could be amazing. Remember Bernard? He's out there. Maybe he'll let us sleep on the floor."

"As long as he doesn't join us!" A spark lit up in Nataly's heart.

"Oh my God!" her mother said later on the phone. "Which hotel should we stay in?"

In May, Dr. Roeg stopped making an appearance at her station. Nataly thought about that. She thought so much about it that once, while Eric the manager was in the kitchen, she logged onto the reservation screen and scrolled through the book. There, going back into February, March and April, was Dr. Roeg, with his phone number and her table number on every Thursday night. But there was nothing for May.

In between waiting tables, paying her bills and working on that small woven sketch, Nataly went to the bars with Yesenia. She liked Al's, tucked off a dank dirty street. Inside it was dark. And noisy.

Sometimes she and Yesenia would go to the bars in swank hotels and scowl at the men dressed in their business suits. No one there she or Yesenia would ever consider dating. Sleep with? That was a different question.

Late May, Yesenia announced she was moving to New York. "It's a career move," she said with a wide smile, her thick black lashes fluttering. Yesenia wore a fuchsia scarf that matched the fuchsia tips of her hair.

Nataly was stunned.

"You'll visit," Yesenia said, tugging at her arm and giving her a hug. "Look, nothing's happening here for us. And you can expect more of the same. This is a window of opportunity, a limited time offer. Come with me, *chamaca*. None of us, Nataly, are going to be young artists forever."

Later Nataly said to her mother, "Can you imagine? Basically she's telling me I'm going nowhere. I don't even know if I want to see her again."

"Can I visit you in New York?" her mother said.

Eric kept asking her out, and Dr. Roeg had not been into the restaurant in what seemed like weeks and weeks. Probably on a luxury cruise with his wife and kids. Probably staying at the Ritz in Paris or London or river rafting the Amazon. *Probably not thinking about me at all. At all, at all.*

Her therapist said, "You realize you're being neurotic."

Nataly said, "Of course I realize I'm being neurotic! That's why I'm here with you!"

The Thursday after Yesenia's going away party, where Nataly had made the mistake of bringing home an overly-impressed-with-himself musician, Nataly stepped down from the bar with her tray of sidecars, seabreezes and Belvedere vodkas and almost missed a step. She recovered swiftly, held onto the tray tight and passed Dr. Roeg at Table 12. She smiled in his direction, but his eyes were closed, and he was rubbing his forehead.

She set the cocktails down in front of the four middle-aged businessmen. Nataly had figured out long ago how to identify an alcoholic: he checked out the size of his drink before he sized up her breasts. This party was evenly split.

She passed the doctor, smiled and said, "I'll bring that vodka gimlet right out." He nodded and said, "Make it a double."

As she placed the order at the bar, Eric murmured in her ear, "I see your boyfriend's back."

Nataly smiled, hoping for enigmatic.

Eric said, "I figured out why some women don't like nice, simple guys."

Some women meaning me. Nice, simple guys meaning you."

Eric nodded. "They don't want nice, simple. They want exciting, complicated."

"Imagine that."

"Their loss," he said, with no smile on his face.

Nataly thought Eric looked quite handsome at that moment, with his stubby pony tail and that wisp of wistfulness on his face. Was he really that interested?

"You know, Eric, if I had your inflated ego, there'd be a waiting list a mile long for my art work."

He smiled. "You haven't seen the best part of me inflated."

"Thank you. You forget that I did. And I almost liked you there for a minute." Nataly set the doctor's drink on her tray and stepped down to the restaurant.

"Hello, stranger," she said. "Ready to order?"

There he was, those perfectly broad shoulders, the clean manicured hands, the hair spiking upwards. But he didn't look the same, not really. The creases across his forehead seemed deeper. His eyes appeared weary. And something else. He looked so piercingly at her that Nataly glanced down at the tablecloth.

He cocked his head and said, "Did you miss me?"

Nataly glanced back into those eyes and found herself unable to speak, the way he looked at her. What color were they? Gray. Green. The color of sex, colored by loss.

He cleared his throat. "Yes. Well. I'm not in a hurry tonight. Let me think about it."

Nataly nodded, walked away, a kind of furious activity going on deep in her rib cage—hidden, she hoped, from everyone else.

It turned into a busy and lucrative shift. Nataly didn't have time to personally deliver his salmon caviar on blinis drenched with clarified butter and a dollop of crème fraiche. Or his dover sole. After the rush had subsided, she was able to make her way to his table to see if he wanted dessert.

"How about a decaf espresso?"

Nataly noticed that he nursed the espresso for half an hour. She set down his credit card and lingered as he tabulated and signed his receipt.

He reached inside his wallet, pulled out a business card and scribbled something down. "If you ever want to talk," he said. "Just talk."

Later that night Nataly again inspected the small, beige business card, cut on heavy stock.

DR. PETER ROEG

CHILDREN'S HOSPITAL LOS ANGELES

PEDIATRIC ONCOLOGIST

His office number was listed, as well as a pager number. On the back he had written a third number and under it *private*. She set the business card on her night stand next to her phone.

That seemed like too much of an invitation so she slipped it in her night stand drawer. She pulled it out to investigate his handwriting. Eleven numbers and one word. She decided she couldn't tell much. She decided not to think about that gold band on his hand, which actually told her everything.

Jolene, that was the name of the waitress, Nataly recalled. Blonde, with thick eyelashes, heavy mascara and hot pink lipstick. It wasn't just the way she touched him, but the way her father looked at Jolene. What did you do with that awful knowledge?

She certainly didn't tell her mother.

Nataly went into her work room. She had been pleased with her model and was now making progress on her piece. Working on her loom, she got into a rhythm with the heddle and shuttle and fell to thinking of her father, always full of surprises. During the divorce, Nataly had pitied her father. It had been easy to do. The bluster of his well-tailored suits, the sheen of their fabric, never masked the doleful eyes he had when he spoke of Mercy. He was turning into a pathetic figure, and her mother remained beautiful. Once he had been gold, and her mother had been silver. Before Jolene. During the divorce he was a smoldering brown.

The divorce had proceeded without outward bitterness or acrimony. When Nataly talked to Celeste, Celeste was so cold, blaming their father for mismanagement, possibly malfeasance, practically accusing him of being a criminal! Then blaming their mother for being blind. When Nataly spoke to Sylvia, she, pregnant with Miriam at the time, was appalled that her mother had joined two dating services. All of the daughters had penciled the date the divorce was to be finalized into their agendas. *Two against one,* Nataly thought. *Two for their mother, one for their father.*

The surprise came on the day her parents' divorce was finalized. That day Nataly had picked up a bottle of champagne and driven from Pasadena to their old home, now her mother's alone, in Orange. She didn't want her mother to be alone and depressed in that huge and empty house which had been remodeled while she lived there—five bedrooms, three baths, one inhabitant. She didn't want her father to be alone either, but figured he was with one of those women of his. The glimpses she had caught told her they were of a type: white, lean, hungry. What a crock of shit marriage was if you could live together for thirty years and never know each other. Unless, of course, her mother did know her father and accepted him anyway. And what did that unpleasant information tell her about her mother?

She gnawed on this during the forty-five minute drive south on the 5, the ugliest highway in southern California. Past the dying factories, the industrial areas zoned for smog, noise and waste.

What did that tell her about her mother? Nataly was nauseated. It was a combination of the drive, the diesel fumes, the traffic and the thought that her mother was a willing participant in this marriage now dead. She put her hand on the bottle of champagne. It was warming up in the sunlight coming in the front window. She moved it into the back seat under a serape while she kept her eye on the road.

Nataly parked in the driveway. Her 1967 VW bug dripped oil and grease. Her mother would just have to deal with it. She should just sell the damn house anyway. Hadn't Celeste told them all that already? To cover all the debt her father had run up.

Nataly rang the doorbell. Her mother didn't answer. Maybe she had gotten caught in the afternoon traffic. She let herself in, stepped into the entry, punched in the security code. The house felt still, cold and clammy without her mother in it. Nataly put the champagne into the refrigerator, one of those high-end, oversized glossy models that her mother would have to sell with the house. Nataly stepped over to the phone to check for messages when she heard footsteps overhead.

"Mom?" Nataly hung up the phone and went upstairs. "Hey,

Mom, I rang the bell but you must have been in the bath—" Nataly stopped. It was not her mother upstairs. It was her dad. His hair dark and thick, his unlined face smooth and guileless. Strong chin, jaw, the same brown skin tone as her own. He was wearing a very expensive suit with a tailored shirt. Why was he dressed like that in her mother's bedroom? Something was very wrong. The hair on the back of her neck stood up. Her lower intestines started gurgling.

"Sweetheart," he said in that soothing maitre d' voice, the voice he had used in restaurants for decades. "I didn't know you'd be here. I was waiting for your mother."

He's stalking her! Nataly thought. She still wasn't able to say anything, but found herself backing her way downstairs. She could smell the alcohol. She wondered if it were possible that bottles were still hidden around the house. His right hand was clenched around something. *Oh my God, it's got to be a weapon.*

He staggered down the steps towards her. He said, "I was in La Verne, thinking about your mother, thinking of our lives together." She continued back down the steps. "She doesn't know what she means to me," he said.

Nataly stood in the entryway by the front door. Her father fell onto a sofa in the living room. He put his feet on the coffee table.

"Get me a drink, sweetheart, would you? It's up in our room. Your mother's room. It was always her room even when I lived here." She exhaled. He wasn't here to stalk her mother. He was here to cry and wail and gnash his teeth.

She went upstairs and found the bedroom as neat and tidy as her mother would normally leave it. But it smelled of him. On the dresser was a bottle of vodka and glass filled with melting ice. She grabbed it all and was about to head back downstairs when something caught her eye.

Nataly sucked her breath in quick, then stepped into the bathroom. On the counter were ten empty pill bottles. One was aspirin. Nataly knew you could overdose on aspirin alone, and that it was slow and painful. She leaned closer. The first container label read Prozac, the second Valium. She stared in the mirror at the store brand bottle of vodka that she held and put it down.

She walked over to the phone in the bedroom and dialed 911. As she waited on the line, Nataly told herself she would not scream. She would not cry. She would get help. She would get help for her father. She heard him call up to her. "Do you remember when I drove the Mustang?"

Nataly gave the dispatch her name and the house's phone number. She held on. She would not scream. The dispatch came back on the line and told her paramedics were on their way. She walked downstairs. There he lay, looking up at her as if she were a marvel.

"Do you remember all those Sunday brunches? You, your sisters, your mom coming after church. Every one of you, so different, so beautiful."

"Dad, it'll be okay. You're gonna be okay. I promise." *Please God, agree.*

"You know, it's a beautiful life. I was happy the way this house was, but your mother wanted more. I was happy in our first home, where you three were so tiny, so sweet. She's a hard woman, Nataly. Nothing was ever enough, ever. And then she turned you all against me. Where's that drink?"

The room swirled black, gray and brown around her. Nataly promised herself she'd scream at the hospital after he was checked in. Not now. Her father closed his eyes and lay still. Christ, was he dead? Was she going to watch him die?

"Daddy?" she said.

He opened his eyes, focused them on her, then continued, "I love your mother. I thought she was gonna be here. What are you doing here? But I don't regret anything. I'm just sorry she had to take it out on me the way she does—sounds like someone's in trouble."

The piercing screams of the ambulance announced that it had pulled up in front of her mother's house. Nataly opened the door to two men in uniform and pointed at her father. The taller man asked her father questions. The third paramedic, a small Asian woman, pulled Nataly aside and said, "What do you think he took?" Nataly led the woman upstairs and pointed at the empty bottles.

"Did he tell you he took these?"

Nataly shook her head. She sped downstairs and watched the paramedics strap her father into the stretcher.

"Tell your mother she's the only woman I ever loved."

Nataly sat up front with the driver while the other three rode in the back with her father.

"Nice place," the driver said. Nataly caught the appraising glance from behind his wire-framed glasses.

"That your husband back there?" he said. Nataly shook her head.

"Real nice area." The driver swung onto the highway towards the hospital. "Boyfriend?" *I will scream,* Nataly thought.

The ambulance pulled up to the emergency entrance of Hogue Hospital. The noise of four people jerking open doors and shuttling her father from car to doorways jarred Nataly. She trailed the gurney, spoke to an abrupt and cross nurse while she checked her father in. He disappeared into the hospital.

Nataly found a bathroom and wept. She scooped water from the sink faucet and washed her face. Outside of the hospital, the air was clammy, misty, scented with salt. Nataly felt like she was encased in gray rust. *So here we are,* she thought. I have no idea where my mother is. And my father just washed down a shitload of pills with half a bottle of vodka.

People die everyday, she told herself. They die in car accidents, of long illnesses, at the hands of someone else. They die in their sleep. They die surrounded by their loved ones. They die alone. Oh God, was her father dying in there?

After twenty minutes alone, she realized she needed to find a phone. First she checked her messages. There was her mother's voice, bright and cheerful, "Nat, I'm going to be late getting home. A couple of women at work just, you know, Lynn and some others, well they insisted on taking me out for a drink, in celebration. I'll be home about an hour late. Bye!"

Then another message. "Nat, this is your mother. I'm home."

Then another message, "It's your mom. Call me."

Nataly punched in her phone card number. Her mother picked up after half a ring. "I'm at Hogue with Dad. We were at your house. He tried to kill himself." Nataly said this with as little emotion as possible. And then, since her mother didn't quite grasp what had happened, she repeated herself. "I'm at Hogue. With Dad. He tried to kill himself." Silence.

"Sweet Jesus," her mother said, followed by a sob. "I'll be there in fifteen minutes."

Nataly punched in Sylvia's number. As she was leaving a message on the answering machine, Sylvia picked up. "What?!" Sylvia demanded. "What?!"

"Dad tried to kill himself."

Sylvia said, "Why?"

"Their divorce was finalized today?"

"Is he going to be all right? Is he going to be okay?"

"I don't know. They didn't say anything to me. Can you…can you call Celeste? I don't think I'm up to it."

Nataly waited at the emergency entrance. She sat down, closed her eyes and was flooded with gray. A wall of gray nausea slammed into her so hard, she opened her eyes. A halo of maroon approached her. It was her mother.

At nine o'clock, the emergency doctor attempted to take Mercy aside, but Nataly refused to budge.

"He's going to spend the night here, recovering. Worst-case scenario, there may be possible long-term liver damage."

"He's not going to die," Mercy said, clutching Nataly.

"No, ma'am," the doctor replied.

"Thankgodthankgodthankgod," Mercy murmured to Nataly.

Nataly stood in the hallway corridor while her mother went into her father's room. Nataly peered in. There was her father, looking at her mother, looking like he really did love her. She waited a moment. Mud. That room, her father, were the color of mud, not gold, and her mother still shimmered silver. Did her mother still love him? It appeared she did, and it was a mass of tangled knots and threads within her, a malevolent tumor growing within. She stepped inside the room, patted her dad's arm and said, "I'm glad you're going to be all right."

Nataly and Mercy waited for Celeste and Sylvia in the hospital cafeteria. The empty chrome counters gleamed, the display cases shone light. There were vending machines for coffee, soda, candy, chips, wrapped sandwiches. Nataly could see that her mother had been especially beautiful for today, her hair and nails recently done. She still wore the makeup she had put on this morning. Nataly picked up her mother's hand and held it between her own.

"Your father," Mercy said, little tears slipping from the corner of her eyes, "is full of surprises. Always has been." Then she shook her head of wavy hair sideways, wiped at her eyes and nose with a cafeteria napkin and looked back at Nataly. Hazel eyes, golden brown and green. "Thirty years of marriage," her mother said. "This is shit."

Nataly saw Sylvia out of the corner of her eye. It was hard to miss her. Somehow this pregnancy inflated her twice as much as other women. After her marriage, Sylvia had been flush with smiles and kindness. Now, even before tonight, she just seemed sad. *Why get married? Why have children?* Nataly thought. *Why willingly walk straight into misery?* Marriage and motherhood were two languages Nataly was never going to learn how to speak.

Celeste strode in right behind Sylvia. A surge of sadness and anger swept through Nataly. The Celeste she loved had moved to Humboldt with Michael and never returned. This Celeste was all adult and professional sheen. She emanated metal gray, steel, no nonsense. Compassionless. Her hair was pulled back taut, her face looked intelligent, elegant and her clothes probably cost more than Nataly's rent.

The Amado women, gold, steel and earth. What was she, then?

Sylvia and Celeste had been up to visit their father. Now all four women sat in the hospital cafeteria, nursing bitter black coffee, looking at each other, and looking away.

Sylvia stirred her coffee. "I'm really sorry, Mom."

Mercy shook her head. "We all are."

Sylvia continued. " How hard it must be for you, how hard it must have been to start the whole process."

Their mother shook her head. "After a certain point, it wasn't hard at all. But this?"

Celeste said, "A blatant, manipulative ploy for sympathy." A small tremor shook the women.

"Just shut up!" Nataly said. "Who do you think you are? Like your life is so terrific? Like you're the only one to make the right choices? You come breezing in here when it's convenient to you, flaunting your wraps and your coats and your bags and your wallet."

"Stop. We're just upset, we're all upset right now," Sylvia said.

Nataly ignored her. "You don't live here, Celeste. You don't talk to Dad, you barely talk to Mom, you have no right."

Celeste gave a bitter laugh. "You don't know that. You don't know anything. And I'm not going to explain or justify my choices to you."

"Who in the hell do you think you are? You already ran away from us, once, twice. You have no patience for all of our messes. Fuck you, Celeste," Nataly said and stormed out of the cafeteria.

Nataly stomped her way back toward her father's room and stood in the corridor. *Celeste had moved so far away so long ago. If Celeste had loved any of them at all she never would have left. She would have found a way to make it work and she would have stayed…*

At eleven the next morning, Nataly went into her father's hospital room. The brown sheen on his face had turned slick green. He had a look of relief on his face when he saw her.

"Is your mother coming?" he asked.

Nataly shook her head. "She's at work. They told me as soon as the doctor makes his rounds and gives you the high sign, you can check out. They told me you're not fit to drive, so I'll drive you home."

"To your mother's?" he asked.

"No, Dad, your apartment."

Edgar looked up at the ceiling and lay quietly. Nataly sat down and flipped through the *National Enquirer*. An actress she admired was a recovering alcoholic. Edgar flipped on the overhead TV.

When he was ready, Nataly pulled her car up to the entrance. She watched her father struggle to right himself in the passenger seat, then fumble around for the seat belt.

They drove along in silence before she flipped on the radio and punched different stations until she was satisfied. Bono of U2 sang something profound and deeply felt. Probably because his soul was profound and deeply felt. She glanced at her father, his face slack, eyes closed. Nataly glanced at herself in the rearview mirror. *Shit.* She looked just like him, the deep set, soulful eyes. Eyes that cajoled, persuaded, betrayed. She looked tired, the highlights in her hair were fading and incipient wrinkles were forming in the corners of her eyes.

Nataly, who had never been to her father's apartment before, had to check her *Thomas Guide* a few times rather than interrupt her father's snoozing. He still smelled of the hospital, something sour dipped in antiseptic. Forty minutes later they arrived in Azusa.

Nataly helped him out of the car. At first he refused her help, wouldn't lean on her, but when he lost his balance pulling himself out of the car, he changed his mind. "Just a little bit farther," Nataly said.

It was a one-room studio with a sink, refrigerator, small stove. There were candy wrappers, fast food wrappers, empty bags of chips scattered about. The unmade bed took up most of the floor space. A tiny TV set stood on a makeshift nightstand of a cardboard box. How had he come to this? She closed her eyes. *I will not feel sorry for him. I will not feel sorry for him. I will not.* She pitied him despite herself.

The two of them shuffled into the small room, and Edgar collapsed onto the bed. He said nothing at all.

"So," Nataly attempted, "You have to go to therapy or something?"

He nodded his head. "Something like that."

"Interesting place here," she said.

"It's all your mother left me."

"Mom did all this, huh?"

"Don't kick a man when he's down," he said.

"I just don't understand," she said. "You want me to get you anything before I go? I can run out to..." She looked around and spotted the wrapper, "Del Taco?"

"No, thanks," he grimaced.

Nataly stood at the edge of the miniature sink. It was hurting her to look at him. A better woman than she, a better daughter than she, would be the one to make this mess all better. Could snap her fingers and the memories of all his affairs would evaporate and fill the bank accounts with all the money he had spent. All his put downs and insults would be smoothed away.

But this was the best she could do. "All right, then" she said. "I'll be seeing you." She stepped over the scattered papers, leaned down, patted him on the shoulder and pecked him on the cheek. His skin was sweaty. "Love ya, Dad. Please, please take care of yourself. Please. And call me if you need something or want to talk about anything."

"Sure" he said. "Don't worry about me. Just know, you've all been such a disappointment to me. Especially you, Nataly."

When she remembered that moment, nearly a decade ago, sitting there in her workroom, Nataly's fingers froze at her loom.

May means Open House at Santa Ana Unified. Mercy and her best friend Lynn were eating lunch after the early dismissal. That morning, Mercy's students had cleaned out their desks, scrubbed the tops with 409, swept the floor and thrown out trash. This year, as she did every year, Mercy offered premiums for students whose families came with their kids—bonus points, homework passes, a class party. Now she had a minute to relax with Lynn before going home herself to rest, shower and arrive tonight in time to greet the families.

On the walls were the autobiographies her sixth grade students had written, the math quizzes they had taken, the science posters they had worked on in small groups. On one wall, Mercy's wall, was the Poem of the Week followed by the prompts that never changed, What is the author trying to say? What images does the author use to support this? Why do you agree or disagree? Her authors were Edna St. Vincent Millay, William Carlos Williams, Octavio Paz.

This week it was Langston Hughes' "Mother to Son." Life hadn't been gleaming chrome and crystal for that narrator—her students would understand.

Near this was a laminated fluorescent poster that Nataly had redone for her. *Opportunity favors the prepared mind.* —René Descartes. Nataly had decorated the poster with soaring planes, a podium, a stage and a cap and gown. In another, Walt Disney spoke about accomplishing your dreams. A plain posterboard proclaimed, *El respeto al derecho ajeno es la paz.* —Benito Juarez. *Respecting the rights of others is peace.* What a revolution it would truly be if the world listened to that humble man.

Some days these posters cheered her, prompted her forward, other times they mocked her as a hypocrite. Today she peered at the posters, turned to Lynn and said, "Swear to God, one year I'm gonna put up, *Might makes right* and *Money talks and bullshit walks.*"

Lynn laughed and nodded. As Mercy wiped her hands on a napkin, she saw that Susana and Olga were tapping at the door, sure that there was something they could help with in the classroom. If just a few of her students grew up to be teachers, Mercy counted herself a success. As she opened her arms to hug the two girls, she wondered how it was that Sylvia, her own daughter, never got the hang of this? Inside a classroom you belonged to your students. You could earn reverence and adoration. You were somebody.

"Girls, go home. Go on. We're all ready for tonight." The girls argued, smiling, wanting to be welcomed in, but left after another hug.

As far as she was concerned, only death would stop her from teaching.

Mercy sat back next to Lynn, "Did I ever tell you how I got into teaching?" Lynn shook her head.

Mercy said, "From a bad babysitter to a teacher. Sometimes I can't believe it."

It was Christmastime. Nataly was four. She carried a tattered knit dolly with her everywhere. Mercy's mother had given it to Nataly when she was an infant, and it had been slobbered on, drooled on and puked on. Then Mercy would wash it and, over the years, repair it. Stitches taken up and rewoven in, hidden threads tightening together gaps. The doll had cross stitches for eyes and nose. The mouth gave the dolly a look of constant surprise. Mrs. Fuerte had knit the doll a red cape to go with the red apron, but the cape had disappeared underfoot years ago.

Celeste was an all-knowing and skeptical twelve-year-old who attended Bible classes and enrichment for gifted kids after school on alternate days. She would not discuss Santa Claus with Sylvia or Nataly.

Sylvia was in fourth grade and had her heart set on the solo part in the school program. She admitted to her mother that she kept hoping the soloist, Alma—her best friend—would die. Or at least get really, really sick.

"For me, it was *el tiempo fregado*, the fucked-up time of the year."

Lynn clucked her tongue in recognition.

"Where we lived then was probably our worst home together. Edgar's parents owned this two-bedroom in Compton. When the previous tenants were evicted, leaving it decorated with insect carcasses and rat poop, his parents had offered it to us. The only reason I agreed was because it had a yard. A yard for Celeste and a yard for Sylvia to scramble around in, to use their hula hoops and cap guns and wading pool. So Edgar and I scrubbed the floors and the walls, ripped out the carpeting, painted the two tiny bedrooms, mowed the lawn, hacked at the overgrown shrubs. I still remember the curtains I sewed, very sixties, astrological signs in vibrant colors."

It was their labor that paid for everything. And finally, when the stench of the previous tenants had evaporated or was obliterated by bleach and Pine Sol, Mercy decided it was time to move in. She began taking in infants and toddlers during the day to make money.

There were vicious dogs across the street. They kept Mercy up until three in the morning. No. She was lying. Waiting for Edgar until three in the morning kept her up. And then he slept through the breakfast, the babies having been deposited, his own children sent off to school, and Nataly hanging onto her little dolly.

On their right were tall highschool boys, getting older every year, whose music and clothing and eyes frightened Mercy. To the left was a woman who looked even older than Mercy's mother. Was that humanly possible? Her house was shrouded in vines and shrubbery. Mercy visited her once. Her house stank of cats and spilled wine.

She found things to be grateful for. Tony at the corner store who gave them credit. Edgar's parents, far in Arizona, even though they kept a running record, wouldn't ever evict them, no matter how many jobs Edgar decided were unsuitable for his many talents.

"I saved every bit of money I could, hiding it in a coffee can I was sure Edgar didn't know about. Then there were two coffee cans. Then three. Four." Four coffee cans filled with coins and worn bills. Even now she could feel the sting of not being able to open a bank account without her husband's signature. And the hot shame and anger at what followed.

"This was my world: my daughters, the two small bedrooms, the yard, the babies who got older and then were replaced by new babies. Collecting bottles and exchanging them for the deposits. My daughters' school. Nataly. Nataly coloring and coloring and coloring, but never reading or listening to the stories I read to the babies. Between Edgar's jobs, my babysitting paid for the ground beef, the utilities, the fabric I stitched into clothing for the girls.

"I got this idea that one day we would own a house. I wasn't babysitting for the experience of changing diapers or inviting strangers into my home. Our home, the one I was saving for, would have four bedrooms. Four bedrooms! And closets. And two bathrooms. And it would be in a neighborhood where at last I could let my daughters wander next door or across the street and even into other people's houses.

"When Edgar was out of work, a new coffee can would take forever to fill." That fateful Christmas, Edgar had slept late, ironed a pair of slacks and shirt and taken their car.

"Remember their Christmas program is tonight," she called after him.

"What time?"

Mercy subtracted an hour. "Six o'clock. If you're back by five, we can have dinner together, then drive to the school."

Edgar nodded, kissed Mercy on the mouth, and left.

In between feeding and changing the babies and entertaining Nataly, Mercy stitched golden yellow rickrack onto the sleeves and hem of Celeste's angel costume. The teacher had sent home a halo, so that was taken care of. The rickrack, which should have taken ten minutes, ended up taking an hour because one of the babies needed soothing and the other needed to be played with. The thread on the bobbin broke three times. Mercy had to rewind the whole damn thing. She finished sewing the costume, pressed it, then hung it off of Celeste's bunk.

"So that afternoon I went to put the fifteen dollars a client had given me in the coffee tin which I kept hidden high up in my closet, next to the others, away from the kids, away from Edgar. I had taken enough out for the Christmas gifts and for the tree. The money that was left would be for our house."

Mercy looked at Lynn. "Of course it was gone. All of it. Every can was empty. Not a goddamn bill or penny. I sat down on our bed and cried. Nataly toddled over and patted me on my back, exactly the way I patted the babies' backs. All the cans had been nearly full."

Edgar had told her he was working.

Nataly had said, "Mommy not cry, mommy not cry."

It was her own goddamned fault for keeping the money in the house. She heard Sylvia and Celeste come in through the front door so she locked herself in the bathroom, ran the water—resented the rust streaks around the fixtures and down the sink—flushed the toilet and stepped out to greet her daughters. All that money.

By five-thirty her girls were fed. All that babysitting.

"Do you think he even showed up for the program? Of course not. And he had taken the car, so we walked."

By six o'clock, Celeste paraded out in her costume, Sylvia wore a bright red sweater her grandmother had knit for her, and Nataly was dressed in a crushed velvet jumper that Mercy had sewn for Celeste. Mercy wore a shimmering gray suit she had sewn five years ago, new hose and elegant black high heels. Then she put on her makeup. All that money.

At six-thirty, the four of them set off for Franklin Elementary School. Mercy kept thinking about the empty coffee cans.

Nataly despised strollers, wanted to walk with her sisters. But after a block, she was too tired so she wanted Celeste to carry her. Celeste clutched her for five and half blocks, then handed her off to Mercy.

By the time they reached the school, Mercy's feet ached and there was a run in her hose.

But the auditorium! It was packed with the mothers Mercy occasionally saw and waved to. And with fathers, infants on laps and in strollers, in the aisle, gray-haired grandmas and grandpas looking crisp and smelling of mothballs. Everyone was chattering with anticipation, noise to the ceiling, from which hung red and green and gold garlands. There were silver garlands draped from the edge of the stage and wrapped around the podium on the left.

Mercy wished her mother were here to see this.

Sylvia and Celeste had seen their friends, squealed, then run off.

Mercy smiled tentatively at no one in particular, picked her way through the aisle, looking for a single seat.

An older gentleman with graying blond hair cut into a crew cut looked at Mercy, eyes widened, looked again, then stood and offered his seat.

"Thank you," she murmured, setting Nataly firmly on her lap.

"I regret I have but one seat to offer you," he smiled, then moved to the side of the auditorium and leaned against the wall. Mercy felt his gaze and ignored it.

"Besides my daughters, besides losing all that money to Edgar who was probably using it in a bar, I'm sure, I never asked, what was the point..."

When the audience had reached a high pitch of impatience and anticipation, the principal stepped up to the podium and cleared his throat. Mercy held Nataly tight on her lap as the immaculately groomed black man of an indeterminate age cleared his throat and greeted the audience.

"Thank you, parents, teachers, and friends, for bringing all the joy of the season here to this auditorium. As our small charges tie laces, tuck shirts in and tune up, I want to welcome you and thank you for being an important part of who we are."

Mercy was distracted by her daughter and the decorations as the principal spoke about school business and PTA business. She thought about Edgar, with a slow burning deep within her chest. The principal's tone changed, and Mercy looked back up at the stage.

"Tonight is perhaps the one night I will see many of your faces," he said, gently, but sternly. "We all know our schools face challenges, some from within, some from without. I can sense love and goodwill within this room. I know the passion of parents. Will you bring that passion with you throughout the rest of the year that follows?" He looked across the audience, and Mercy was momentarily convinced that he was staring right at her. She could say she was doing the best she could. But she had a withering sense of disappointment—this best of hers was not enough. It could never be enough.

"Come be a greater part of Franklin Elementary. Come work in our classrooms. Come be a teaching assistant. We need you."

That burning inside of Mercy lit like kindling, and a flame grew. A teaching assistant? A teacher's assistant?

Then Mercy lost herself within the earnest faces of the pageant, the smiles of her daughters, the look of anxiety on Sylvia's face and the sweet guileless expression of Celeste's, made more vivid by the garland halo above her.

Edgar arrived in time to drive them all home. Mercy had three girls circling her—Sylvia wanted to know if Mercy could hear her sing during the chorus, Celeste wanted to know if the halo was on right.

"Can I be an angel too?" Nataly asked Celeste. Celeste removed her halo and adjusted it so Nataly could wear it home.

The three girls chattered in the back seat while Edgar and Mercy said nothing to each other. Mercy could smell the alcohol on his breath. *The first one to speak loses,* she thought. She was always the first one to speak. But it didn't matter. Because tomorrow, while Edgar slept, she was going to drive her daughters and the babies to Franklin, and apply for that job.

At home Mercy put three very excited little girls to bed. Except Celeste was not so little any more, and Sylvia was charging up right behind. Nataly remained her baby, and at four still slept in the oversized crib they had bought new for her.

Mercy reached into the crib to remove the halo from Nataly's head, but she cried so loud Mercy was afraid the girls would never get to sleep, so she relented, removed her makeup in the bathroom, went to her room to change into her pajamas.

Edgar lay asleep on the bed.

She adjusted the polyester nightie around herself, pulled on the blankets. Her mind was racing. She would pay someone to watch Nataly. Or simply enroll her in preschool, just like she did with Celeste and Sylvia. Despite both her mother's and mother-in-law's needling, her oldest girls had thrived at preschool and taught Nataly the songs and games they learned. Yes, they might even have the money for that.

"So this is what I thought that night, Lynn. I thought, I will not sleep through my life. I am going to live it awake. I don't care how much it hurts. And it hurt.

"I became a teacher's assistant and couldn't believe they paid me for doing it. An older teacher told me how to get my AA at Compton Community College, a professor at the college showed me how to get a credential. Looking back it seems like magic. Looking back, I can almost forget how much it cost me."

A month after his suicide attempt, Nataly met her father for lunch. All his maitre d' elegance had evaporated. Instead of sleekly brushed, the hair on his head was untidy, like a rumpled bed. He was slouched in the booth when she walked up to him, staring at the odd pattern on the table. He wore a brown polyester shirt with lapels that were too wide, his mustache betrayed seeds of gray. It needed a trim. His eyes were bloodshot. The only trace of the father she had loved was his skin, the color of a single-malt scotch.

"Seedy really doesn't suit you," she said, sitting down across from him.

"I just thought you might know how she's doing."

"You could call her and ask her yourself," Nataly answered. "So, since you've managed to skim so much money, is this lunch on you or on me?"

"Money?" He used the word as if it were something exceedingly abstract and incomprehensible. "I don't know what you're talking about."

"Right. Well, that impacts my dining choices here." Nataly ordered the grilled cheese with fries. Cheapest thing on the menu. It would get her through her six-hour afternoon life drawing class.

So how much is Mel claiming you stole from him these days?" Nataly asked when her sandwich was placed in front of her. Her father sipped at his coffee, pouring crinkly packets of artificial sweetener into it. He had been gaining weight, she noticed.

"Now I know why there are anti-Semites in this world," he said, nodding his head sadly. "The way I figure it, he's pouring onto my head all of his problems with the IRS. He's out to make Edgar Amado his scapegoat."

Nataly nodded her head. Denial as coping mechanism. It had been able to carry her father throughout his entire life. Always thought he was brown because he drank chocolate milk. Always thought he was better than the dumbass busboys or waiters or anybody who had walked across the border because he could speak English without an accent. But it hurt even Nataly's ears when he rattled off his pathetic Spanglish.

Out the window was a gritty street scene. City traffic, signals, an occasional pedestrian. Unrepaired potholes, banners of graffiti decorating the street corner. Pretty wasn't in this part of the country. Gentrification, reurbanization were fads for other parts of the world. That's why her rent was so cheap, that's why she could eat lunch out.

It occurred to her that she and her father fit right in. The thought made her feel nauseated and colored the restaurant a sickly yellow green. If she looked too long at her father, his outline began to blur, turn brown, then gray, then black. She always knew where he'd been in their house, leaving bleak traces of himself behind. Dirty dishes, food wrappers, vodka bottles. She was beginning to suspect that there was a shadow of him within her. *Son of a bitch.*

"So, does your lawyer think you'll go to prison?" Nataly took a ferocious bite out of her sandwich. She made herself eat. She'd be miserable the rest of the day without food, and this was her only opportunity. If the question made him squirm, it wasn't apparent to Nataly. He hadn't answered it, just flagged the waitress down for more coffee.

"Prison's for street kids, gang members," her father answered. "You know, it would look a lot better if your mother was there in court. Every day during the trial. Remember DeLorean and his beautiful wife? Everyone said that her just being there impressed the jury." He sipped his coffee. "Nobody needs to know we're divorced."

"You mean, besides the fact that you embezzled funds from Mel, ran up thousands of dollars on your cards—"

"He claims I stole money. I didn't steal anything. As far as credit cards, your mother never understood how much the remodeling was gonna cost us—"

"I don't know, Dad, maybe you got a chance there. You'd have to ask her yourself."

Edgar smeared his hamburger bun with mustard and mayonnaise. "That's why we're having lunch, Nat, that's why I'm askin' you. You're the one who can get through to her. She won't listen to me, she'll think I'm lying to her—"

"Funny that she would think that," Nataly said. She poured a pool of ketchup on her plate. She wished she could dunk her father's head in it. "Wake up, Dad, you fucked up big time."

"Watch your language, I'm still your father."

"Yeah, that's right, you are. And that's something I have to live with. I don't suppose you can divorce your father, can you?"

Her father looked away. "You hurt me, Nataly, you really hurt me."

There was a pain under her rib cage. She had meant to hurt him. Unfortunately it seemed to rebound within her. The pain in her stomach and heart seemed to pulse gray and green and yellow. *Goddammit!*

He continued, "I thought if there was anyone who might understand, who might still be willing to meet me halfway—." He looked at her, eyes red and watery, "You know I always loved you most."

Jesus Christ, anything but that.

"I don't know what you want me to say to that."

Her father winced. "I see."

The only sound from their table was her father's chomping. *Nothing made him lose his appetite*, thought Nataly. She pushed more fries into the ketchup and made herself eat them. She hated waste. Wasted food, wasted money, wasted talent, wasted lives. The pulsing colors and pain within her were making her ill. The image of her father seated across from her, the view of the urban blight from her seat, was all making her sick.

Her father wiped his mouth and crumpled his napkin onto his plate. "Well, I gotta go. If you hear anything about your mom, you know, if she's gonna change her mind and stand beside me on the off chance there is a trial, give the old man a call, will ya? You got any money on you?"

She handed him a ten-dollar bill. Nataly saw he knew better than to offer a peck on the cheek. Instead he squeezed her arm and headed towards the register.

Nataly pulled a few dollar bills out of her pocket to leave for the waitress. She watched her father stop, making small talk with her until both of them were laughing. Then they glanced in her direction. Nataly took the bills off of the table and shoved them back in her pocket.

She concentrated on those colors within, soothed them, smoothed them down and tried not to think of her father who acted as if nothing had to do with him. *But the worst thing*, thought Nataly, *was that if he had done all these rotten, grubby crimes, why did she feel like hell inside?*

Stupid to be thinking about this at four in the morning. Nataly had nipped at alcohol, but still she was awake. She had warmed milk in the microwave, stirred in a teaspoon of sugar, sprinkled cinnamon on it like her grandmother used to make it, but still it didn't work. So she kneeled in her second bedroom, removing the scrap of material that had failed her and threaded the warp again.

What if this were all meaningless? No, no, no, why not simply accept that it *was* all meaningless? Self-doubt at three in the morning was an excruciating way to spend a night. Her fingers kept screwing up the tension of the yarn. When that happened, she'd try to go back to bed and rest against the overstuffed pillows and the smooth sheets. Tonight the sheets were burning.

She wouldn't tabulate the number of men she had slept with, but she did like to think about them, at least the few that she enjoyed summoning. She loved rough-edged boys with that wild, unpredictable energy. Like Bernard, who was doing very well out of his loft in New York. She could probably stay there with Yesenia if she asked in a nasty enough way. Then he'd laugh, tell her about the past three girls he'd slept with, and take them out to the best place in the city for breakfast.

She had learned quite a bit about people as she waited tables over the years. She couldn't count how many times she had been asked, "Where are you from?' or, "Where were you born?" or, "Where did your parents come from?" At first, at the coffee shop, she was offended. Hadn't these people ever seen a tanned brunette before?

"My people, are a people of the dessert," she would say, smiling and handing them a dessert menu. But some people insisted.

"No, no really. Are you Serbian?" Or Italian. Or Iranian. Or Hawaiian. Pakistani? Polynesian?

"My grandparents came from Mexico a long time ago."

She kept a pleasant expression on her face as her interrogator's mouth dropped, and he or she said, "Mexican?" or, "But you don't look Mexican" or, "Which side?" or, "Spanish, right?" or —Nataly's personal favorite—"Are you sure?"

Not much you can say to that and still expect a tip and a job at the end of the day.

One evening while she was working the bar at the steak house, a man with dark hair that hit his shoulders, skin the color of pale ale and wide Asian eyes, asked if she were Filipino. Nataly felt the bristling starting up inside and tried to smooth it away, but her voice betrayed it. "No," she said flatly. "Are you?"

"I'm just plain old Mexican," he said, his eyes cast down.

"Me too," she said, smiling, this time meaning it. Not Cuban, not Spanish, not Filipino. Just plain old Mexican.

What would she do with Peter Roeg? He was now Peter to her, Peter with the planes of his face slightly scuffed by worry and experience. How would his face feel next to hers? She must have fallen asleep. Next thing she knew it was nine a.m. Wednesday morning. She dug his card out of her nightstand drawer. She dialed his number. She had had his card for almost a week.

She hung up before it rang. She went into the kitchen, got a glass of water, turned on her TV set, turned off her TV set, wandered into her art room, wandered out, picked up his business card, picked up her phone, dialed his number, cleared her throat and let it ring.

"Dr. Roeg."

Nataly said, "So, how are you? And, how long is this heat going to last?"

"Ah, yes, that's the question of the moment, isn't it, Nataly?"

She sighed inwardly. He knew her voice.

"I mean, I was just wondering if you had any thoughts on it," she said, staring at her unmade bed. What had she wanted him to say to that? What a stupid thing to say. Why was she on the phone? She should just hang up now before she made a further idiot of herself.

"Actually," he said, "it's a bit inconvenient to discuss it now."

There you go, you idiot. You've fallen from the waiting-table goddess to a table scrap of inconvenience. He interrupted her train of thought. "What if we discussed it over dinner tonight? Seven-thirty?"

"Hold on, let me check my calendar." Nataly put the phone down. She wandered out of her bedroom with its florid orange walls into the living room with its pastel yellows. From the living room window, she could see the trailing vines she hung from the balcony. A neighbor across the courtyard was leaving for work, dressed in her scrubs. Nataly stepped back into her bedroom. What was she doing?

"I'm busy till about eight," Nataly said, that wild thumping in her chest starting up again. "Where should I meet you?"

"Why don't I pick you up?" Peter said.

After Nataly gave him her address and telephone number, she hung up the phone and fell back onto her bed. This was not a good thing. However, if you looked at it from a completely different angle, squinted your eyes, made sure the scene was back lit, this could be a perfectly innocent dinner. Perfectly innocent.

Nataly went into her art room and cut sheets of newspapers into long strips and divided a trail of strips into groups of four. She wove these four strands of strips into a long braid.

Some people smoked, some people drank, some people ate chocolate. Nataly made braids. It kept her fingers busy and her brain empty.

At five o'clock. Nataly realized that she had no idea where they were going out to dinner. He seemed like the swank type, but it would be a bit obvious to make that assumption. She gnawed at her lip and cast clothes onto her silk comforter, onto the bed that she had just gotten around to making.

Jeans? Black leather? Mini-skirt? Heels? She finally decided on a black lace sweater she had trimmed in glittering blue thread and beads. She rummaged through her underwear drawer for the perfect pair, then wriggled into her sleekest jeans and placed the ankle boots at the ready. She wriggled out of everything and took a long, steaming shower.

This doesn't have to be a sexual thing, she said to herself in the shower. This could be a—meeting of minds. Purely intellectual. A lower voice running through her head said, "You chose tonight's underwear on a purely intellectual basis?"

Seven-thirty came. Then eight.

Nataly hadn't eaten anything, but at eight-fifteen she made a mini-quesadilla. Depending on where the restaurant was, it could be forever.

At eight-thirty, he rapped on the locked screen door. Nataly leapt up from the deep sofa, wobbled on her ankle boots and opened the door to reveal Peter.

Look at that face, Nataly thought. Iconic.

Peter smiled at her through the screen door. It was a wide and friendly smile that softened the creases on his forehead. To Nataly, he looked young and wise, with a capacity for foolishness. He wore a lavender polo shirt under a light summer sports coat.

He said, "Are you still talking to me? Look, I feel terrible about running so late."

Nataly unlocked the screen door and grabbed her bag, "Where to?" she asked.

He said, "Do you mind if I step in for a minute and catch my breath? Three miles of solid traffic."

She stepped back as he walked in and sank down into her sofa. "Could I trouble you for a drink of water?"

Nataly walked into her tiny kitchen, opened two or three

cupboards before finding a clean water tumbler. She chose one, blew into it, hoped he hadn't noticed, then filled it with tap water.

She set the glass down on the coffee table in front of him and sat as far into the opposite corner as possible.

He drank the glass down in a gulp or two.

"All right. Thanks. I think we're ready," he smiled at Nataly. He stood, offered her his hand and pulled him up to her. It was a strange sensation, being helped out of one's own couch, but Nataly had little time to reflect on that. She felt his warm hands on the sides of her face, pulling her towards him, and his lips on hers. They were the most marvelous lips that had ever pressed against her own. Just as she realized what was going on and began to respond, he pushed her back and said, "I've been wanting to do that for such a long time." Then he pulled her back towards him.

When he touched her, her body shivered. Every nerve ending was alive. The room shimmered gold. Out of the corner of her eye, she watched the beaded fringe of her sweater sparkle and dance as it sailed overhead and fell to the floor. Then she closed her eyes to better feel the cascading red that exploded from deep within her. And then watched as the red scattered into a shower of purple shards.

Oh my god, she thought, *was it because she had been so long without a real man or was it simply him?* And then he began with her again.

Afterward, afterward, afterward, when particular parts of her body were sore and tender and satiated, when he was clutching both her breasts yet breathing deeply, she sighed. There he was, in her bed, at her side. His hands had been on her face, on her body, and hers on his. What longing. What longing. Then there was his body, from the light covering of hair on his arms, to the thicker layer on his chest, to the toned chest and back muscles. Everything about him was magnificent. Then he murmured in her ear, softly, in a way that thrilled her senses, "How's this? Or this?" Then light kisses down her neck and onto the nether regions.

Wasn't that what all art was about? Wasn't it, she thought. As she tied and knotted and created, wasn't that all in the hopes of creating something similar to what transpired here in her bed?

Maybe not all art then. Maybe just her art.

He emanated cool, hip, edgy. She could introduce him to every single one of her friends. and they'd be forced to admire him. From his air of control and command, to his intelligence and wit. He'd never embarrass her at a vernissage. She winced. He might even upstage her.

It had been better than her fantasies. How many things could she say that about? She peered at him, face slack from sleep, black gray gristle sprouting at his cheek. She delicately removed one hand, then the other. The gold band glinted in the room's light. That gold band.

Nataly had already decided what that meant. It meant that Peter was hers—and hers alone. She wouldn't be able to introduce him to her family, running their gauntlet of approval or disapproval. She wouldn't have to drag him to familial celebrations. He might even turn out to be a reprieve from some of those.

He was hers and hers alone. He stirred long enough to roll over and clutch a pillow tightly. Nataly hobbled off to her bathroom, her body aching.

Those muscles must have atrophied from lack of use, she thought. She caught herself in the mirror, makeup smeared, one earring missing. She washed up, pulled her hair back. Then the phone rang. And rang. Nataly sprinted out of the bathroom as the phone blared in her bedroom. Peter had pulled a pillow over his head and contracted his body into the bed.

"Hello?"

"I was wondering if you'd seen your mother lately." Christ, of course it was her father. "How's she doing?"

"Hey. Hey, Dad. After midnight is so not a good time for me. It makes me think somebody's dead. Let's talk tomorrow." Leave it to her father to insert himself into her magical evening. Just add this incident to a long list of others. She shook her head and started back to the bathroom when Peter's hand slipped out of the covers, grabbed her hand and pulled her towards him.

"If you don't want him to call after midnight, stop taking his calls," Peter said. "Always works for me." He started at the side of her neck again, while stroking her breast, then reaching downwards.

"You're telling me something I should know?"

"Yeah, Nataly. You're incredible. You know that you are. Amazing."

Then the world, her father, her sisters, her pathetic job and his wedding band melted away for the third time that night. He left at two in the morning, after kissing her hard on the mouth.

"I'll see you tonight," he murmured.

Nataly lay in bed, listened to his footsteps as he walked out of her apartment, listened to the door shut, then the screen door fall back.

She was starving! No, she was incredible, amazing. She smiled at the thought. She put on her flannel robe, walked into the kitchen, started a kettle for tea, then swiftly scrambled three eggs. As she heated a flour tortilla over the gas flame, she laughed. They didn't even make it to a restaurant. He had had other things on his mind. And so had she.

Another voice within her said, *God, that was a cheap date.* She set the slightly charred tortilla onto a plate. She scraped the eggs out of the skillet and onto the flour tortilla. She opened a bottle of green tomatillo sauce and poured it onto her eggs, then added dollops of sour cream, sprinkled it all with salt. She was ravenous and this burrito was too hot to eat. Had he eaten before he got here? What did he mean, see you tonight?

The tea kettle hissed. Nataly poured hot water into a mug, set a teabag of Prince of Wales tea to steep and ate half of her burrito. She removed the tea bag, added milk and sugar, waited for the tea to cool, then sipped at it while she finished eating.

Today was Thursday, she realized. She'd see him tonight at Rimsky's. She felt like buying him something. Something he could look at and remember her by.

But as she thought about it she realized that she really didn't know anything about him, other than that he loved sex as much as she did. Right before she fell into a deep satisfied sleep, she realized that she had been right about the underwear.

A Saturday morning in August. Celeste woke up early. It was misty outside and she couldn't remember if it was winter or summer or if Christmas had passed or was coming soon. She had a sense that time was slipping around, and she was on the wrong side of it.

She ground her coffee beans, put them in the gold filter, added a pinch of cinnamon like her grandmother sometimes had, set the timer. Too bad she couldn't open a bottle of wine to shake away the dread she felt wrapped in.

Another birthday.

She slipped into her gym clothes, tied on her shoes and jogged for forty minutes. Twenty less than her usual route, but, hey, it was her birthday.

When she got home, she smelled the brewing coffee, scented with cinnamon. She showered. Decided on the casual pant suit she had just picked up at J.Jill, comfortable, but nice enough to maintain her image in front of Victor. Coffee. Makeup. She refilled her coffee mug and dashed out. It was funny, she never saw this guy on the weekends.

At the restaurant, something small, but cozy and plush that Victor had found and where they occasionally met for breakfast or lunch, they chatted about the overlap of their clients. He looked so unfamiliar this morning in his navy blue sweatshirt and worn jeans. Suddenly vulnerable—this serious lawyer who made men worth millions shudder.

"You must be proud of your daughter," she said, as he finished recounting his daughter's success at Boalt.

"It's an adventure. And, the honest to God truth is I can't take the credit. You know my hours."

"And your divorce rate," Celeste smiled.

"Her mother made sure it happened. You should try it sometime."

Celeste shook her head. "I told you before, I'm never going to have kids."

"I hear about you. I hear you're at the high schools, talking to girls about controlling their money. That's nice."

Celeste squirmed.

Victor sighed. "You've made your decision. I'm not gonna try and talk you out of it. You of all people should know the trajectories that we plan for ourselves, well, sometimes they kinda get derailed. Happy birthday." Victor finished up his Belgian waffle, then, with a sparkle in his eye, gave her a small blue box. Tiffany's.

"What is this?" Celeste said, smiling. "A gift?"

A shrug.

"Can I open it now?" She felt like she was ten years old. She felt giddy and lighthearted.

Inside, two X-shaped slivers of sliver with small diamonds in each corner.

"This is too much, Victor, too sweet."

Victor looked at her, then out the window. "Will you keep them?" he said.

"No. You know I can't."

"You're my friend, Celeste. If I can love a girl I'm never gonna kiss, you're the girl. I just want you to think of me fondly."

"I do. I already do think of you fondly."

"Then keep them."

She squeezed his hand, a fat-fingered hand that had never known manual labor. Then she put the earrings on. And she didn't dare stand up and lean over to kiss him on the cheek, because something she didn't want to happen, might.

Back home, it was still too early to drink. Instead, she chatted

·with her mother on the phone, not telling her about the earrings, not wanting to give her that to cling to. Or to parry her questions about it for the next few months. But, as she listened to her mother talk about her students, Celeste thought about Victor.

Why couldn't she just decide to be with him? Wouldn't that make things so much simpler? She wondered if she'd hear from Nataly. Hell, she hadn't called Nataly on her birthday last April, just sent off a fancy boxed gift of papayas. A corporate gift. Which should have arrived trimmed with gold for what it had cost her. Nataly had sent her a terse thank you note months later.

After she hung up with her mother, she put on a Judy Collins CD in commemoration of a life she no longer led.

Once Celeste had recovered from the shock of being married, from the jolting direction her life had taken, she realized it was a beautiful summer. For a long time afterwards, its sweetness had been difficult to endure. There had been no warning shots.

On the drive up the coast, the blazing silver and orange U-Haul trailer behind them, they listened to Michael's tapes of Bob Dylan, Johnny Cash, Leonard Cohen, bluegrass, and Celeste's Beatles, Joni Mitchell and Judy Collins tapes. Mainstream radio played disco, edgy stations played the Ramones and Talking Heads, but Michael and Celeste were in their own musical universe.

They argued, then settled, then argued again about the pending baby's name. They schemed five, ten, fifteen, then—*brave souls*, Celeste thought—twenty years into the future. It had made Celeste cold to think how old she'd be, but warm to think of Michael even older. Always. She smiled.

"Kiss me," she said.

It was an eight-hour car ride up the coast. They had purposely decided to drive past the craggy cliffs, the trees deformed by wind, the brilliant gleam of the sea instead of zipping past the inland oceans of pesticide-laden fields. Every time Celeste passed such a field, she squirmed inwardly: there but for the grace of God went— her entire family.

Near Morro Bay, they pitched a tent at a state park between families beginning their summer vacations. This was Celeste's first time camping. The wind whipped at her ears till they ached. She blinked her eyes against the scuttling sand and bit her lips, praying that the sun would soon set.

And when it did, Michael turned to her and crooned Bob Dylan.

With just a sheet of thin nylon between them and the rest of the wild world—the sound of strangers, the babble of children's voices, their arguments and music—Celeste and Michael made love on two sleeping bags. The wind and the sand and the stars all conspired to force Michael even deeper into Celeste, and she groaned with pain with pleasure with love with lust with despair, she squirmed and ached and loved him. And she wouldn't ever let him stop, ever let him go, ever forsake him.

The next morning Michael pumped at the gas camp stove, lit it, filled a saucepan with water and heated it up. He pulled a cast iron skillet out of the cardboard box he had packed, retrieved the bacon out of the ice chest and laid the strips on the skillet.

"Got to make sure you'll be willin' to do this again, you know."

She wore his windbreaker to watch and admire him, then gave up and wrapped the sleeping bag around herself as she shuddered near the stove.

One hundred yards away, waves hit the shore and gulls circled while the heavy clouds bred a mist that kept everything damp and cold.

"Good morning, husband," she said, kissing him on the mouth.

They arrived in Trinidad late that night, after eleven. It was exactly as they had left it late April when they had found it, put a deposit down, and begged the freckled fifty-year-old landlady not to charge them till June. She ended up charging them half of May.

Celeste stood in the shower and rinsed all the sand and grit from her skin and skull. Oh, her back ached from the hard tent floor the night before, her nipples ached from Michael and her pregnancy. She walked sideways, like a monkey. But when she was clean and toweled, she lay naked against the cold clean sheets and waited for her lover who was now her husband.

She couldn't remember at that instant for the life of her why she hadn't wanted to get married, why she hadn't wanted to be pregnant, why she hadn't wanted the baby at all.

It was a long, lazy summer. She used the money she had saved for college to help with the rent. She didn't bother looking for a job since the baby would be coming soon. But she did start the paperwork for California State Humboldt. Not exactly the same ring as Reed College.

But honorable, she told herself. There was no shame in it.

She applied for a Cal grant, for an Educational Equal Opportunity Grant, for anything she could scavenge up. They would need another car by January when she planned on attending college at least part time. Maybe even full time if she could swing enough night classes.

Michael sometimes drove off in the station wagon to Portland or Seattle. The window still needed to be replaced. It was summer, it could wait. She didn't want to go, but he didn't exactly ever invite her either. When he performed in Trinidad she sat at the back, never at the front. It was too overwhelming. She watched as he chatted up the audience, strummed at the guitar, sang, and balanced it all even as he accompanied himself on the harmonica.

She wasn't going to be jealous of his music, of his travels, not yet, she decided. They were grownups. She was going to revel in this opportunity called solitude.

On the weekends when Michael was away, Celeste walked along a public pathway that lined the coast of Trinidad. She practiced making soup. She visited a knitting shop, where the owner was friendly and curious. She splurged on wool for her baby and old used books for herself.

Then she'd hurry back to their apartment, burrow into her room. While Michael was away, it was her very own room.

Her mother visited, then left. Celeste mourned in anticipation the arrival of the baby which would banish her solitude and quiet moments. She'd probably dig up a group for new mothers. She'd learn the second language of diapers and nursing and baby food and other things new mothers talk about. She would wait and see.

Years back, when her mother started community college, it had been she, Celeste, who had made sure Nataly got to school, did her homework, ate. Sylvia could always take care of herself, but it was Nataly, with the high forehead and prominent front teeth, who needed cajoling. She could do this. She'd done some of it before.

Then the Puritan within her said, *Life is not an endless summer.* It couldn't be. Not for anyone, not for you. Later, she thought, you are allotted only one summer like that per lifetime.

If the beauty of Trinidad had been spectacular in the summer, with its low clouds skimming the coastline, seals in the distance, jutting rock and swooping gulls, it was thrilling in the fall. Celeste loved the smell of wet foliage, damp earth, misty air and the chill that enveloped her. She loved this excuse to stay in bed, now nearly due, loved the reason for steaming hot soups. She refined her dough-kneading technique, had hours to let it rise, come back again, punch it down, knead it again.

College would have been quite different from this, she thought, not knowing exactly how outside of what she'd seen in the movies. Michael cancelled all performances that required him to travel out of town the month of September. She read baby books. She knit. She crocheted. She distilled all of the hours she had spent with her mother and her grandmother into small, neat booties, bonnets and soft, pastel-hued baby blankets. Her mother came up again and clucked in disapproval over the baby room, which made Celeste laugh.

"Mom, this baby won't have to wait until it's thirteen, like me, to have a room of its own."

"But why does Michael have to store his music junk in there?"

"You know, Mom, you might just have to cut your trip up here short. I think Nataly and Sylvia and Dad miss you desperately. Yeah, I feel it in my bones. You know, this mother's intuition business, it's contagious." Celeste smiled.

Her mother stopped needling her and stayed another two nights. After Mercy left, Celeste read more baby books. She knit. She crocheted. She got bored. Her body was unbearable and she could no longer stand Michael's touch.

But the night before she went into labor, she started to sob and let him pull her close, his arms around her, the huge bulge of the soon-to-be baby between them.

"What's wrong?" he said, stroking the small of her back and the side of her face. "What is it?"

"I'm afraid, I'm afraid, I'm afraid," she sobbed. "I feel like I'm going to die. This isn't what I planned."

"Baby," he said, pulling her close and whispering softly in her ear. "Only a fool wouldn't be afraid. You're not a fool. But we're going to have a wonderful baby. You're going to be a wonderful mother."

When Celeste went into labor and entered the hospital, she had some sense of what it would be like—she'd read a lot of books. She felt calm. Michael had laughed at her thoughts of mortality and her fears had evaporated.

They were going for a natural labor. Michael stated this to every nurse, doctor or technician who entered the room.

It was obscene how often she was checked there between her legs. By the admitting nurse, the room nurse, her doctor, the attendant, all with a natural wish to know how far she had dilated. But still, it was obscene. Michael hovered. Taking a break from proclaiming the room a drug-free environment, he smiled like an idiot, and then scowled as Celeste groaned with the labor pains.

She remembered his face, the sheen of concern on his cheek, a sense of excitement. He wanted that baby.

Her water broke. Now the contractions began in earnest and while Michael urged her to go natural, that she could do it, Celeste screamed at him. The pain was intense, horrible, torturous.

For an hour she was in a pit of physical misery, grimacing, moaning—

Then something went wrong.

The instruments that monitored her were indecipherable to Celeste, but she heard a whoosh and saw the cloths being tented over her belly, saw, rather than felt the IV swirling in the room, the needle jammed into the back of her hand. She watched as Michael was moved out of the room, and that was when she felt the panic. She heard a clatter of instruments, of metal hitting metal. She waited, the panic building. She waited, seeing nothing, hearing a dull roar in her ears. She waited, while something deeply important to her took place where she couldn't see.

And then. The doctor was talking to her, but all she could hear was the clatter of instruments. The doctor looked at her with concern.

"I'm sorry, Celeste." she said. "This was a still birth."

This was a still birth. What did that mean? What had she read? What happened? Celeste took a deep breath. "Is it a boy or is it a girl?"

They were all looking at her. How many people were in that room? Michael wasn't. "A girl."

"Let me see her," she said. What had happened to her daughter? The baby was blue, covered with the slick sheen of birth. The baby's hands were tiny tight fists, the face a blue pucker of lips. No air, no milk for those lips. Her eyes were closed. Couldn't see her mother that way. She reached for the baby and lay the tiny body on her chest.

"She can't see me." Celeste touched those tiny, tiny finger tips. "She can't see me, but she will be with me." She stroked the slick hair on the baby's head. She thought of the name Skye. That's what she would call her, so she could always look up and see her. "Hello, Skye," she said.

Later, Michael held her hand as they both wept, facing away from each other. The doctor had said the baby had strangled on its own umbilical cord. In her heart, Celeste felt sure that she had done this. She had killed the baby she had never really wanted .

Skye Amado Niedorf.

I t had been months since the worst day of her life and months since Celeste had confirmed that the money was gone. And still she had done nothing about it. Sylvia lay in bed staring at the ceiling. She had kept her promise to Tamara—Tamara, who knew what to do in any situation. Tamara who knew Sylvia's secret and loved her anyway. Tamara who kept her secret and yet wouldn't pressure her to move forward, to file for the divorce. For months, shame had kept her from telling her best friend about the money.

You had to parcel out your secrets, you couldn't trust any single person with the entire, authentic you. That was far too risky. But that moment with Becky, everything between her and Jack had vomited out. Today she would tell Tamara she was ready, ready, ready to push for a divorce. Celeste would put her financial house in order. She and the girls would thrive, instead of merely survive.

Sylvia packed the pool bag with a towel for herself, her cover up, two identical white-and-pink striped towels, and two identical San Diego Zoo t-shirts. It had taken Sylvia quite a while to catch on. If she bought two cans of Play Doh and gave blue to Miriam and red to Becky, they cried as if they had just undergone some psychic trauma. Each girl pined for the other color with a passion verging on hysteria. They whined about injustice and frustration until they realized the elegant solution was right in front of them. They traded.

It had taken Sylvia ages to figure this out. Now she just bought two of everything. In her mind, two different items expanded the girls' possessions and two identical items limited it. But it also limited the bickering.

She started packing a lunch for the pool club. Now there was a battle she *had* won. When Jack had shown her the plans for a pool in their back yard—complete with sauna, whirlpool, cascading fountains, lush tropical landscaping, all for a beginning price of sixty thousand dollars—she fought him, hard. Thinking about it now, months later, she figured there must have been a reason he let her win.

Jack was out of town again, leaving Sunday night, back in New York for just a few days. It made no sense to Sylvia that he had to travel over a three-day weekend, but she didn't need to argue about it. Big company acquisition. Big company bullshit. According to Jack they were flooded with cash. According to Jack, he was shoveling it into the bank.

Not according to Celeste.

Sylvia went upstairs to wake the girls. They were spending Labor Day together at the pool, it would be crowded with other families, the girls would splash and Sylvia would be with Tamara.

A lovely day ahead.

Miriam's room was tidy, organized, with no sign of the eight-year-old who lived there. Becky's room was chaos, with her tiny body still under the blankets. Sylvia sat on Becky's bed. Becky opened her eyes, saw her mother, stretched her arms out and wrapped them around Sylvia, hugging her close. Sylvia wished she could keep that feeling with her always, that feeling of being needed and adored. So easy to make her smile.

When Becky let her go, Sylvia asked, "Ready for breakfast?"

Becky smiled and nodded, then winced.

"Something wrong?"

Becky shook her head, closed her eyes and pulled the blankets up.

Downstairs in the kitchen, pouring the milk over the cereal, Sylvia knew it was time. Time to say goodbye to the overwrought kitchen countertops, the hideous landscaping, the furniture Jack insisted on picking out and buying.

Could she do it?

Miriam was in the family room watching morning cartoons. How fierce and proud Miriam was of everything she did. Miriam, soon to be a third grader, had been setting her own alarm for a year. Every night before bed, she planned and laid out her clothes for the next day. In the morning, she spent twenty minutes on grooming, made and ate her own breakfast and kissed her mother good bye—all before the car pool arrived. She informed her mother that she no longer needed to be tucked in. But Sylvia continued to sneak in at night anyway, watching her daughter read or study or draw or sleep. As much as she impressed Sylvia, she also inspired a smattering of fear and dread. Miriam reported any misstep or mishap to Jack at length.

Because who had the power? Jack did. And Miriam wanted to be on the winning side. Through Jack's eyes, she and Becky were weak losers. She had to change the way Miriam saw her.

And when people asked why, when her friends, their friends, her family asked why, what would she say?

There was nothing she could say that wouldn't make her look *como una tonta*. Like an idiot, a stupid victim. Because *eso no le pasa a todos*. This didn't happen to everyone, the implication being it was her fault. They would all think that. Even her family. Especially her family.

Sylvia shook her head. How would it look? God, how would it look? What the hell would she do? What did she think she could do?

How easy Becky was, compared with Miriam's constant struggling. Becky could never, for the life of her, keep her drawers organized. The T-shirts were with the underwear, the socks mixed with the shorts, pajamas mingled with her sweats, and all of this was scattered between six separate drawers. *She's only six, for God's sake,* her mother's voice whispered.

But it irritated Jack. Thank God he'd been traveling so much. No time when he got home to make a bedroom inspection. Miriam always won anyway—and beamed and boasted in a way that made Sylvia uncomfortable. Not only were Miriam's drawers perfectly neat, separated into their appropriate categories, but they were also color-coordinated. After these inspections there was no question which little girl Jack loved better, and that always made Sylvia's heart pang.

Sometimes she felt like God gave her more than she could endure. But he also seemed to have snuck in an escape pod. *Adios, Jack. I don't need your money to leave you.* She'd make those calls. What was she waiting for? It was time to start the upheaval of a divorce. Far past time.

Miriam sat at the kitchen table with the paper open to the comics and a bowl of cereal. "Mom?"

"What?"

"When can we get a dog?"

"Your father's allergic to dogs. Where's your sister? Why didn't she come down?" Sylvia asked. Miriam shrugged.

Sylvia walked upstairs and found Becky huddled back in a ball. "Come on, baby, we're going to the pool today." But the ball under the blanket didn't move.

Sylvia tugged on the bedding, but instead of Becky's blissful face fringed with lashes, there was her baby, scrunched up tight.

"What's wrong?"

Becky said, "My back hurts."

Sylvia panicked for an instant, but reminded herself that Becky wept over paper cuts. "Come on, I've got a great day planned." Sylvia picked her up to cradle her, but Becky winced at her touch and tears streaked down the sides of her face. Like Becky was holding it in, trying to be brave.

"What's up, baby?" Sylvia said. "What's wrong?"

"Dad says it's all in my mind."

That stupid fuck. "Let's see what's wrong," Sylvia said scooping Becky up, feeling the slickness of her pajamas, the tenseness of her body. She called the doctor.

Two hours later, after watching nearly all of *Toy Story 2*, a nurse called out *Rebecca Levine* into the waiting room, and Sylvia carried Becky into the office.

"We'll be back in a minute," she said to Miriam, patting her on the head. Miriam ignored her and continued to read her book of fantasy, four inches thick.

A diminutive Filipino nurse weighed Becky. Sylvia carried Becky to a small room where she helped Becky take off her clothes and change into a drab and faded hospital smock, then lay her on her side on the examination table. She stroked her daughter's hair.

"Mom?"

"Yes, baby?"

"Don't do that."

Sylvia stopped, stood up, and wandered around the room.

Their regular pediatrician, Dr. Ariz, was on vacation. Sylvia read the newspaper postings about childhood obesity, the risks of second-hand smoke and a diabetes f.a.q. sheet three or four times. She read and reread them while Becky squirmed and fussed on the table. *Becky was going to die, wasn't she? Becky had bone cancer that had eaten into her spine, and Becky was going to die.* While Sylvia plotted divorce, the cancer cells had spread and poisoned her daughter.

A rap on the door, a whoosh of air and in stalked a tall stern young man. He greeted Sylvia and then leaned over Becky. Becky was now sobbing.

"Why's she crying? What's going on?" he said.

Becky immediately stopped crying, rolled onto her back and opened her eyes.

"What did you eat for breakfast?" he asked.

"Nothing," Becky snuffled.

"Does it hurt here? Here? Or here?" His tone was skeptical and mildly menacing.

Becky shook her head no matter where he pointed.

The pale young doctor cleared his throat. "I honestly believe she just needs to eat more. She's underweight. There's nothing to worry about here."

The stranger left before she could think of an articulate question. Becky lay hunched over, still in her smock. Sylvia smoothed the hair on Becky's head and whispered, "Why didn't you tell him where it hurts?"

"I didn't want him to be angry with me," she said.

Sylvia walked up to the nurse, the one who had just weighed Becky. "I need to see another doctor."

"I'm sorry, ma'am, but—"

"I need to see another doctor. I will sit here until I do. Or I will sit in the lobby yelling and screaming and crying until you find someone."

Thirty minutes later, a Dr. Kaplan moved Becky's legs and arms, listened to her chest, prodded her lower back, depressed her flat tummy.

"We need a couple of blood tests," Dr. Kaplan said.

Sylvia watched Becky flinch as the technician drew blood. Sylvia saw that Becky was trying not to cry.

Instead of going to the pool that afternoon, they got ice cream. At home Sylvia called Tamara and told her about her long, confusing day.

"What do they need blood tests for?" Tamara asked.

"I have no idea," Sylvia said. She told Tamara she was going to move on the divorce today, this very day, and now it was the weekend.

"It's okay. You need to concentrate on Becky right now. It's all right. Do it on Monday. Let me know if I can do anything."

"You've done enough." Sylvia breathed in. "I can't ask for more."

"Yes, you can," Tamara said, gently. "Any time."

Nataly plucked her eyebrows. She liked them short but not too narrow. She liked the way a well-plucked brow made your face clean and neat. She was never going to be Frida Kahlo. Nataly snipped and thought about Peter. It was good she didn't know too much about him. (Besides that wedding band—and really, she'd prefer not to think about it now, thank you very much.)

After Celeste's thing—that's what they called it—*Celeste's thing*, but no one said that to her—after that thing, Nataly decided she would never, ever have sex.

That didn't quite work out. As soon as she could, she got a prescription for birth control pills. A friend of hers hadn't because she said she didn't want to gain the ten pounds everyone told you you would gain. After three months of using a diaphragm, that friend got pregnant. So much for diaphragms!

One thing Nataly was sure of was that there was no way in hell she was going to be ensnared by the material trappings of men. Look at where Sylvia had ended up—Sylvia and Sylvia's friends—with their heavy engagement rings and their diamond studs, their oversized cars and their oversized homes.

Not this woman, Nataly said. And they were all so fucking impressed with themselves. Those women married men who after a few years turned flushed and florid, men who had figured out young that what they really wanted to do was to make a lot of money and have the accessories that went with it. And so they did. Men who spent their money in appalling ways. Everything they owned gleamed, while none of it—in Nataly's eyes—had any character, any soul, any scratch or sign of meaning.

You're just jealous, said the voice. Jealous of their money and their clubs they don't invite you to. *Fuck their clubs,* Nataly thought. And their money. So uninteresting, in and of itself. Strange to have two sisters so consumed by money. So strange. Their mother had never been like that.

Nataly had already removed the mini tapestry and begun the full-blown picture. She knew what she wanted now, she had the emotion behind it, she had the colors, the image exploding in her mind. And the way she would drape it, once done, the physical shape it would take. All there.

As she raised the heddle and passed the shuttle, she didn't think of Peter. She concentrated on the work in front of her and of the image she carried in her mind.

Her home phone rang, but Nataly ignored it. Then her cell began: "Did you want to do a show together or not?" Yesenia said, in that scolding voice of hers.

"Yesenia! What? What did I do?"

"Where's your portfolio? You think I can string the owner along forever? He's got to figure out the calendar, the dates, the spaces. Are you smoking crack, girl?"

Fuck. Being with Peter had pushed it right out of her brain. "I can get it together. I can send you everything, soon."

Just do it. Hell, hand carry it. He'll take one look at you and sign you on. Why do I have to beg you to be the artist you are? What are you waiting for?"

While Yesenia spoke, Nataly watched the motes of dust sparkle in her living room. Then she said, "You know, I have something I'm going to bring out there. It's just going to take time. I'm looking at hundreds of hours on this one. It's something, it's the next step." The loom she'd leave here. LA was where she lived, was where Peter lived.

"Don't wait to come out here, Nataly. Don't put it off another month, another week, another minute. Shit, then I need to get off the phone and let you get back to work. But not yet. Who is it?"

"Who's what?"

"Who's keeping you tied to LA?" Then Yesenia laughed. "Like I don't know! I can't leave you alone without you getting yourself into trouble. Bad Nataly. Bad, bad, bad Nataly. Are you having fun?"

Nataly sank into her sofa. "More than you know."

"I'm not sure I like that heartfelt sigh. Don't let him distract you from your main purpose in life! But on the other hand, he's older, right? It'll definitely help you work through those father issues."

"I don't have any father issues." The glittering dust went dull. It felt as if Yesenia had dragged a knife through her tapestry.

"Yeah, and I'm Paris Hilton. Hey, did I tell you that I saw her at a club last week?"

Nataly recovered enough to say, "You and Paris Hilton in the same room does not compute."

"Yeah, I know. And she looked at me like I should be bussing the tables. Bitch!"

"I do not have father issues," Nataly said again.

"Look, don't let him keep you there. You really, really need to be out here. I mean it."

"I'll get it together," she said.

The first week of school, Mercy and Lynn started talking about today's young mothers.

Mercy declared there was too much freedom today. When she was a girl, it was very simple: only tramps slept with men before they were married. The risk of pregnancy made the stakes so much higher. Hence, she had been a tramp.

As her children grew, Mercy had met quite a few women who had also lied to their children about the date of their marriage. That had been a revelation. It's so easy to think you're the only fool in the world.

Not that Mercy ever seriously thought too much about anyone else. There was too much work to be done. Children to be raised, bills to be paid, money to be saved. And then, that miraculous item that had cost Mercy *gritos y lagrimas*—a college degree and a teaching credential.

Edgar had kept himself quite busy too. Between the woman at work, skimming that money and laughing at how seriously Mercy took her classes, her job, he had been quite occupied. Mercy had not known about the money, but had known about the woman, had endured it, while he laughed at everything she attempted, not realizing he had been responsible for what she'd become. Now here she was.

What had he really wanted on the day their divorce was recorded and he made what might have been a final gesture? Pity?

He hadn't wanted her. That had been clear their last years together.

Lots of time and a little bit of youth left. Just a little drop.

Should she thank God for the last layer of beauty he had left her? Was it a blessing? Or was it a curse? Was he punishing her for her pride in her appearance, for her vanity? Was he taunting her with it, allowing it to attract the slightly demented? She thought too much about God's motivations. She decided to concentrate on her own.

How do you sort through all your options? Too many men. All she really wanted was just one. She hadn't met him yet. Neither had her daughters, for that matter.

Really, she had to stop worrying about her girls. They were all grown now. They were fine. Or, as far as she could tell, they were fine. They didn't need their mother weighing in or meddling. Fact of the matter was, once they hit high school they didn't seem to need their mother at all. Oh, for those sweetest moments when they loved her best of all, when they needed her more than anything to make their world just right.

That time had ended. *They have their lives, and I have mine, right?* Time to focus on my own life now, that strange life free of children and husband. What was the word? *Pamper.* Yes, I need to *pamper* myself.

Stop worrying about the rest of them. That was the American way. They have their lives, I have mine.

Mercy's sister Lydia lived in Fresno. Close enough to visit, to share holidays and birthday celebrations. But, of course, they never did. Mercy had tried when the girls were young, when the girls were growing, but now she and her sister never, ever spoke. When she watched the similar decay between Nataly and Celeste, it was too painful. To have everything—*everything*— and not recognize it. Wasn't that the way with all of them?

She had thought her daughters would remain hers forever, would need her always, would adore her when they were adults just like they had as small intense children. Celeste, tall and thin and so funny until she lost the baby. Sylvia, a smile for everything, for everyone, lighting everyone's heart. Nataly, with those clear eyes and vision for everyone but herself.

At work, she told anyone who would listen how successful Celeste's business was and namedropped a couple of those Northern California celebrities who were part of Celeste's client list. Her entire grade level had celebrated Nataly's first showing. And to anyone within earshot, Mercy would recount the misadventures of her grandchildren. She might as well get some credit for doing things right, occasionally. Mercy sighed. Sylvia still hadn't called her back. Nataly had cancelled their coffee this weekend. Celeste lived so far away.

But that's what they were supposed to do, right? Grow up, grow wings, and explore.

She got dressed and headed out the door. She had decided to check out the synagogue up the street. Maybe she'd change her luck. Find out if there were any singles mixers. A bit old for Parent without Partners. How about Grandparents Without Wrinkles?

By early September, Nataly had spent two months with Peter, months that sparkled gold and white with an undertone of elemental darkness. At work she found herself shuddering with memory and desire. If she had ever known, she had forgotten what it meant to ache in this way. She reveled in the parts of her body that ached—from previous disuse or from current overuse—gentle, intense, agonizing lovemaking.

The summer had turned out to be very full. When she wasn't sighing in bed with Peter or earning her rent at Rimsky's, she was exploring textile tension in her second bedroom/art studio, and dreaming about this piece she was working on, her breakthrough piece. She would escort it off to Yesenia in New York. Then return, gloriously triumphant, to be with Peter.

"What's gotten into you?" Eric kept saying, looking her up and down.

She burned all over. She'd go into work with her finger tips and toes tingling, almost fifteen minutes late because he wouldn't let her go, even though she would wait on him later in the evening.

She loved having him in her station, solitary, nursing his drink and occasionally catching her eye. Their private joke. Oh my God, his body was as handsome as his face, something rough hewn about it, rugged, and knowing—*oh my god*—so knowing. There would be no one for her after him. This she knew.

She noticed that he never removed his ring. Nor did he speak of his wife, although at times Nataly listened as he spoke to his wife. From his side of the conversation, filled with rapidfire medical jargon, statements bordering on brusque and confrontational, Nataly inferred that Peter's wife was a doctor too, working in his field, but with a conflicting perspective.

He was perfect in all ways. In all ways, except this, where it mattered.

For obvious reasons they rarely went out. First off, he seemed to know people everywhere, but circles removed from Nataly, circles filled with money and endowments and benefactors, the kind of people who ate frequently in those trendy restaurants of Pasadena or the West Side. So the two of them never ate out.

She worked in her art room and called out to him, "Why don't we ever go to Pink's or Phillippe's? I bet no one would ever recognize you there." Nataly stood and walked into her room. He was sitting on her bed, tapping at his Blackberry. "Have you ever been to Casa del Sol on Olvera street? The best carnitas and champurrado. Or we could go to Guelaguetza and have the molé my mother never made. We could go to the beach. The movies."

He raised his gaze from his PDA to her. Gray and green in his eyes. He put his gadget down and said, "Come here." She went.

He held her close, kissing her neck. "If that's what you want, we can do that. I just thought this is what you wanted."

Yes, yes, yes, this was what she wanted.

She really couldn't bring him to the parties she attended. She wasn't allowed to introduce him as her angel or investor. On the nights they didn't spend together, Nataly either worked at Rimsky's or worked at home. She seemed to be using a lot of purple and red these days. Shimmering red yarn, sparkling purple thread, bordered with an earthy physical brown.

She made the best of their time spent indoors. She didn't see a lot of her mom or her nieces or Sylvia or friends. Even if it had been possible, it was too wonderful to share, and something about their arrangement made it even more exciting. Like that Whitney Houston song, she was saving it all for him. *This is the one,* she said in a voiceless mantra to herself. Peter maybe just hadn't figured it out yet, for himself. And she needed to get her act together with that portfolio. *Shit. Why was she dragging it out?* As she pulled herself away from him, her phone rang. Sylvia.

"Please come here," Sylvia said. "Please. I need you—to be here with Miriam. I'm taking Becky to the hospital, as soon as you get here."

Nataly heard panic in Sylvia's voice. "Why does she have to go the hospital?"

"It's a long story. I took her in last week to urgent care, they ran some tests. They called with the results just now."

"What results?"

"I don't know! I don't speak their language." Sylvia lowered her voice. "Look, I have to tell the girls soon, before you get here. How long will you be?"

"Twenty minutes. I'll be right there." A six-year-old in a hospital? That didn't make any sense to Nataly. "I'm sure it's nothing."

"They don't put kids in the hospital for nothing," Sylvia said. "Please. Please hurry."

"I gotta go," she said, after hanging up with Sylvia.

"One day I'm going to have to meet this family of yours," Peter said. When Nataly heard him, her heart started pounding. He drew her face close to his and kissed her mouth with a forceful tenderness that always left Nataly breathless and gasping for more.

"What?" she said, still flustered.

"You always dump me for them," he said, slightly scowling, then kissed her again.

"Like when?"

"You take your father's calls."

"Shut up! You take your wife's!"

"Your sister calls, you drop everything. It doesn't seem... appropriate."

Nataly glared at him. "I'm picking up my niece. My sister is checking my other niece into a hospital. And I hope you feel like the jerk you are."

Nataly stalked off into the shower to rinse him off of her body. When she stepped out he was still there, sitting on the bed, looking up at her. As she wriggled into her sweater and jeans Nataly read regret and lust in his eyes and promptly forgave him.

"I'll call you," she said. As she leaned down to kiss him, he pulled her down on top of him. "What do they put kids in the hospital for?" she asked.

"Plenty of things," he said. "Mostly nonfatal." She glared at him. "Nah, really. Infections, injury, trauma."

Nataly drove north on the 2 Freeway, then east on the 210, keeping her attention as much as possible on the San Gabriel foothills. It was that time in the afternoon when the hills reflected the yellow and orange of the sunset. Dusk and the gathering clouds transformed the hills into a smoky deep purple.

"Thanks for coming," Sylvia said. She loaded a carry-on into the car, then went back to retrieve Becky.

"I'm sure it's nothing, probably some dumb doctor's mistake," Nataly said, watching her sister move in and out of the home. There was nothing wrong with Becky, maybe just a cramp, all you had to do was look at her to figure that out. Just flushed. Just a fever. "I'm happy to be here for you." Hell, Sylvia looked worse than Becky by a hundred years. She didn't tell her sister that. She just wondered why she always looked so damn tired. She hated thinking that, after two kids, Sylvia was letting herself go.

Sylvia motioned for Nataly to follow her. Nataly trailed Sylvia into the laundry room. Sylvia closed the door tight behind them.

Sylvia's face was drawn. Terse lines pulled her mouth downwards. "If Jack calls here, just tell him to call me, please. I want to be the one to tell him."

Nataly nodded, pulled Sylvia to her and hugged. Sylvia was wire and knots underneath Nataly's arms. "She's going to be okay, I promise."

"I need a doctor to tell me that."

"Nothing bad is going to happen to Becky, I promise."

"It's not your promise to make, Nataly." Sylvia shook her head.

"Bad things happen. You need something to eat, just rummage around," she said, opening the laundry room door.

Once they left, Nataly shook a pillow out of its case and started asking Miriam to get her pajamas and clean underwear. Miriam would have nothing to do with the makeshift overnight bag. Instead she spent the next twenty minutes hunting down a child's suitcase, her own, emptying the stale toys stored inside and then filling it with her dolls, a purple stuffed frog, her pajamas for the night, and clothes for tomorrow.

Becky is going to die, Sylvia thought the entire drive to the hospital, choking up as Becky sang "All I Really Need" along with Raffi. The hospital room was clean, bright, and private. Becky played with the bed controls. An attendant took more blood, then poked a thick needle into the back of her daughter's left hand. *Don't they have enough blood already?* Becky whimpered, as the attendant taped her small hand to a flat board.

Sylvia held Becky's free hand. She hated that horrible hospital smell: illness masked by medication, the threat of decay and disaster, neatly wrapped inside an antiseptic ointment.

She really should call Jack. This is what husbands are good for. This is what they're supposed to support you through. As she dug for her cell through the Burberry handbag that Jack had brought back from London, a paternal-looking older man with pink skin and white hair walked into the room, smiled easily and peered at Becky, then back at Sylvia.

"I'm Dr. Johannsen. I'll be in charge of your daughter while she's here." Then he gave Becky a brief examination, moving Becky's arms and rotating her legs at the hip, having Becky pull her knees up, one at a time as close to her chest as she could, then having her roll on her side, prodding her bottom, this time taking care not to disturb the IV. He explained that right now they were treating Becky's illness as an infection, and the IV was to introduce massive amounts of antibiotics. They would see how she responded to that treatment and then make decisions from there.

"Decisions?"

"Yes, how to proceed with the treatment."

Sylvia braced herself. She said, "Should we go into the hallway to talk?"

Dr Johannsen smiled very broadly. "There is no reason," he said emphatically, "for us to discuss anything in the hallway. This is an infection, and unless something alters drastically, that's what it will remain. Now, has she had a fever recently?"

Her daughters were never sick. And if they were, they snuffled around with plenty of Kleenexes or threw up and got over it quickly. In other words, Sylvia had no idea whether Becky had had a fever or not. Sometimes she ran hot, like all kids. Sometimes she ran cold.

"No. I don't remember her having a fever recently."

He smiled kindly, but Sylvia followed him out the door.

"I have read," Sylvia began, "about bone cancer. The first symptom can be back pain."

"Good heavens, absolutely not," he said. He patted Sylvia's shoulder gently. "Absolutely not."

Sylvia exhaled all the knots within her. *Thank you God, thank you God, thank you God.* "Thank you," she said. She had phone calls to make.

While Becky discovered the joys of a remote with no older sister around to veto her choices, Sylvia remained in the hallway to make a call to her mother.

"Mom, I'm here at the hospital with Becky. I don't know how long we're going to be here. Nataly's with Miriam. I know you would have come. I'm fine. It's going to be fine," Sylvia exhaled. "It's an infection. Antibiotics. No, I'm going to call him when I hang up with you. Yes, that's right, I called you before him, you're the most important person." Sylvia smiled. "Look, if Becky's here for a while, can you stay with Miriam? Thanks, Mom. Thanks."

She dialed Jack's cell. Voice mail picked up. She said, "Please call me, I don't want to leave a message. It's important. I'm not at home, call my cell."

If she said it's about Becky, he might never call back.

She called Nataly. "How's it going?"

"Fine. We're watching *The Emperor's New Groove*. I like all these brown animated characters. And crazy colors. Set in a Latin American country. Impressive. Made popcorn for dinner. How's Becky?"

"It's just an infection. She's not going to die." Sylvia attempted to laugh at herself but couldn't quite manage it. "By tomorrow or the next day they'll tell me, here, take these three little pills and go outside and play."

"There, see, didn't I tell you?" said Nataly in a tone managed only by those who didn't yet know how bad things could be. "FYI, I brought Miriam home with me. I left your husband a note. I'll get her to school in the morning."

Sylvia called Tamara.

"Honey, I would've taken Miriam. In a New York minute."

Sylvia could picture Tamara's face displaying affectionate concern. She smiled. "I'll keep that as a backup in case Nataly doesn't work out."

Jack didn't return her call.

That Tuesday night, she shared a hospital bed with Becky. The noises of the night staff were partially mitigated by the steady breathing of her daughter. The lights from the corridors leaking through the blinds at least allowed Sylvia to glance at Becky's features. They always seemed a work in progress. There was the nose, not prominent, not delicate, still waiting for its destined shape. And the eyes—as Becky slept her eyelids and lashes seemed larger and longer than humanly possible. Something out of a Japanese cartoon.

Sylvia picked up Becky's free hand and kissed the back of it. A nurse walked in, checked the fluid container, the machine hissing next to it, glanced at Sylvia and Becky and stepped out again.

Her instincts had been right, and that arrogant doctor had been wrong. She thought of Miriam, staying with Nataly. Now, that should be an educational experience for both of them. Sylvia briefly wondered if Nataly would tell Miriam the facts of life—according to Nataly, of course. Would she show her her thong underwear?

At seven the next morning, Jack finally called. Sylvia had been up for an hour, stiff from her contortions in the hospital bed, reading and rereading the picture books Becky had packed.

"Hey, sweetheart." Jack's voice was unfamiliarly hearty. It was the voice he used for his good buddies at work, the voice he used on people who could be useful to him. She couldn't remember the last time he had spoken to her that way. *Red alert.* He was going to ask for something. "Sorry for calling early, but I just wanted to get to you before I got swept up on my way. I tried calling you at home. Are you running around already?"

Apologies? Concern? Consideration?

"No, actually, I'm not. As a matter of fact—"

"Good, good, glad to hear it, you work too hard as it is. Look, I'm calling because it looks like this trip is going to be extended."

"Oh. Really? I thought you were coming home tonight."

"No, no, no, no, not tonight. That's all changed. I emailed you the schedule."

He may have. She hadn't checked.

"So even that schedule's being changed. Look, they love me here. Love me. And I love them. The two of us really ought to come here some time. You'd love the restaurants, Sylvia, the energy. You'd love the people. They want me, Sylvia. They got this terrific development project starting up here, they really want me."

"This is something. You've never asked for permission before."

"The thing is—" He paused. Sylvia figured he was trying for the correct spin. "The thing is, this company here, they're wooing me. I can tell. They want me. And I don't want the folks at home to know what's going on. I don't want them to know I'm here on an extended business trip. It'd smell to them."

"Are we moving to New York?" Sylvia asked, incredulously.

"Well, no, not right away, in any case, and that's not a decision I would make without you." His voice turned impatient and harsh. That was the tone Sylvia was used to. "You're missing the entire point," he said. "There are invaluable information and contacts to be had here. And if they're wooing me, I can't say no."

"I am not moving to New York," she said. Why was she arguing with him? *Let him move. Let him go without her, without the girls. Let it all go.*

"This is the life, the lifestyle I've always wanted, I'm telling you. But we'll talk about that later. I'll be here this weekend and all of next week. I should be home a week from Sunday."

A week from Sunday. Every muscle within Sylvia relaxed until she realized where she was. "It's seven in the morning, I've spent the night in the hospital with Becky, I don't understand why you're calling me for permission if you've already made up your mind."

"I'm asking you not to blow this to the home office. They can't know a thing. I'm on vacation, that's my story. Visiting relatives in the city."

Sylvia said nothing.

He said, "What's this horseshit about the hospital? Were you testing my hearing?"

"Becky's here, plugged into an IV and another machine that makes a lot of noise." Sylvia stepped out into the corridor.

"What the hell did you do to my daughter? What happened?" he growled.

"The back pain you told her was in her mind is real." Sylvia told him all that had happened. He only interrupted when she told him Miriam was with Nataly.

"You left her with your crazy sister?"

"My sister loves my daughters." And would never hit either of them with a spoon, wooden or otherwise. Why didn't she just say that?

"Okay, okay, okay," he said. "I'm sorry I lost my cool there. Sylvia, you did a terrific job. I'm glad Becky's going to be fine. Are we square on this home front deal?"

Let it all go. Let him go. Keep Becky. "Square."

"And you'll keep my story covered?"

Keep Becky. "Will do."

"I love you, Sylvia. You're a terrific woman." He hung up before Sylvia could say a word. And it would have taken her some time. I love you? Normally that was something he doled out, like a bargaining chip. Had he been drinking? He was worked up about Becky. At first Sylvia fought against it, but inside she felt proud of his approval.

Later that morning, Nataly brought Miriam to visit. When Miriam saw the IV on the back of Becky's left hand, she froze. Panic moved across her face, and she looked at her mom, then back at Becky.

"They have Nintendo here," Becky said, her face and arms a silky golden color against the drab of her hospital gown. "Look, this is the button for that. And we can move the bed up and down. Wanna see?"

Nataly had braided Miriam's hair. It made Miriam look younger than Becky and just as tender—right up until she socked Becky for not sharing the Nintendo controls.

"Miriam can't stay with me tonight," Nataly said. "I gotta work, and later, I gotta—" Nataly, standing in her pencil thin jeans and a red lace sweater Sylvia was sure Nataly had crocheted herself, actually squirmed. "I gotta date."

"Good for you!" Becky was fine. Becky was fine. "Mom'll be here soon."

When Mercy arrived, Sylvia watched Becky's face light up. Sylvia's mother wore a sleek gray velour gym suit and just enough makeup for the nurses and attendants to think that there were three sisters in the room. This now seemed like just an excuse for a party. *Celeste should be here,* Sylvia thought, but then the party would get a bit tense. Sylvia watched her mother fuss over the girls and compete for their attention with the video game.

There. It wasn't as bad as all that. She had called Tamara and told her it was a little jolt out of their routine—like salt in a brownie recipe, to make sure you paid attention to the sweetness.

The days for them now became a routine of temperature, blood pressure, blood tests, IV bags—interrupted by x-rays for Becky. The daily menu card loomed large. Becky made a huge production out of choosing this, that or the other thing, while Sylvia headed down to the cafeteria for food supplements of grease and salt, sugar and fat.

As soon as Dr. Johannsen had said not to worry, she had felt so much better. Even hungry. Becky's back still ached, but less, and she bounced on the hospital bed as she played Nintendo or strolled to the children's area of donated books and board games. Nataly or Mercy or Tamara brought Miriam to visit. Miriam monopolized the Nintendo— until Nataly or Mercy or Tamara took her home.

It was Thursday afternoon when, instead of Dr. Johannsen—who always made the morning and evening rounds—three other people came into their room: a young Asian woman in a white coat, whom Sylvia had noticed had accompanied Dr. Johanssen previously; a young man in a white coat; and a third man in street clothes, very hip street clothes— Sylvia could tell by the shirt's neckline and the trendy cut of the sport coat and pants. He had an au courant haircut, sort of buzzed and spiky on top. And he was a handsome man. Sylvia viewed him with dread.

The spiky-haired doctor headed towards Becky. He was friendly and Becky smiled easily. "How's that back?" he asked.

Becky bobbed her head sideways. "Okay. Still hurts. Just not as much. Mom says that means I'm getting better, and I should be out of here soon."

"That's good," he said, gently lying her back, rotating her legs in their sockets, bending her right knee towards her, then stopping as she said, "Ow."

He smiled at Sylvia and said, "Can we go talk in the hallway?"

No. No. Let's not, Sylvia thought. *Really, let's not.*

There wasn't haze or mist or a film before her eyes. Not yet. The picture in front of her was perfectly clear. She had always known she would be following a doctor into the corridor.

So she did. The four of them crowded the empty space near the elevators, far from Becky's room.

"You need to know," the man in the sports jacket said, "that the antibiotics are not having the desired effect. That was further confirmed by your daughter's most recent x-ray. There's a mass near her spinal column at her lower back. We can't tell if it's soft tissue or bone. At this point we do not think it is an infection."

Sylvia blinked at him. Now all she could see were his gray eyes.

"I'm forgetting my manners. This is Dr. Hom and Dr. Singh. I'm Dr. Roeg."

Sylvia's mouth was dry. There was a buzzing right behind her ears. She couldn't bear it. She asked anyway. "What's your field?"

"Pediatric oncology."

The three doctors stared at her. At the base of her skull, the buzzing grew louder. Dr. Roeg's mouth was moving, but Sylvia heard absolutely nothing. *Pediatric oncology. Becky had cancer. That's why the pain hadn't gone away. It was in her bones.*

Couldn't they, couldn't they please, couldn't they please stop looking at her, couldn't they please stop hovering, couldn't they please stop?

"So, Monday morning," she heard, "we'll do an MRI. On Tuesday morning, we'll be doing the biopsy. There will be the chance that we don't get enough of a tissue sample to give accurate results. I really refuse to speculate until we have the results of the biopsy."

If there was concern in any of those faces, Sylvia couldn't see it. They were strangers, after all. How do you decipher the face of a stranger? A rational person, a polite person, a good girl, would continue to stand here even if the world was swirling out of control at her feet, while the faces of three strangers watched and waited for her response. A good girl would stay and try to make sense of everything— the glances, the faces, the words.

"I can't hear you," Sylvia said. "I can't hear you, I can't understand you. You're going to have to talk to my husband."

Sylvia rushed into Becky's room and pulled her cell phone out of her bag. She headed back towards the elevators and the hovering doctors, punched in a number then and handed it to Dr. Roeg.

Dr. Roeg stood there for a moment. "Shall I just leave a message?" Sylvia nodded. The doctor turned and spoke into the phone for a few minutes.

He handed the phone back to her.

"Right. So, Tuesday morning. They will have to prep her at six. There's an entire procedure protocol. The nurse will explain."

As Sylvia stepped back into the room, Becky said, "Mom, they said they're going to have to take a blood sample."

"Yes, sweetheart."

"Will you be here, Mom?"

"Yes, yes, yes." Outside she saw the smog glowering over the landscape.

Becky was going to die, and when it happened Sylvia was going to die. If she stayed here a minute longer, Becky would know too much. "Look, baby, I need to take a walk. I need to talk to your dad. I'll be right back." Sylvia walked back down the corridor to the elevator. The doctors had vanished. She took the elevator to street level. Out of the building, she crashed into a poster display. Some sort of colorful and way-too-cheery health fair was being held on the steps, with balloons and popcorn and punch.

She dialed Jack's number and walked up the street. Past the construction, past the two homeless women with their respective shopping carts. Past the coffee shop, the Mexican restaurant. A horrible orange haze shrouded the streets. The din of the moving buses, the stench of the diesel all sickened Sylvia.

Jack's voice mail picked up. "Jack, Jack," Sylvia choked. "Call me, call me please, as soon as you get this. Oh my God, Jack, they think Becky has cancer. They're doing the biopsy Tuesday morning. Jack, if she has cancer…I won't, I won't be able to…" Sylvia hung up, turned around, passed the same assortment of ugliness this time in reverse order, passed the health fair, watched the floor tiles give and sway as she walked from the elevator to Becky's room.

Becky started to cry. "You said you'd be here! They took blood, Mom, and you weren't here and it hurt!"

Thirty minutes into her new identity—mother of a seriously ill child—and already she'd failed.

Later that day, while Becky ate everything on the lunch tray—the day-glo orange macaroni and cheese, the diced cubes of canned pears, the chocolate milk, the stale brownie—Sylvia punched the numbers again. God DAMN, where was Jack? His cell voicemail continued to pick up, while his voicemail at work was full. She left a message with his secretary, Faye. When Faye returned the call, Sylvia got his "vacation itinerary." God knows what kind of marriage Faye thought they had. Whatever she thought, she'd be right. Since he wasn't answering his cell, Sylvia called his hotel in New York. Over and over again, she got an automated response she didn't have the patience, or the mental resources, to navigate.

Shouldn't he be the first to know? Didn't he deserve to know before her mother, before her sisters, before Tamara? She waited for him to call.

She walked Becky and her IV to the playroom. Becky struck up a conversation with a fragile looking little girl, pink and bald.

Later, back in the room, Becky laughed in delight at something Daffy Duck had just done. Her little body shook when she laughed. It had been three hours, three hours and no whisper from Jack!

Was she being punished? Had she been so self-absorbed that she'd been oblivious to Becky's symptoms?

Or for daring to contemplate a divorce? Had she called this upon Becky? Was all this somehow her fault, and if so, what now?

Sylvia stepped out of the room and called Nataly.

"Call Mom and tell her to come. I need her. They think—," Sylvia paused, because she didn't want to voice it, "they think Becky has cancer." There, she said it. It was now alive and real.

There was a chasm of silence between Sylvia and Nataly. At last Nataly said, "They're wrong, Sylvia, they're wrong."

"Nataly, if I hope that and instead they're right, I'll die. I have to—prepare myself." Sylvia cleared her throat. "Tell Mom. Tell Celeste. They can call me here."

Sylvia wanted a tranquilizer. A drink. Her mother. Her sisters. Her husband, Jack. Anything that would get her mind out of its loop. Caring for Becky, caring for Becky, and then no more Becky. Sylvia could see only darkness after that. A divorce. And Miriam? Anything to stop thinking about this. Anything. Getting pissed off at Jack helped here. She didn't know which company was interested in hiring him. She hadn't listened that hard. What the fuck did he think he was doing? New York?

Celeste sipped her third glass of wine and was reading *The Economist* when her mother phoned.

"Has Nataly called you?" she said.

The question made Celeste's stomach churn. What, to say something vicious? To misconstrue or misinterpret everything that Celeste had done before?

"It's Sylvia," her mother continued. "Becky's having a biopsy Tuesday. They think it's cancer."

"What?!"

Her mother continued, "Jack doesn't know. Sylvia won't leave it on his voicemail, and he hasn't called her back."

Friday morning Celeste caught a flight to Burbank. It was a brief, unhappy flight. Celeste thought about money—Sylvia's lack of an emergency fund, Jack's debts. The 529 funds Celeste had set up for Becky and Miriam. Their 529 balances were spectacular—Becky wasn't going to die. They didn't even have a diagnosis yet.

Celeste had thought she was being so clever. A rainy day education fund for her nieces, started when they were born, moved and managed according to the varying tax laws of the varied presidents. Even

Celeste's capacity for fine shoes, wallets and handbags had a limit. As Jack's ludicrous financial situation became more and more apparent, Celeste quietly added more and more to Becky and Miriam's war fund.

Celeste had already contemplated what would happen if Sylvia and Jack died. Celeste was the person, who, after all, insisted they draw up a will. Jack's mother was to have custody, but she had passed away. Sylvia had asked their mother, but Mercy said she wouldn't even think about her only grandchildren as orphans.

Nobody mentioned Nataly. Jack had no siblings, so Celeste agreed to take on the children in case of their parents' deaths. But no part of Celeste, no part of her analytical, evaluative, assessing mind, had ever contemplated a strategy based on one of the children dying. *Pretty well blocked that one out*, she thought.

God, she hated brooding about this. She ordered another Bloody Mary from the stewardess. She'd looked Michael up online recently. He was packing them in, in Tulsa and Austin and Tupelo. Singing his original Christian music to tiny packed concert halls. His website showed his wife and two boys. Christian music. That definitely would never have worked out.

Celeste rattled the ice in her cup.

That night Mercy washed her face, brushed her teeth, stepped out of the bathroom and sat on Sylvia's guest bed when Celeste rapped on the door and came in.

"Aren't you beautiful," Mercy said, looking at Celeste in her satin pajamas, her skin freshly scrubbed and perfect. "Sit next to me."

Celeste did, and Mercy could smell soap and alcohol.

"You're more beautiful now than you were as a girl," she said.

Celeste shrugged. "I'm glad you think so."

"Nataly's picking us up in the morning."

Celeste nodded. "I know."

Everything in Mercy tumbled out before she could stop it. "Both of you damn well better get over your scratched feelings and come together. Whatever you two feel is nothing compared to Sylvia right now."

Celeste said nothing.

"Goddammit, you're sisters. I don't know what happened

between you two, but I'm not going to stand around and watch it deteriorate over…over what? Hurt feelings. Everybody has hurt feelings. Get over it!"

Celeste picked up her mother's hand and kissed the back of it. "We will. I'm sure we will. For you, for Sylvia—"

"No, for yourselves!"

"Yes, Mom."

Mercy's eyes filled with tears. "What are you fighting over?"

Celeste wrapped her in her arms and said what she had been pondering for years now, almost afraid to say it out loud. "I really think she thinks I abandoned her when I went to Trinidad. Not that I got married, but that I never came home." Celeste waited for absolution.

"Well, you did." Her mother said, matter-of-factly. "It was painful for all of us, but it's what you had to do."

Celeste sat there shaking her head, telling her mother this was supposed to make her feel better, not worse, there was supposed to have been some kind of consolation or realization that Nataly was wrong. But there it was, once again, it was Celeste who had been wrong.

Her mother pulled her close, ignoring Celeste's resistance.

"If we wanted you back home with us, doesn't that tell you how much we love you?"

After Celeste kissed her good night, Mercy crawled into bed, said her prayers, prayed for Edgar and all her daughters and especially Becky. Ah, God, the babies of the family always had the charm. Even Joey.

How is it that the babies of a family always possessed some kind of wild charm, some endearing personality that captivated, enchanted, intoxicated? Nataly had it. Becky had it.

When each of her babies was born, she didn't have that sense of the miraculous as she had heard so many other mothers talk about. Instead, it was a sense of redemption. With each of these girls, she was born anew. With each child, she had a clean slate. And Edgar—well, thank God for Edgar, for he had made it all possible.

"And I do," she said to herself, as she tugged at the comforter in Sylvia's guest bedroom. "I thank God for Edgar every day." Even if he didn't pay the slightest bit of attention to how it had all turned out, he had given her three daughters.

She felt cold, got out of bed, and started poking around in the closet for more bedding. What she found made her step back. It was the granny quilt made by Mercy's mother, the same quilt that lay across the back of the sofa for years and years in the front room where Mercy grew up. Mercy stepped towards the closet, pulled the quilt down and inspected it.

Sylvia had kept this? She shook her head as she poked at the squares and found more than a few places where the yarn was unraveling. Mercy thought that she should take it home and stitch it up. How could Sylvia have this? Why? Mercy folded it up quickly and shoved it far back into the closet, then found a fleece throw she had bought for Sylvia at Mervyn's and wrapped herself in it.

Still, even knowing that the quilt was in the closet oppressed her. Sylvia would have too much on her mind to notice. Maybe Mercy would sneak the quilt out and burn it.

Mercy lay awake in bed, brooding over the quilt. The quilt was her mother, her childhood, Joey. Mercy lay in bed, trying to fall asleep, thinking she heard the wind again. It was the wind of Lompoc, she remembered, as it beat against the trees, rattled the windows, flew in through the cracks of their home. It was the wind that chilled her, even though she had been cold long before.

On a plate in front of her rested a homemade tortilla, fresh from the griddle on her mother's stove, slightly charred. Her older sister Lydia, ten, already imperious and miserable, had cried at the wretchedness of the burned patches on her buttered tortilla. In frustration, she had stormed out of the kitchen and off to school, slamming the back door loudly behind her.

Mercy ate her sister's breakfast. It was delicious, especially the crisp, charred bits. Her mother made sure the stove was off, put a wool hat on and wrapped herself in a shawl. She spoke to Mercy in Spanish, "I need to finish this dress for Mrs. Lansdown. You're going to stay home this morning and take care of Joel. I'll be back in an hour." As her mother slammed the back door, the wind rattled against the kitchen windows, and Mercy stood, watching the wind beat against the oak trees. Her mother said the baby's name more like "Ho-ell."

Mercy and Lydia called him Joey. Mercy stared at the bright sun, the blue sky and the flailing tree branches for a minute, then walked back through the house. She walked through the front room, with its sofa, radio, rocking chair and sewing table. Often her mother was the fixture that accompanied the sewing machine, pumping the treadle, pins between her pursed lips, tugging, pulling, rearranging fabric on her machine, the fine lines of wrinkles on her face echoing the threads she worked with. A granny quilt, made from years of knitting and crocheting scraps, lay across the sofa.

Mercy went into her bedroom and pulled out her doll, Amalia. When she tilted this doll, as Mercy did now, she said, sweetly, plaintively, "Mama!"

Mercy hugged the doll close to her. She walked by her brother's room. Joey was in there, but he was quiet, and Mercy wasn't going to bother him. Mercy brought her doll into her mother's room. Her mother slept in a huge four-poster bed. It was neatly made, covered with a patchwork quilt made of scraps. A small braided rug lay at the side of the bed. Mercy propped her doll against the pillows and pretended to serve her breakfast in bed.

Mercy's favorite room, besides her mother's, was the kitchen because it was slightly warmer than the rest of their house, and the aging wood under her bare feet felt smooth. The kitchen had a small breakfast table. Her mother extended the table with a panel only on extremely formal or important occasions, like the afternoon Mercy's father was buried. Her mother had widened the table in order to hold the serving bowls, casseroles, dishes and desserts that his parishioners had brought in his honor to sustain his family.

Mercy brought her doll into the front room and sat down with her on the rocking chair. She rocked back and forth for a moment. She stared at the radio in the center of the room, just under the windows. The wind continued to rattle the windows, shake the branches. It was howling now, and drafts entered the house.

Mercy looked at the radio and decided not to be afraid. She was absolutely strictly forbidden to play with the radio. Her mother's scolding voice replaced the broadcasts of music, sermons and episodes of *The Shadow*, telling her and Lydia how many dresses the repair would cost her—how many hours of careful measuring, cutting and stitching.

She turned it on anyway. The music she heard was light and playful and filled the small living room. Mercy recognized the exciting trill of a clarinet, and decided she needed to practice her clarinet more. It was the same music they played at the white steeple church where they held the dances on Saturday nights, the dances she and her sister spied on. Mercy loved to watch everyone dance—the women were so beautiful, the soldiers so thrilling. That's what she would do when she was old enough.

That was, however, beneath Lydia's dignity to even contemplate. "They're just a bunch of nobodies from nowhere, like us," she said. "When I get out of here I'm going to dance with somebodies. I'm gonna be somebody. Look at those dresses! Half of them were sewn by your mother! When I grow up, I'm gonna buy everything from the store. Brand new. Everything."

Mercy knew that Lydia, at ten, could already neatly sew a skirt, although she still needed her mother's help with the zipper. Lydia always referred to their mother as "your mother," as if that was the only way she could bear that piece of information.

Mercy went into the back room to check on Joey, music trailing behind her. He lay in his crib on his back, a trail of drool sliding down his cheek. Her mother had said Joey was a good boy, a sweet boy, one of God's innocents. Joey was born after their father's death. Mercy knew that, although her mother may have called Joey a blessing from God, he was not like other three-year-olds. He never crawled, he couldn't walk. She and Lydia spent a lot of time hauling him from one part of the house to the other so he could watch and join in their play. His smile was truly heart-stopping. It made his eyes sparkle. Anyone he aimed his dazzling smile at involuntarily responded in kind. Everyone knew Mercy was his favorite.

He also cried at the most unexpected times. Right at the most crucial part of *The Shadow* where the identity of the beautiful jewel thief was at last revealed. Or early in the morning, before the birds recognized the coming dawn and had begun to sing. Or just as their mother placed the last quesadilla on the hissing griddle. His shrieks were alarming, he was inconsolable. They passed and patted him, hummed to him and sang, until Mercy's mother finally shouted in exasperation, "Ya no mas, mi hijito, ya no mas!" Then he would stop and sleep for fourteen hours.

That must have been what happened last night, thought Mercy, which explained why she, Mercy, was watching the drool trickle down Joey's cheek instead of being where she belonged in Mrs. Ganz' third-grade class. When Mercy went back into the living room, the radio had turned into a terrible drone of tedious adult language. Mercy looked at it. She knew she wasn't brave enough to find another program so she simply turned it off.

It was later than she thought, eleven-thirty. If her mother didn't get home soon, Mercy would have to figure out something for lunch and something for Joey.

She sat on the rocking chair and was halfway through the second chapter of *Toby Tyler or Ten Weeks with a Circus* when she heard Joey move around. How he smiled when she appeared at his crib. He looked up at her, sparkling and shiny with pleasure at the appearance of Mercy's face. She noticed the mocos accumulating in his left nostril and went to get a handkerchief to clean him up. He tugged at her wrist as she wiped his nose and face. His diaper was heavy, but Mercy decided to let her mother worry about that. She hauled him up and over the crib rail and carried him around the house.

Joey had a wide face and huge blue eyes that made him look younger. His hair was long, brown, stringy and curled upwards just past his ears. He was the palest child in the Fuerte family.

Mercy propped him up in the kitchen in his high chair. He slid in his damp diaper against the white slats and lightly pounded the tray with his pink fists. Mercy diced cheese and placed the cubes on his tray. She couldn't find any leftover tortillas, even though she knew her mother always had a few safely hidden from her children, so instead Mercy struck a match, lit the stove and heated a pot of beans. When the beans were lukewarm, she placed a few spoonfuls into a saucer and fed Joey. He liked grabbing her wrist and gnawing playfully at her fingers before clutching the spoon and savoring the beans.

When the beans were hot, Mercy served herself some, then

dropped the diced cheese on top. She wished she could find those tortillas her mother had made last night. Joey played with the cubes of cheese on his tray, knocking half of them onto the floor. Mercy patiently picked them up, rinsed them off, then gave them back to him. It was two o'clock. At this rate, Lydia would get home from school before their mother got back.

Mercy was still hungry. She looked at her baby brother pawing through the bits of mashed beans on his tray, pushing the cubes of cheese back and forth.

She went back into her mother's room. Her mother had a huge wooden trunk at the foot of her bed. It served as a resting space for Mrs. Fuerte's clothes before they were pressed and hung, never as a space for her children to sit and visit or play. There were no clothes on its surface now, just the smooth sheen of polished mahogany.

This was very serious. Mercy was in her mother's room, going through her mother's things. Not the jewelry boxes, not the lingerie drawer, not the closet with is assortment of hats and shawls and dresses and throws, but her mother's treasure chest.

Mercy tilted the heavy lid towards the poster bed. Underneath were gray woolen blankets and piles of fabric tied neatly with another scrap of fabric. Keeping the lid propped up with her left arm, Mercy poked around and beneath the woolen blankets, the bolts of cloth, the miscellaneous linen napkins and tablecloths. She felt waxed paper and heard it rustle. She pulled out the neatly wrapped packet and stared at it. She knew it! Half a dozen flour tortillas. She unwrapped the package carefully. They smelled almost as fresh as they had last night. She took one out, rewrapped the package and placed it back between the linen napkins.

In the kitchen, Mercy heated the griddle expertly while Joey watched. She sprinkled a few drops of water on the surface and when they exploded and sizzled, Joey laughed. She heated her tortilla, watched it bubble and collapse, then put it on a plate and smeared a lump of butter on it, watching it melt and trickle around.

Joey was quite interested now, but Mercy was hungry. He gaped at her with an open mouth, his way of begging for more. She tore off a corner, placed it in front of him, and ate the rest of hers quickly.

Joey picked up the scrap and swallowed it. He looked at Mercy, his mouth open and started moving his head from side to side. He banged on the tray with both his fists. He waited for more.

"Let's go play, Joey," Mercy said, to change the subject. She began to unstrap him from the high chair.

"Ah ah ah ah ah ah ah ah," he said, softly. As she pulled him out of the high chair, he began to scream and wail.

"All right, all right," she said, strapping him back in.

But now Joey was on his way. Little red patches of anger spread over his face. He began crying and wailing and fussing so hard that he started to cough. As he coughed and cried and wailed, Mercy patted and cooed and sang, but he would not be calmed.

Mercy gritted her teeth and headed back into her mother's bedroom. This time the trunk lid felt heavier, but now she knew where the waxed paper package was. She unwrapped it carefully, taking out another tortilla, and carefully rewrapped the package before placing it back in the trunk and lowering the lid. Her mother would know this time, her mother would certainly know this time. Mercy wasn't ready to think about the consequences as Joey continued to wail and fret and pound on his tray.

She hadn't remembered to turn the griddle off so it was too hot, and Joey's tortilla had a lump of char, but he didn't seem to mind now that it was slathered in butter. Joey grabbed it greedily and shoved it into his mouth. At least he tried to shove the tortilla into his mouth, the whole thing, but it wouldn't all fit. He started to cry again, mouth agape, crammed with food, nothing going down, nothing coming out. As he cried, he began to cough. Mercy rushed over and started pulling the tortilla out of his mouth, but Joey fought her, slapping at her hands and holding onto the food in his mouth and crying and coughing and suddenly choking.

Moving in some kind of strange distorted time where her arms seemed heavy and her own breathing stopped, she tried, she tried so hard, to unstrap him. She pulled him out of the high chair, but too slowly it seemed, too slowly turned him upside down, thumped at his back, whacked at his back, but nothing more came out of his mouth.

Finally she righted him, and there was Joey, his face purple blotches, his eyes wide in wonder and astonishment. And then—the worst part—nothing more at all.

In his eyes Mercy read, *How could you do this? How could you let this happen to me?*

Joey's body quivered then heaved, and a mass of vomit landed on Mercy's chest. He was alive!

Mercy held him back to look at him. His eyes were open and motionless. His mouth covered in a smear of mashed food. He was dead.

Mercy ran outside. She watched a familiar figure approach. It was her mother, covered in her hat and shawl, carrying her huge fabric bag up the dirt road. Mercy stood in the middle of the road, buffeted by the wind, and waited for her mother.

"What did you do to him?" was the first thing her mother said.

That night—after the scolding stoicism of her mother, her questions, the curiosity and hysteria of the neighbors, the doctor's visit, the stunned silence of Lydia—Mercy went to bed. When Lydia was told to go to bed, she cried and stamped her foot and swore that she wouldn't ever sleep in the same room with Mercy—the murderer—again. Mrs. Fuerte relented and allowed Lydia to sleep in her bed.

Alone in her room, Mercy clutched her dolly tight, but when it startled her with a mewling *Mama!* she heard the accusation and threw her onto the floor.

Too sick, too miserable, too lost to cry, Mercedes Alvarez Fuerte lay on her back on the cold sheets, listening to that wicked wretched wind until she fell asleep.

Saturday morning, Celeste woke up in Miriam's bed. Miriam had pummeled her back with her size-five feet all night long. *Wasn't sleeping with a young child supposed to have some kind of sedative effect?* wondered Celeste as she rubbed at the small of her back and then stretched.

Celeste let Miriam sleep. She rummaged through her overnight bag and pulled out a gray sweat suit, the new suit with the delicate ribbing. She had sent Becky the cookies. She had stopped at the airport and bought Sylvia a pair of pajamas. New pajamas always cheered up the Amado girls.

She ran her fingers through her hair, put on the new sweats and tied the laces on her shiny white cross trainers. Celeste was ready to tackle her mother *and* Nataly and be with Sylvia and Becky, all in that order. No makeup this morning, just the moisturizer with the sunscreen.

Celeste glanced again at Miriam who had moved and contorted herself across to the other half of the bed. *Now, why couldn't she have done that last night?* Wisps of hair escaped from her niwce's braids. *Miriam's lashes seemed longer than…than Nataly's when she was a kid,* thought Celeste.

Well, she wasn't a kid anymore! She went to the guest room and rapped on her mother's door. No answer. She rapped again. "Mom, are you up?" Celeste, suddenly nervous and wary, opened the door and stepped into the room.

It was shrouded in darkness. The blinds were closed, but Celeste could make out a granny square quilt tossed onto the floor, and a lump of a body on the bed. "Mom?"

"Oh, Celeste."

"What? What's wrong? What is it?"

"I'm not going."

"What do you mean?" Celeste sat down next to the lump. Her mother had been crying.

"I can't go. I won't be any good at all for her. I'll stay here with Miriam."

Celeste stroked her mother's hair, brittle and dry from all the coloring and blow drying. "Come on, Mom, Sylvia needs you. Probably only you. I'm just going to show up with a lump in my throat. She needs you there too."

"You didn't kill your baby, Celeste."

There was a terrible pang within Celeste, and it seemed as if Sylvia's dark guest room had gotten even darker. They hadn't talked about this in at least fifteen years, and she sure as hell didn't want to step into that whirlpool now. She moved away from the lump under the blanket.

"Have you been thinking about Skye all night long?"

"No, I've been thinking about Joey."

"Who the hell is Joey?" should have been the next words out of her mouth, but Celeste couldn't do it. She had Nataly and Sylvia ahead of her. The lump on the bed trembled. She could see her mother's body shake with the little sobs.

"Oh, Mom, don't cry," Celeste finally said.

"I feel like everything I've done wrong is visited on you and your sisters. Everything."

"Oh, Mom." Celeste lay down against her and hugged the body under the bedspread. "Then, if that's true, all your successes will be visited upon us. All of them."

"It's all my fault," Mercy said a moment later, her voice a pale whisper.

"How much power do you have, Mom," Celeste said, "that everything could possibly be your fault?"

Her mother still didn't come out from under the covers. Celeste pulled a corner of the bedspread down and kissed her mother's cheek, just like she would kiss Becky or Miriam. Just another little girl, as if she were her own. And suddenly her heart was so suffocated by the thought of so many little girls in distress that Celeste left the room—and her mother—by herself.

Saturday morning Nataly drove up to Pasadena and parked her Altima in front of Sylvia's house. There was always something odd and garish about the stucco job Jack had chosen, and the landscaping was as if they couldn't decide between lush, tropical or xeriscape. Nataly hated the energy of this house. It was painted an angry orange, and that's how it felt inside. Only Miriam and Becky transformed it into yellow.

Except that Becky was not here now. She was at the hospital looking like a public service announcement with the IV up her arm. *You'd think they would have figured out a way to spare kids that ugliness,* Nataly thought. She unlocked the front door. She saw baggage tags. Christ. Celeste was here.

"Anyone home?" she said.

Nataly heard Miriam call from the master bedroom. Suitcases in the entry way, papers strewn across the dining table, half-filled take-out cartons scattered across the kitchen counter. Nataly started putting dishes in the dishwasher and wiping down the counters. She stacked the papers on the dining table, cleared the crumbs off.

So much easier tidying someone else's house. So much easier doing anything besides walking upstairs and seeing Celeste. She had just started sweeping the kitchen floor when she heard the stairs creak.

"Auntie," Miriam said, "Why don't you stay with me? I don't want to go to the hospital. Did you see that thing on her hand? I hate it."

Miriam looked up at her. She was wearing green cotton shorts and a yellow t-shirt. Those eyes challenged Nataly to disagree. *Didn't everyone hate hospitals?*

Nataly scooped her up and hugged her close. Just skin and bones, smooth skin, little bones. Were they really all that way once?

"I don't know," she said.

Out of the corner of her eye, Nataly saw ice cubes. Snow. Blue ice. No, just Celeste's profile—the sharp chin, cheekbones and nose. She had done something different with her hair, oh yes, she had let it grow and gotten highlights. It suited her. Made her look precisely as she was. Successful.

Then Miriam wriggled free and was gone from her arms. She said, "We could watch TV."

Celeste said, "Miriam, your grandma's not feeling well. Why don't you hang out with her, watch some cartoons in your mom's room. Just remember to check in on your grandma after each show."

Miriam smiled and nodded and ran upstairs.

Nataly looked down at the granite countertop. She should have wiped it down with Windex.

"Thanks for cleaning up," Celeste said, coolly.

"You're welcome." Nataly aspired to be equally icy. "Where's Mom?"

"In the guest room."

Nataly went to the room, knocked, then opened the door. She cleared her throat. "I can't leave you here, Mom."

"Yes, you can. I'm not going anywhere," her mother said. She was still under the blanket. "I'm not getting out of bed. I don't want to be there when Sylvia finds out Becky's going to die. I don't want to be there when Becky dies."

"We don't know that's going to happen."

"We know God fucks up," Mercy said.

"Mom, sit up. Sit up and look at me."

Mercy sat up, her eyes awash with smeared makeup and sorrow.

"It's my baby brother. Joey," Mercy said, as if Nataly should know.

"Mom," Nataly said gently, "What brother?"

Her mother shook her head, "Joey."

Nataly put her arms around her mother as Mercy sobbed.

"I think it's everything, Mom. It's just everything." Nataly rocked her mother back and forth. Was this whole Becky thing pushing her mother over the edge? Was she losing it? Nataly felt two stabs of pain of betrayal, one for thinking it, the other for the possibility of it being true.

Celeste's voice came through the door. "Sylvia's on the phone. She wants to know what time we'll be there."

"I'm not leaving Mom alone," Nataly scolded.

Mercy wiped her eyes. "You won't be leaving me alone. I'll be with Miriam. Now go. Be a sister, for my sake."

Nataly hugged her mother again, then stepped out of the guest room. She nodded at Celeste and said, "Let's go."

Nataly picked up her car keys and watched as Celeste locked Sylvia's front door. "This is quite a detour for you, from your place," Celeste said.

Nataly was surprised Celeste had even noticed. "I didn't want you to worry about renting a car. I mean, I didn't want Mom to have to drive." *What did she mean?*

Celeste looked admiringly at Nataly's Altima. Nataly was suddenly conscious of the fabric remnants cramming up the back seat, the box of buttons she was planning on returning, the wrappers of fast food she hadn't bothered to clean out. *Just like the rat's nest her father used to drive around in.*

"Nice car," Celeste said.

Nataly shook her head. *There she goes again,* she thought. So goddamned condescending. She'd call her own car slick, elegant, wild. Mine's nice. Diminutive. Insignificant.

"I like to think of it as cutting edge," Nataly said. They drove south towards the freeway, past the camphor, carob and oak trees. Past the homes inspired by Greene and Greene. Past Spanish mansions, Arts and Crafts bungalows. Humble homes, elegant homes, apartment buildings, shops, industry. Then onto the freeway, through the hills of Glendale, south towards Los Angeles, on to Children's Hospital. Nataly tuned the radio to her World Music station. She could feel Celeste's eyes roll.

They were practically into the parking garage when Celeste said, "This is hard on Mom, on Sylvia. Do you think we could try to get along?"

Nataly pushed the button, pulled out a ticket and drove up the ramp. The space was narrow, so Nataly kept concentrating on the turns.

"Nataly. I mean it. Can we?"

Nataly kept looking for a spot. Visitor parking? Patient parking? Definitely not staff. She pulled into the first empty spot and stopped abruptly.

"I get along with everybody."

"Why is it every goddamned thing I say irritates the hell out of you?"

"Why is it every goddamned thing you say is so goddamned irritating?"

Nataly stared at Celeste, then turned off the goddamned irritating music. She turned off the engine.

Celeste said, "Come on, Nataly, we used to be able to talk to each other."

Nataly said, "You want to talk? After all these years? In a parking garage? I don't think so." Nataly got out of the car. "Get out," she said, then "You have to get out or I can't lock it."

Celeste emerged slowly from the car, shutting the door firmly. "This is hard on everybody," Celeste said, "I thought we could make it a little easier…"

"Jesus Christ, Celeste, do you think I live in a bubble? Do you think I'm an idiot? You see us all, what, three or four times a year? In your fucking expensive clothes looking down at my car and you want to fucking make this all a little easier? Jesus Christ, you're so much like your father." Nataly glared at Celeste. She couldn't read a damn thing on her face, the parking garage was so dark. She glared as Celeste looked at her watch. "Fuck you and your attitude and your money. Fuck you." Nataly slammed her car door.

Silence. Celeste said, "I am going for a walk now. I will be up to visit Becky in an hour. Please don't be there. I will take a cab home." Then Celeste walked past the elevator doors and towards the exit signs.

For a brief instant, Nataly wanted to shout, "I'm sorry! I'm sorry! I'm an idiot! I miss you! I've missed you forever!" Since the day Celeste had driven away with Michael, since Skye, since she realized Celeste wasn't coming back, ever. For an even briefer moment she wanted to run after her. But she didn't. Instead she strode over to the elevator and punched the up button towards Becky's wing.

One of the elevator lights wasn't working. She was shrouded in darkness.

On her way to Becky's room, she passed several corridors. The walls shimmered with pastels, watercolors, nature scenes, cartoon characters.

Nataly shuddered against the forced cheerfulness.

No one wants to be here, she thought, even if the frescoes were by Michelangelo.

She caught a glimpse of Becky from the glass window of the playroom. The IV hovered protectively next to her. Becky wore a faded blue hospital smock over a pair of green flannel pajama bottoms. She was playing Break the Ice with a little girl who seemed to be a bundle of pink. Pink nostrils, pink ears, pink-rimmed eyes. Pink scalp. No hair. Becky showed the pink girl how to tap an ice cube in without breaking the ice.

This is…not happening, Nataly thought, and turned to look for Sylvia. Nataly passed the nurses' station, passed the thirty thousand snapshots of recovering or diseased or deceased children, entered the third door on the right. Sylvia sat in shadows, the blinds shut, the television set emitting an obnoxious glare and hiss. She was hunched over a phone in the corner, but when she saw Nataly, she turned, shook her head and snapped the phone shut.

"I don't know where the hell he is," she said.

Nataly came over and hugged her sister. She felt the softness of Sylvia's face, of her fleece sweatsuit.

Sylvia sat back in the chair. Nataly twisted open the blinds. Out the window, a blanket of orange haze lay over everything. It shimmered rage and despair and hatred.

If this were her view, she'd keep the blinds closed too. But instead, she opened them for the light, sat on Becky's hospital bed, smoothing out the covers while she thought about how to respond to Sylvia's comment about Jack. She hadn't been worrying about Sylvia and Becky, actually. She was preoccupied with Celeste.

The two sisters sat in silence. The only thought in Nataly's head, which she couldn't push away, was that if Sylvia hadn't married Jack this never would have happened. It was irrational, irrelevant and ridiculous, but reason couldn't keep the thought from repeating itself.

Look at Sylvia in her worn sweats, her hair frizzy and unbrushed, generally unkempt and miserable. She didn't look thirty-eight, she looked fifty-eight. She looked older than their mother.

"Where's the rest of you?" Sylvia asked.

"Mom's with Miriam in your house."

"And Celeste?"

Nataly waved her hand, looked away and said, "We got into a fight on the way down."

"Well, that's progress," Sylvia said. "I didn't know you two talked enough to argue."

"Yeah, well, anything to take your mind off your own problems."

"Christ, here comes one now."

Peter Roeg walked into the room, glanced in Nataly's direction, then smiled at Sylvia.

Could Sylvia see? Would she know?

He said, "The nurses tell me you wanted to see me?" Sylvia nodded. "In private?"

Nataly slid off of the bed.

"No, this is my sister, Nataly Amado. She can hear anything we are going to say." Peter nodded in Nataly's direction again, then back to Sylvia. "How can I help you, Mrs. Levine?"

"I want this biopsy done as quickly as possible."

"Absolutely."

"Why do we have to wait till Tuesday?"

The rest of the conversation was lost on Nataly. She watched Peter at work. It never occurred to her she would meet him here. He now listened without emotion, without expression, as Sylvia spoke, her voice sounding more distressed, demanding something. Nataly moved closer and hugged her sister as Sylvia wiped a tear away from the corner of her face. Peter nodded again and patted Sylvia on the shoulder before leaving. He also patted Nataly on the way out. It seemed to Nataly as if her hearing had returned.

"I hate that arrogant prick," Sylvia said. "You think if it was his daughter they'd be waiting for a space in the schedule? I swear to God, one phone call from Jack…And what's he doing touching me? Or you? Who the hell does he think he is?"

"I imagine he thinks of himself as a professional, doing his job."

Sylvia glared at her. "That is so like you, Nataly. You always take the man's side. God, no wonder you were always our father's favorite. You were the only one who defended him."

It was Nataly's turn to feel angry and assaulted. Before she could sputter out a retort, Becky walked into the room trailing her IV behind her, catching Nataly's eye, her face lighting up.

"Auntie!" she said, hugging Nataly with her free arm. Becky's arm was warm, slim, light brown, and her touch light and gentle. All this love in one light touch.

Nataly said, "I'm just saying that you've probably got the best doctor they have."

"So, of course he's arrogant. Fucking arrogant bastards. I hate him on principle. But if he so much as threatens to hug me, so help me God…" Sylvia smoothed the covers and helped Becky into her bed.

"Did you bring me something?" Becky said.

The Greatest Gift of All!, said Nataly, in her best Whitney Houston impersonation.

"Oh no," said Becky, knowing the routine.

"Love!"

"Oh, no thanks. I think I've got enough to hold me for now."

"Put it in the bank for a rainy day," Nataly said, pulling Becky onto her lap, while keeping an eye on the plastic tubing. It looked like there was a stiff metal needle feeding right into one of Becky's slim veins. So much to ask Peter about. What was going to happen to Becky? What would happen to them all? Weren't tragedies supposed to draw you all together? Shouldn't she and Celeste have kissed and made up and put up a brave, united front for Sylvia? And now she was pissed off at Sylvia. *The man's side.*

The man she considered hers acted as if they had never met. That's how she would have played it, right? Was she with the wrong man? Was this just another stupid choice of hers?

Nataly played Super Mario Brothers with Becky. Nataly kept falling into abysses, missing ledges, not jumping high enough for the gold coins. Becky beat her every time.

"So that person I can't get a hold of," Sylvia said, "had better be missing a limb when he shows up,"

Becky said, "She means Dad," then deftly had her Mario somersault and catapult into another world.

"I don't know what to say," Nataly finally replied.

"As long as none of you say, 'I told you so'—as long as none of you say that—we can still be sisters."

"I do *not* take the man's side," Nataly said.

Sylvia sighed, "Yes, you do, you don't even realize it."

"No, you're wrong. What I said about Mom and Dad was that after thirty years of marriage, I don't think one person can be wrong. It takes two people being wrong to last that long."

"Get back to me on that one when you've been married thirty years."

"Keep that up and I *will* say I told you so."

Nataly only realized an hour had passed when she saw Celeste in the door, smiling at Becky.

"Something for the mom," she said, handing Sylvia a gift bag.

Sylvia stood, giving her older sister a hug. Nataly felt jealous and stupid. She hadn't brought anything for anybody. Now Sylvia pulled out nubby white chenille pajamas. Celeste had the money to throw away. *Why am I so hateful*, Nataly thought. Celeste didn't look at her once, as Nataly, flustered, gathered her things and said goodbye to the three of them.

"Stay!" Sylvia said.

Nataly waited for a cue from Celeste who was completely focused on helping Becky unwrap a cookie. *If she had told me to fuck off, I would have yelled back! Stayed and fought—she's ignoring me. That's how little I mean to her.*

"I have to get going." Nataly stepped out of the hospital room into the despairing shimmer of fluorescent lights. She stopped at the nurses' station. "My niece's doctor came by, about an hour ago, Dr—"

"Roeg."

"Right. Is he still around? I think my sister has another question for him."

They pointed her in the direction of a corridor. It was lined with doctors' cubicles, not patient rooms. She saw Peter in a doorway immediately, his spiky hair made him taller than the group of three white-cloaked people clustered around him.

"Dr. Roeg, is it?" Nataly said, feeling both stupid and clever.

"Excuse me," he said to the group of white-cloaked people.

Nataly raised her eyebrow at him. "Wow. So this is you. At work."

He had that slightly smug smile on his face she'd seen before. Here he didn't look tired or worn at all. He looked fully charged, excited, electrified. And maybe, even happy to see her.

"This is me, in all my glory," he said. "Come into my office."

She followed him through the doorway. She glanced at the diplomas but what she was looking for were photographs. *Ah, there was his wife.* Attractive blonde, too practical for makeup and contacts.

"Your kids?" Nataly asked.

Peter swiftly shook his head. "Patients."

Nataly nodded, looked again at the photograph of his wife. She could be a knockout if she wanted to be.

She turned back to Peter. His sense of purpose excited her. A little stubble on his cheek, reeking of masculinity. The spiky hair, the smug smile, the rugged face, that perverse twinkle in his eye. "Is she going to be okay?"

Peter shook his head and Nataly felt an elevator plummet within her.

"I can't talk to you about this. The biopsy will tell us what we need to do next, and your sister can tell you what she wants you to know."

Nataly pulled him toward her and kissed him. He didn't fight, much.

"This fell out of your purse."

Nataly heard Celeste's voice and looked in its direction. Celeste stood at the doorway, holding Nataly's wallet between her fingers, looking neither at Nataly nor at Peter but at the floor. Nataly took the wallet without a word. Celeste walked back down the corridor. Peter tilted his head at her. Nataly frowned and shook her head in response.

If she were with the right man, would she feel this much embarrassment and shame?

On the drive back up Vermont towards her apartment, Nataly trailed a dusty pickup. On the driver's window, a sticker read "Juan 3:16." On the passenger side a sticker read, "Yo corazon Cristo." Then she felt the shame of Celeste not even looking at her. What could Celeste be thinking? Her steps swirled in gray, in green, in pink, in shame, shame, shame. Nataly walked up the concrete step, pulled open the screen and unlocked the front door. Stepping into the darkness, she realized that she was the one who had turned into her father.

To order her feelings about Nataly, Celeste set up a mental spread sheet with debits and credits. That Nataly was her sister should have outweighed any debit—but that she was clearly involved with a married man (ring, photographs, even Nataly should have been able to clock that)—that *was* definitely a debit, was it not? That Nataly angrily rebuffed her attempt at a truce: debit. That Nataly caused her such pain: debit. That Nataly felt she was in a position to judge the world, but more particularly Celeste: debit. That she came when Sylvia needed her: credit.

Nataly's sex life was none of her business. Celeste knew the only reason she was now obsessing over Nataly was to avoid thinking about Becky. Nataly was lost to her. That had been clear for a very long time. Being a successful financial planner meant knowing when to cut your losses, to not let sunk costs drag you down with them.

Sunday morning, Celeste slipped into the tan Tahari suit and the low tan Tod's heels she had packed. She brushed her hair, dusted her face with makeup, and smelled a familiar scent of oil being heated, of tortillas being fried. How many times in the poor side of San Jose had she trailed that scent and found herself in a tiny restaurant with plastic tablecloths, unsteady tables and chairs? Searching for her mother's cooking—invariably disappointed, occasionally surprised. In the kitchen, she watched her mother fry corn tortillas strips, drain off the oil, scramble half a dozen eggs, salt them, pour the eggs into the skillet on top of the tortillas strips, scoop around quickly, add a dollop of sour cream and dish it out to the three of them.

Miriam scrunched up her nose. She wore a red floral summer dress with rickrack on the collar and hem. Celeste recognized it as her mother's purchase. It had the familiarity of her own childhood.

"Can't you or Mom ever just make white people's eggs?" Miriam asked, stabbing her fork at the center of a tortilla strip.

"How would they do that?" Celeste asked, curious.

"You know—dry and flabby, just eggs."

Mercy laughed. Celeste sipped her coffee. The three of them sat at the granite island. It was ice cold to the touch. Her mother stretched out her hands, and both Miriam and Celeste took a moment to realize that Mercy wanted to pray.

"Dear God," Mercy began, "thank you for being here with us. Keep us together always. And be with Sylvia and Becky. In Jesus' name. Amen."

At the word Jesus, Miriam yanked her hand away and shook her head. Mercy pointed her chin at Miriam. "You keep that up, and there will be no ice cream for you after church."

Miriam ate her migas and drank her orange juice. *Children are just alien creatures*, Celeste thought, *just like everyone else.*

Celeste drove her mother and her niece to Mercy's church in Orange. Celeste watched out of the corner of her eye as her mother put on her makeup on the drive down the 5 Freeway. Her sixty-year-old mother wore a blouse and skirt in the style that women in their twenties and thirties were wearing. Her mother's hemline was shorter than her own. "Looking very curvy," Celeste said.

Mercy pushed up the visor. "I've been thinking," she said. "After this all settles down," she waved her hand, "you know, once everyone realizes Becky will be fine, I thought I'd come up and visit you."

Celeste heard that funny tone in her mother's voice. The resolute tone, as if she were announcing her plans, not asking permission. And just underneath it, the counterpoint of a plea in her voice, in her words. Celeste felt all scrunched up inside. "That sounds delightful," she said, stretching her mouth.

"Oh God, don't act as if I'm killing you," Mercy said. "I'm not planning on staying long, just a week or two. I mean, come on Celeste, you must know some fellow who's set. Someone who doesn't mind the sadder but wiser woman?"

Victor Resnick was the only name she had at the back of her head, and she smiled reflexively. Her mother was not exactly the age bracket Victor targeted.

"Those men," Celeste answered, "I keep to myself, Mom."

Calvary Church reminded Celeste of the churches of her childhood. For as long as she could remember, their mother, dressed in something snug and stylish that she had sewn herself, feet jammed into life-threatening heels, dragged her three daughters from church to church, from neighborhood to neighborhood, from denomination to denomination—looking for something. Sunday brunch was their father's excuse, too busy to be able to take the morning off from the Mexican restaurant he managed.

Methodist. Baptist. Presbyterian. Quaker. Looking for something. They learned a lot of hymns. "Standing on the Promises," "Deep and Wide," "In the Garden." Mercy went through a phase of Spanish-speaking churches, where they learned "Solamente en Cristo." Nataly screamed every time Mercy took them to the Spanish church in Santa Ana, so they stopped.

Even today, Mercy kept taking them to churches. However, it didn't cost Celeste anything to be here today, alive between the warmth of her mother's and her niece's bodies. Miriam sat prim and attentive, not bothering to use the pencil and paper Celeste had packed for her. She had already announced she was ordering strawberry ice cream. They stood to sing "Standing on the Promises." Her mother sang harmony.

Celeste watched the pastor, Reverend Covarrubias, as he sang earnestly. She was used to, for many many years, turning off her analytical mind when she entered a place of worship. But today the questions percolated in her mind. *What would it have been like,* thought Celeste, *to be a believer two thousand years ago? One thousand years ago? What would it have been like to listen to these stories when they were fresh and new? To believe the Kingdom of God was at hand? Instead of listening to these sermons as stale reruns, like an annoying television theme song. Like* Gilligan's Island *in black and white but without the humor.*

Maybe she could have been a believer back then. Maybe she would have been passionate. Maybe she would have been willing to die for her beliefs instead of barely tolerating the religious hand she had been dealt. God as new, revolutionary, embued with meaning.

Once, in the Baptistry in Florence, Celeste had felt that the inspiration of God was indeed awesome. She looked up at six-hundred-year-old mosaics. She saw the face of Jesus and she also saw the adoration of those artisans, the gifts of the parish that paid for that house of worship, the beauty that had surrounded God made flesh in the world. *Wherever your treasure is, there lies your heart also.* Their faith was alive and vivid. Not a cultural relic.

Reverend Covarrubias' sermon was titled "The Prodigal Son," given in his Texan-Mexican lilt. The sermon was always the prodigal son, it seemed to Celeste. Preachers seemed to think by telling this story they would bring in those masses of sinners running rampant in the real world. When would ministers realize that the prodigal sons weren't in their congregation? And that the God-fearing of the congregation might actually resent the fact that their good deeds and reverent ways were constantly being upstaged by the penniless, now contrite, sinner? Besides, with credit cards it was increasingly difficult to be penniless, much less contrite.

Enveloped in her own thoughts Celeste caught the last words of the reverend's summation. "Unconditional forgiveness. Let us pray."

Hard to stop the scorn for the concept of unconditional forgiveness forming within herself. Celeste wrote a check anyway and placed it in the offering plate. Writing checks often smoothed out her interior struggles.

At the end there was a special offering of prayers. Halfway through, Celeste's ears tingled.

"Dear Lord," the pastor said, "in the tradition of 'ask and ye shall receive, seek and ye shall find, knock and it shall be opened unto you,' we gather now to ask, to find, to understand. Lord, remember the sick ones, sick at heart, sick in soul or sick in body. We ask a special prayer for Becky Levine. We ask for your guidance, Lord, and your understanding. We ask for the reconciliation of family members, dear Lord…"

Mercy squeezed Celeste's hand, then whispered, "My heart will break for all of us if—," then hugged both Celeste and Miriam.

Monday they did another MRI scan to verify the precise site of the "mass" everyone was talking about.

Becky moved slowly off of her bed and around onto the wheelchair as far as the plastic tubing of the IV would allow her. An orderly pushed her, Sylvia followed. They were taken into the Magnetic Resonance Imaging Lobby.

There was a young black girl strapped to a wheelchair that leaned unnaturally backwards. Her forehead was misshapen. Her young eyes rolled around the room, but Sylvia had no sense they took anything in. A tall woman stood over the wheelchair, regal, wearing a purple wrap over her dark suit. She looked only at the daughter sprawled in her wheelchair.

The orderly left. Sylvia nudged Becky's wheelchair farther into the lobby, then sat down next to her while Becky gaped at the TV suspended high on the wall. Sylvia glanced left. From another door, a young boy used a walker to cross to the nurse's station. A heavy woman in a faded paisley print dress hovered, walking slowly behind the shuffling boy, speaking to him in low tones in a language Sylvia assumed to be Armenian. On her right, across the aisle, a young woman with eyebrows the width of a straight pin spoke to the nurse. She looked like one of the bad girls from Sylvia's high school, one of the fast girls who wore makeup early, got pregnant and dropped out.

"Date of last seizure?" The nurse waited for the young woman to answer.

"She didn't have none since the last surgery," the young woman said. Both women were referring to the child in the stroller, a young girl about four, babbling upwards to her mother, who kept patting the toddler's leg.

"Yeah," the young woman said, snapping her gum, "she had like ten seizures between her second and third surgery. I think the electrical stimulation worked. And the Depakote." The young woman nodded, but the nurse would neither confirm nor deny. "I think we're on top of things," the young woman continued, "considering her anatomic abnormalities." Sylvia listened to the technical jargon. Maybe next week or next month, she too would be using a new vocabulary.

The young woman had her medical terminology down. All because her daughter—delayed at God knows what stage of development—was now the centerpiece of this woman's life. As were the other children who surrounded Sylvia, each one the very purpose that propelled their mothers along. She wanted to flee this room, this rainbow coalition of misery.

Now Becky would be her life. That's what Sylvia understood in this room. The mothers at their school would say, "Have you heard about Sylvia Levine's daughter?" And they would tremble and be grateful that it was not them.

Just her and Becky.

Then there was Miriam. How in God's name was that going to play out? *There's the kid with the sick sister? The sister in remission? The dying sister? The sister who passed away?* Sylvia closed her eyes. She was going too fast. God only gave you what you could endure.

She could endure Jack. She knew she wouldn't be able to survive this. But she had to get herself sorted out inside. She had to get to someplace where she could handle it, one day at a time, one hour at a time. Otherwise she'd just be a weeping pillow for her daughter and not much good for anything else.

Tamara, like Nataly, didn't believe it. Couldn't believe it would be true.

"They always tell you the worst case scenario. It must be some kind of mandate to avoid malpractice suits. You can't believe it's true."

"But if it is, Tamara," Sylvia said, "if it is—" Sylvia paused. "Look, when I know, you're going to have to call and let everyone know. I'm not going to be able to do that. I'll get a list together for you. Just not yet. Just not now."

"Of course. Of course."

God only gave you what you could endure. Becky had been talking to her. "What, baby?"

"Do we go home after this?" Sylvia shook her head and squeezed Becky's hand.

The cluster of ill children thinned and re-formed while she and Becky waited. Then they were led to the MRI, where Becky, with an easy compliance that now angered Sylvia, got onto the bed and smiled up at the technician. As if she were loved, as if these strangers were going to care for her.

During the thirty minutes of what sounded like gunshots, rifle shots, artillery, going off over and over again, Sylvia worried about Becky and wondered about the poet Anna Akhmatova. Had she ever lost a child, that woman who had lost so much? The noise of artillery shot through her bones. What about Becky's bones, she wondered? What about Becky, inside this machine? After this was over, Sylvia told herself, she'd never think about the divorce again. What had happened no longer mattered. The money didn't matter. All that mattered were her daughters.

Maybe Jack could commute to New York. She could live that way. She would even be grateful.

Back in the room that night, Becky slept, face slack, eyelids displaying tiny pink veins across them. Sylvia pulled an orange frosted leaf from the cookie bouquet and unwrapped it. Leave it to Celeste. Sylvia had never even heard of such a thing. A dozen cookies in autumn shapes. A leaf, a pumpkin, a pine cone. Sylvia chewed her frosted leaf slowly. It was gritty with sugar.

Dr. Johannsen no longer made the rounds in Becky's room—Dr. Roeg did instead. The nurses no longer stayed and made small talk. They probably avoided mothers with grief-stricken faces in sheer self-defense. Her mother said she was just being paranoid, but Sylvia recognized self-preservation when she saw it.

When Mercy put Miriam to bed Monday night, she asked to hear her prayers. Miriam recited a prayer in Hebrew. Mercy gathered up Miriam's tiny hands, as she had the hands of her daughters. "Let me show you the way I prayed with your mother."

"Dad won't like it," Miriam said.

"Close your eyes."

Miriam did.

"Dear God," Mercy said.

"Dear God," Miriam echoed. Mercy felt a tingle in her chest. "Please be with Becky in the hospital." Mercy paused and Miriam echoed softly.

"Please bless my mommy and Aunt Celeste and Auntie Nataly. Please God, bless my daddy and have him call. Amen."

"Amen," Miriam echoed.

The tingling was in her heart, her eyes, her nose. "This is my granddaughter," Mercy said, "with whom I am much pleased." Mercy lay in her granddaughter's bed, feeling the girl's little body fidget, waiting for the even breathing, waiting for her to fall asleep. She had done this often with her own daughters but not enough with Becky and Miriam.

Joey's face came to her, the face he had when Mercy had put a book on her head or pretended to snore really loud or pretended to sneeze half a dozen times. The look of surprise, delight and adoration. When would God stop punishing her? Would Sylvia know Becky's being sick was her—Mercy's—fault?

After Joey died, it had taken weeks before Mercy's mother talked to her. Lydia stamped out of the house each morning, waiting in the street for Mercy. Everything took Mercy interminable amounts of time: getting out of bed, getting her clothes on, eating her breakfast. Her mother served the beans, eggs and tortilla to her wordlessly. Silently judging, silently grieving, and all that judgment and grief landing on Mercy's eight-year-old head.

The high chair remained empty and accusing. It gave Mercy a twisted feeling in her stomach to see it. Outside, Lydia screamed for her to hurry up or they'd be late again! Finally, she finished the beans, held onto the tortilla and went out the back screen door silently, without a word to her mother, without a word from her mother. This entire scene, different menu, would be repeated at lunch time. *If only,* Mercy thought all day and all night, *if only Mrs. Ganz would take me home.* Mrs. Ganz was Mercy's third-grade teacher.

One day, weeks after Joey's death, Mrs. Ganz walked home with Mercy at lunch time. On the way, Mercy laughed and babbled and pointed out the houses where her mother sometimes worked. Her beloved teacher, who still talked to her, was coming to her home! Maybe Mrs. Ganz would ask her mother's permission to take Mercy home with her. Maybe Mercy was moving—moving in with Mrs. Ganz. That must be it!

As Mercy thought about this, she continued to point out landmarks: that's where they kept two roosters, can you believe it? We once had a cat and that family still has one of her kittens, Muffin, grown up now. Mercy pointed and babbled. Mrs. Ganz listened and nodded.

Lydia kept as far away from the third-grade teacher as possible. This was serious. *No one else had their teacher walking home with them.* Lydia ran up to Mercy and whispered in Spanish—so Mrs. Ganz couldn't understand even if she could hear—"What, did you kill a kid in class today?"

If she could, Mercy would have killed Lydia.

Mrs. Ganz rapped on the door. It had just been rescreened, and its momentary perfection contrasted strongly against the peeling white paint of the wooden shingles. Mercy wondered what Mrs. Ganz' house was like and if she could take her doll with her.

It must be hard, thought Mercy, *asking someone to give them your daughter*. The whole wide world stretched out behind Mrs. Ganz, the piercingly blue sky, the sweep of birds, the glint of bright sunshine. The leaves were gone, swept away and burned by now. Not even the branches moved in the calm of the midday. Behind Mrs. Ganz was the road they had just walked down, and along it lingered Lydia.

Mercy's mother was in no hurry to reach the door.

"Mrs. Fuerte?" Mrs. Ganz rapped again.

"Who is it?" came her mother's voice, free of any accent whatsoever. By eight years old, Mercy had already noticed her mother's tendency to communicate or misunderstand according to how it best suited her purpose. On some occasions, her mother's English was impeccable. On others, it was worse than the Japanese gardener's at school.

"Mrs. Ganz, Mercedes' teacher." That was another thing about Mrs. Ganz, she always called each of her students by their full names. No familiar nicknames, no nonsense.

Mrs. Fuerte opened the screen door and looked at Mrs. Ganz with a small frown, "Has Mercy done something again?" she asked.

Could her mother look any different from her teacher? That black gray hair braided into a crown on top of her head, the bifocals she peered over perched on her nose, an apron, a needle in one hand, bits of thread on the apron front. While Mrs. Ganz was tall and gaunt, her mother looked shorter, squatter, darker.

"May we come in?"

Mercy bounced into the kitchen, pulling her teacher behind her. Was this the last time she'd be seeing this kitchen? Oh, there was the high chair. She wouldn't miss that, never. Maybe she would miss her mother, a small bit. But she was confident she'd get over it.

"I've sent notes home. I was hoping you would come to school so we could talk."

For the first time in five weeks, Mrs. Fuerte looked directly at Mercy and spoke. "Why didn't you give me those notes?"

Mercy's mouth opened and shut and nothing came out. *I gave them to you! I gave them to you!*

"It doesn't matter," Mrs. Ganz was saying. "I'm very concerned about Mercedes."

Mrs. Fuerte grunted.

"Mercedes was close to being at the top of my class this year. After the tragedy, she's a completely different little girl. I wanted to work with you in helping her through this accident."

Mrs. Fuerte grunted again. It was a sure sign her English was rapidly diminishing.

"Mercedes was, is, the little star in my classroom, Mrs. Fuerte. How can we work together? How can I help? How can I make it any easier for Mercedes?"

In Spanish her mother, for the second time in five weeks, spoke to Mercy. She said: "Why did you bring this idiot to my home?"

To Mrs. Ganz she said, "Mercy is a very willful child. Let me know when she is misbehaving and I will punish her."

"That's not what I'm saying at all! I'm trying to help her survive this tragedy."

"She survived. Joel did not," Mrs. Fuerte said. "Now I must feed lunch to the two children who remain." Mrs. Fuerte firmly steered Mrs. Ganz out of her kitchen, down the steps and closed the screen door against her. Mercy could see Lydia gaping at her teacher as she walked back onto the road.

For the third time in five weeks, Mrs. Fuerte spoke directly to Mercy. "What are you telling her?"

Mercy watched her teacher pass Lydia, who still gaped. So she wasn't moving in with Mrs. Ganz? Well, at least her mother was talking to her again. And it didn't matter, it was only November. She would have Mrs. Ganz to herself until June. After all, she was the little star of her class.

How important that had been to her, to be Mrs. Ganz' star. Now, thinking about it, Mercy knew it had saved her life. God willing, at some point in her teaching career, she had saved someone else's.

In the hospital room, Sylvia had turned off all the lights, but the room still glowed with the monitoring machinery and the light from the hallway. Sylvia wondered whether she had mailed out that last batch of bills on time.

She tried to think about everything else—the scrip drive at school, her plans for the fall planting. Nataly and Celeste. But it forced its way to the surface despite her efforts. What bargain can I make with you, God? What sacrifice will you accept for my child? Then she searched her mind for anything from her childhood that would also mean she was a good Jew. Psalms. *May the meditations of my heart and the words of my mouth be acceptable in thy sight, O Lord, my rock and my redeemer.*

Peter had been patient and consoling Sunday afternoon but now it was clear to Nataly he was bored with the entire conversation. "So tell me again," Nataly said, scrunching up her eyes tight so that every word he said would find a toehold in her brain and remain, fixed and permanent. She needed to remember everything he said.

"Nataly, we're not talking about your niece here. Right now, I don't know what your niece has. They called me in because they're worried. I can't talk to you specifically about Becky, do you understand that?"

Nataly nodded.

"We're speaking hypothetically."

"Hypothetically, what if a kid has a mass in her lower back?"

"A mass in the soft tissue in the lumbar region."

"Her lower back."

"Right. At first they may have thought it was an infection. Then it may not have responded to treatment like an infection should. Some indicators of infection would have been a high fever, but there's no history of that. Also, if pain doesn't respond to treatment, to the massive doses of antibiotics that a child similar to Becky should be receiving, then we have to proceed on the assumption that it is not an infection. And pain like that, similar to the pain that Becky is experiencing, could indicate cancer. To confirm that we need a tissue sample, a biopsy—"

"A biopsy. Tuesday morning."

"Which means taking a microscopic sample from the mass. And then the doctors work from there."

"Negative?"

"If it's negative, there's the possibility that they need another sample."

"Positive?"

Nataly opened her eyes and leaned over to look at Peter. He turned towards her. "Statistically speaking, Nataly, a mass like this in the spine is cancer. The odds of it being anything else are very, very low. I can't tell your sister something like that—but you need to be ready to brace yourself and support her. This is going to be hard."

Nataly rolled away from him. "I don't believe it," she said. "I don't believe Becky has it. How could she have gotten it?"

Peter sighed. "When you figure that out," he said, "you'll be first in line for the Nobel Prize in medicine."

Then he kissed her on the side of her neck.

When Peter left, Nataly rearranged the twine. She had avoided the tapestry and was working on another installation piece. She was dissatisfied with the project she had attempted. It seemed commercial in the worst possible way—Latino iconography without irony, without wit. So serious and literal. And enough to make her rip it all out and start again and that was what she was doing this Monday night.

She hadn't shown Peter her work. Not yet. They rarely seemed to make it out of her bedroom. If Peter did, it was only long enough to put on some slacks and pay the delivery boy at the door. It didn't matter. When he was here, her entire apartment was infused with this golden haze, as if someone was using a soft light and a fuzzy lens.

She ripped out the yellow stitches she had used to embroider a calaca. The grinning skulls weren't so entertaining right now. But that was supposed to be the whole point, wasn't it—death was everywhere, death was now, enjoy this brief moment...

But this was America, and Becky could not have cancer. Not in this family. Nataly had tried not to think about Celeste because all she could think about was how much she must despise her now. But she couldn't know he's married? Sure, not until the next time he makes the rounds and she checks out his ring finger.

Wait a second, she thought, scooping up the scraps of thread and throwing them into a trash container, *wait a second, is this God's reality check? Is this like the beggars at my doorstop? Am I supposed to give Peter up—stop sinning—and Becky will be okay?*

Nataly pushed at that thought like a painful cold sore. Maybe that was her destiny. A secret, personal sacrifice. For the greater good. A small voice laughed from a corner in her mind. You couldn't give him up even if you wanted to, it cackled. Then she thought of the look on his face when she was half naked.

By six o'clock Tuesday morning Becky had already been awakened and prepped for the biopsy. Sylvia had signed the many different waivers. The one that stood out most vividly was that since the biopsy was in such a delicate place—spinal cord, nerves, etcetera—in case of mishap, the hospital was released from liability. *Now that's a comforting thought,* mused Sylvia. My daughter may not have cancer but might be paralyzed from the waist down.

She followed the gurney as two attendants wheeled Becky down the hall, into the elevator, then down to the basement, where Becky continued through another set of doors and Sylvia was directed to the waiting room. She was shocked to see so many people, at least six, waiting as well. They were all transfixed by the TV set, and there was low, furtive conversation. Some idiot pilot had crashed into the World Trade Center. Unbelievable. Was he drunk?

How moronic, thought Sylvia, avoiding the waiting room. She stepped back into the hallway averting her eyes from the TV. At this moment, her mind had room only for one person, Becky, who was lying on an operating table.

For forty minutes, Sylvia paced the corridor, examining the smudges on the hospital wall, the speckles on the vinyl hospital flooring—away from the lobby, away from the television set, all the time feeling as if the biopsy were being performed on her own heart. The floor tiles seemed to shift and move about as she paced. Everything was out of focus.

When they wheeled Becky out, Sylvia could barely breathe. Her daughter's face was slack, slightly discolored. *Had something gone wrong?* A nurse in a blue smock guided the gurney to the recovery room. Other people in various stages of awakening were there. The nurse looked rough and raw, but patted Becky's cheeks gently and firmly to wake her up. "You've got to make sure she wakes up and stays awake." The nurse's voice was sweet and cooing when she said, "This one's a piece of gold. Wake up, darlin'."

Becky did that to people. Brought out their tender side. She fought to stretch open those sleepy lids, then gave up. The nurse prodded her some more. Becky woke up, goggled wide-eyed at her mother, then began to retch. The nurse swiftly held a plastic container under Becky's head.

"She's waking up just fine, Mother. You make sure she stays awake," the nurse said, patting Sylvia on the shoulder. "In about twenty minutes, they'll wheel her back up to her room." Then they would wait some more, Sylvia realized. They would wait for the results.

Positive? Negative? They would wait to see if they had gotten a large enough sample. She had been warned they may have to do this again. Two days? Five days? When would those tiles remain fixed on the floor? When would her world go back into focus?

Sylvia said to no one in particular, "I don't know how I'm going to do this." Then she leaned over Becky, patted her face and made certain her little daughter opened her eyes.

Two attendants pushed Becky's gurney back to the hospital room as Sylvia hovered at its side, talking to her daughter, jostling her, making sure those heavy eyelids stayed open even as Becky tried to nod back to sleep. One of the attendants had family in Manhattan, and the women were talking about two of the towers being hit and collapsing. Sylvia felt no connection to any of it.

Becky was right here, eyes shutting every few minutes, face looking slack and fetal, and Jack was God alone knew where. Sylvia was here too, right here at Children's Hospital, three thousand miles from New York City, surrounded by the smell of disinfectant, decay and despair.

Sylvia was surprised to see her mother and Miriam in Becky's hospital room. She hadn't wanted Miriam to be here.

"I know," Mercy said, "but we wanted to be with you now."

"We've got to keep this little girl awake."

Miriam sat next to Becky, held two cookies and started a conversation between the cookies. Becky looked up at her through heavy eyelids.

Mercy wrapped her arms around Sylvia. Sylvia leaned against her mother and closed her eyes. She wouldn't think about New York City. She had no connection to it. She opened her eyes. *Wait a minute...* Jack was there...in the financial district...she was sure his itinerary had listed a meeting today at the World Trade Center.

"Mom, I've got to get home. Jack's in New York."

Sylvia waited for Becky to be awake enough to wiggle her toes, to smile at her grandma and Miriam. She stayed through lunch and then she drove home. At home the office looked exactly the way it did the evening Jack had come in, menacing her over coddling Becky. It occurred to Sylvia that the computer screens looked like an altar, and that was where she and Jack worshipped. She sifted methodically through all of her emails from Jack, hoping for an itinerary or contact numbers. She found the itinerary. He did have a meeting there—yesterday, today and tomorrow. She dialed his cell phone only to hear his voice mailbox. She called his secretary at work.

I will not panic, she told herself. Back, buried deep, far back, a soft chilling voice, her own said, but what if it's true? What if it's true? Remember the life insurance policy Celeste had you get? And now you'll never have to tell your friends, your sisters, your mother how bad your marriage was. You'll never have to flinch at the sound of his voice or steps or anger ever again. What if it's true? No one deserved that, another voice replied. Not even Jack. And it's shameful, shameful, to anticipate something so horrible.

She found nothing. No contact numbers, no help from his secretary. When she turned off her computer, she heard the faint hum of his computer. The screen was dark, but it was still running. She tapped at the keyboard. In a moment the screen brightened.

Eudora, Jack's email, was running.

She sorted by sender. She sorted by date. She started reading all the emails from mid-June.

Dear Jack:
Reese tells me you missed this morning's meeting. We've already discussed appropriate corporate behavior more than once.

Sarah Garvey
Cc: Bill Claireborne.

>>

Jack:
We're still waiting for your information on the Steiner case.

Hector Salas

>>

Jack:
Return your calls, dammit!

Sarah Garvey

>>

Hey Jack,
I'm going to be thinking about you all day. Till tonight,

Robyn

Well, that's no bloody surprise, is it? Any other day of her life that might have been the end of her world or at least a stick of dynamite, but Sylvia brushed the thought aside impatiently. The emails from Sarah Garvey continued. Apparently Jack's firm had put him on probation and had warned him that a suspension or release from his firm was a strong possibility. There were even emails from creditors. A couple of their credit cards were overdrawn. A couple of others she didn't recognize.

There were emails from Sarah, Hector, and Bill Claireborne demanding to know where Jack was. Or had been.

My God, they're patient with him, thought Sylvia. But they had a reason. He brought them so much money. *So much money,* Sylvia thought, thinking of her own home, her own car. Their trips. And that was never enough.

Was it really just this morning Becky had had her biopsy?

If what she had heard on the radio was true, the Twin Towers didn't exist anymore.

"So, Jack, are you dead or not?" she said to the screen. That gleeful voice from a far corner of her brain was getting louder. *Jack would make it out*, Sylvia thought. He defines self-preservation—Jack would never be slowed down by offering to help someone else, he'd never look back. She looked around the office.

It would be obvious why he hadn't been able to communicate with her. He was too busy saving his own life. She could hear him tell the story again and again—to the business friends they dined with—how Sylvia was obsessed with Becky while he, Jack, waded through the streets of New York City. Yes, that's the way it would turn out. Sylvia thought she was either very calm and had reached that acceptance stage, or she was very numb. She tapped at the screen again, and decided to search by name. By Robyn.

After reading ten emails, the calm had evaporated. She dialed the Amsterdam number she read on the screen.

"Hotel Claire," said a woman's voice.

"Jack Levine, please."

"One moment."

After sixteen rings, he picked up, "Hello?" It was a male voice, masculine—tired or interrupted.

"Jack?"

Now the voice sounded bemused. "This is Robyn, not Jack. Hold on."

"This is Jack."

Sylvia hung up.

Two men, one room. She looked at the clock and added eight. Two in the morning. She redialed the number.

"Hotel Claire."

"Jack Levine's room, please. We were cut off."

This time it was Jack who answered. On the first ring.

"Jack, this is your wife. Becky has been in the hospital for the past week. Last week she had an MRI scan, today a biopsy. She may have cancer. I thought you were dead in goddamned New York City, but instead you're screwing your brains out in Amsterdam. I hope your cock is happy!"

She hung up before he could respond. She let the phone ring over and over again. She went to the office and reread all of the emails. She sorted by name. Emails from Robyn started a year ago. They were graphic, almost violent. Sylvia shuddered with disgust. This, this too? She reached for the phone. Tamara or Celeste?

Nataly had paged Peter four separate times. She had paged him four times, and soon it was going to be five. She tugged at the black ribbon that trimmed her jeans' pant legs. She had sewn this iridescent material on top of all the edging on her pants, her favorite jeans, only to realize she would never be able to launder them. When she realized that, she stitched herself a black bustier out of the same material. That was what she wore when Peter came over.

She called Peter.

Peter Roeg didn't return Nataly's calls.

While it wasn't unusual for Nataly to wait a few hours—or a day even—they had last screwed Sunday, they had last spoken Monday, the biopsy had been this morning and she wanted to know. She wanted to know.

Nataly was at home in her weaving room. In her artist's loft. In her room of dreams—all the different names she used according to her different moods. But she felt brittle and distracted, like she'd drunk too many cups of coffee on top of amphetamines, like she'd taken too many drugs shaken and stirred together.

But she hadn't taken anything. She made herself a cup of herbal tea. And if she was going to start now, between vernissages or openings, she'd never get any work done.

But moving from one room to another, distracting herself with catalogues of yarn and materials, waiting for the kettle to boil and then the water to cool down enough to sip, did not rid her of her restlessness. Nor of the ache for Peter, nor of the anguish for Sylvia and Becky. She felt like she had when she had dieted down to ninety-five pounds that sophomore year in college. Always on edge, always ready for a fight, always ready not to merely bite someone's head off, but to savage it. She wished her father would call right now. She'd be sure he'd never call again.

Kric krac, rick rack, kric krac, rick rack. Now her materials were talking to her, the rick rack making ripples of sound every time she looked at it, the pitch changing as she ran her fingers across it, the iridescent black trim looking at her accusingly, knowingly. It kept saying to her, "This is a shroud, this is widow's weeds, this is a shroud—" while the balls, ribbons, loops of yarn hanging from a post laughed in the tinkling voices of children. She could hear breathing from the bolts of cloth and whistling from the threads.

God is the loom upon which we weave our lives.

Everything had been talking like this since Nataly visited Becky in the hospital. As she worked the loom, the treadle made small muffled noises of pain.

All in all, Nataly's work room was a cacophonous cathedral. In the pit of her stomach, as it churned and twisted, she understood the message she was receiving. *No tiene vergüenza*—she was shameless. Give up Peter, and Becky would be all right. Give up Peter, and there would be no cancer. Give up Peter, because that was the sin her sister and Becky were paying for. Nataly cursed. Celeste had seen them. There were no private sins.

She pulled a drawer of beads out to hot glue against the fabric she had been wrestling onto her work table. The beads clattered to the floor. Black ovals, jewel-like green crystal beads, white pearls. *You are killing Becky*, the clatter said.

Nataly scooped them up, not worrying to sort them back into their slots. If he dumps you first, Becky still loses.

That's why she'd been paging him. To tell him it was over! But she wouldn't call him a fifth time, she couldn't just leave a message, she wanted to hear how he'd take it, what he'd say. Whether he'd be relieved or surprised. Hurt or distracted. That's why her guts were in an uproar, why her head was buzzing, why her materials shrieked at her.

It was Tuesday and she hadn't heard from him. Then the phone rang. Was it Sylvia? *Oh, God*, thought Nataly, *I didn't break up with him. Becky's going to die.*

It was Yesenia. "I'm okay," she said, breathless.

"Why wouldn't you be?"

"Turn on the TV!"

Celeste was on the phone with Victor Resnick, talking about what they had witnessed that morning on their television sets. *Spectacular* had leapt to Celeste's mind. Then, *God bless them, God save them all*. Victor was saying that Silicon Valley would probably be the next target, the seat of America's technology. Call waiting clicked through. It was Sylvia. *No more horrors, please God*, Celeste thought, as she ended her call and braced for Sylvia's news. All the pain she had endured reverberated with the pain she had watched, and now—a dead unborn child, shattered expectations, was one thing. But the fear of losing the child you'd borne, raised and loved for over six years was another. If she had dread in her heart, what was Sylvia feeling?

Sylvia's voice had a quality in it Celeste had never heard before. Celeste couldn't understand what her sister was saying. Sylvia repeated it.

"It's not Becky," Sylvia said, firmly. "I mean, yes, it is Becky, but it's also Jack. He told me he had a meeting this morning, in New York, in the Twin Towers."

"Oh my God, Sylvia."

"But he didn't." Sylvia told Celeste the story, quoting from the emails on the screen in front of her.

Celeste said. "Tell me what you want to do."

"It's over," Sylvia said. "It's been over for a long time, but this time it's finished." Sylvia spoke calmly, deliberately. "I want to end the marriage. But I'm afraid. I'm afraid about medical insurance right now. I'm afraid for Becky. But I want it over."

"You're covered as long as the divorce takes, and we can write the medical into the settlement. Don't worry about that, it can be handled. The very first thing you do is access all of your joint accounts and put the money into your own personal account. Do you understand?"

"Yes."

Celeste was quiet, thinking. "Forward his emails to me." And then, "I know the best lawyer." Victor, of course. Then, "I can fly back down tomorrow, if you like. I can fly down this weekend. You just let me know."

"They won't know about Becky for days. For days, Celeste. And then they might need to do it all over again."

The two women said nothing at all for a moment. Celeste said, "Sylvia, let me help you with this. I'll make the calls."

Sylvia said, "That's what I want you to do. You start whatever you can start. I'll wait till after…you know…after we find out about Becky to worry about it. Like worry about what an idiot I've been for way too long."

"You're my sister. You are incapable of being an idiot," Celeste said.

Sylvia said, "I'm glad you think so." And she meant it, but she just couldn't feel anything right now. Her heart was tethered to an anvil and both were at the bottom of the ocean. That place where heat vents opened up and strange life forms dwelt. The rest of Sylvia was here on the surface, dealing with the misery of being.

Celeste went to bed with a legal pad and a calculator. From what Sylvia had said, Jack was in a very weak bargaining position. The problem was, if he was so self-destructive, he would have no money to pay for alimony, no job for the medical coverage. This was, however, what Celeste could do. Money was wonderfully impersonal and subject to manipulations and permutations.

A thought entered her head as she turned off the light. If he had been killed this morning, his life insurance policy would have ensured Sylvia was set for life. Money was clean. Life was messy.

Six the next morning, Celeste's phone rang. Caller ID blocked.

"Celeste? It's Jack. I'm sorry to wake you, but Sylvia really needs your help. I really need your help."

"You do?" Celeste replied noncommittally, grabbing her pen and legal pad.

"There's been…there's been just a terrible misunderstanding. And it's all my fault, of course. And you know, of all the Amado women, I always thought I was closest to you."

Celeste snorted inwardly. Like the time he pinned her in the closet? And apologized for thinking she was Sylvia? Sylvia had laughed. Jack was just a little drunk, a little toasted, she said.

"What's up, Jack?" she said, feigning a sympathetic ear.

"We're all adults here," he said. "You know as well as I do, no marriage is perfect. And I'm going to be the first one to admit I haven't always acted with—"

Intelligence? thought Celeste. *Honesty, honor, integrity—*

"Wisdom," Jack said. "But now Sylvia's, well, she's not taking my calls. We had an—incident, and now it's blown out of proportion, but I see the error of my ways."

"I'm glad you called me, Jack. You know I love my sister, and I'd love to help you in any way I can. But you're going to have to slow down or something. I'm not following what the problem is."

Celeste heard Jack's sigh. "You know I changed firms a year ago. It was a long time coming, because Fletcher, Luna and Mims just wasn't providing enough stimulation. I know they are the top of the line for my kind of work, but the excitement, the magic, the sizzle was gone. You know how stupid men are, they can't figure out what they're feeling—or why. I'm sure I blamed Sylvia. Even though I made this massive job search and landed quite neatly on my feet at Whitlock and Associates, I kept looking for, um, other forms of stimulation."

"Like?" Celeste asked, pen ready at pad. "What stimulation?" Celeste prodded.

"You name it," he said. "The drugs the office staff discussed, the parties that friends of friends of friends threw. I didn't realize how old I'd become, how much of a stuffed shirt I'd turned into till I went to one of those."

"We do get old, don't we?" Celeste said.

"Half the time I didn't know what they were handing out, whether it was meth or ecstasy, but some of it was rather—exhilarating. Absolutely intoxicating. And the rest of my life—wasn't. And when you added another body, well, suddenly being alive finally meant something."

Celeste listened. He could tell her this on the phone because there wasn't a face to look at, there were no judgmental eyes to hide from. *At last, he found someone he could detail his thrilling misadventures to,* Celeste thought. *Did he want sympathy? Absolution?*

"Which part are you afraid Sylvia overreacted to?"

"Oh Christ, she thought I was in New York, I didn't get her messages about Becky. I was in Amsterdam."

"Lots of stimulation there."

"Yeah. But listen. This morning the fantasy crash-landed. It's over, that chapter of my life has ended. I want to finish the book, the rest of my life, with Sylvia."

Celeste wondered how long he had worked on that phrase.

He continued, "With Becky as she is, I'm just sick, sick, sick that I wasn't there for her. Look, I'm waiting for my flight—but it's been delayed. They're not saying when flights to the U.S. will be running again, but once they are I'm heading straight for my wife and children. As God is my witness, I love them more than my own life. I'll do anything to keep Sylvia and the kids."

His voice was cracking. *He is good,* thought Celeste. She'd never be able to get her voice to crack on cue. "Jack, why are you telling me this? You should be telling Sylvia."

"That's just it. She won't take my calls."

"It seems to me," Celeste said, deliberately, "that Sylvia will come around. Email her. Tell her what you've told me. Tell her, you know, you've sinned and that—" *put it in writing, give Sylvia evidence and ammunition.*

"It's over," Jack said. "I've finished with that."

"You must have had some other conflict in these past ten years, and I'm sure she came around then."

Jack cleared his throat, paused, as if debating how much to reveal, how much to conceal. He said, "Yeah, you're right. She does come around. She sees the light of reason."

"So it seems to me that something you should really be working on is ensuring that your job situation is stable."

"You're not kidding about that."

"I don't really think you want to end that—"

"It would be hell on everyone if I did. And it is a sweet position. I've just been an ungrateful bastard."

"So be a grateful bastard, get your act together at work. Speaking as a sister, it's going to take Sylvia some time to recover. Plan on renting a hotel room and working your ass off." *Give Sylvia possession of the home.*

There was silence as Jack thought about it. "You're so right, Celeste. I'll solidify my position, I'll look like a gold brick to Sylvia, and it'll be better. Thanks, sweetie. I knew I'd called the right person. I better get packing."

Don't call me sweetie.

After the biopsy, it was as if they no longer knew what to do with Becky. Unsure of what they were treating, the doctors discontinued all medication. The following day, they discharged her. Sylvia would await the results at home.

Tamara was at their house with her sons, watching Miriam. The administration feared that Jewish private schools would be the next logical target so their school was closed. Sylvia and Mercy retrieved Becky, the bouquets, the get well cards and the new pajamas. Becky— little dimples on her cheeks, little hands waving at the nurses—smiled at everyone as she left and asked her mom to let her say goodbye to her friend next door, the bald little girl edged in pink.

It wasn't until they were in the Explorer driving north towards the Hollywood Hills, with Mercy in the back seat alongside Becky, that Sylvia let out a tentative sigh. Goodbye to nights in the hospital bed. Goodbye to the hum, click and whir of monitoring machines. Good bye to the IV, nurses coming in at ten, two and four in the morning. Good bye to that, at least for now. *Please God,* thought Sylvia, *please let that be the last time.*

Sylvia parked on Vermont, stepped into a French bakery, and ordered a box full of pastries: croissants, chocolate and plain, almond tarts, chocolate éclairs. She didn't look at the total as she signed the receipt, and she added a ridiculous tip, $5 dollars for loading the pastries into a pink box. *Please God, please God, let Becky be okay.*

Once Sylvia and Becky returned home, Tamara stayed long enough to talk with Mercy, nibble at an almond tart, and make another pot of coffee.

"We should bomb them all," Mercy said, pushing her plate away.

Tamara said nothing.

Sylvia said, "I agree. Although I wonder who would 'they' be. However, the more innocent people we kill, the greater our moral superiority."

Mercy shook her head, "You always make fun of me."

Sylvia kissed the top of her mother's head, "You make it kind of easy."

"Don't do that," Mercy said.

Tamara said, "I wonder what our constitution will look like, a year from now, a decade from now."

Sylvia shrugged. All she truly wanted was for Becky to be alive a decade from now.

Celeste drove down the 5 Freeway, making her time from San Jose to Pasadena a little under five hours, stopping for gas and coffee and food. The planes that typically monitored motorists' speed were grounded—Celeste was not the only one taking advantage.

Sylvia was alone when Celeste got there, the girls asleep.

"You just missed Nataly." Sylvia said.

"Right now, that's probably a good thing. You seem fairly calm."

"I am calm. I'm ready. If Becky's going to die, I am going to do that right. I'm not afraid of Jack. I'm not afraid of anything else. I can take care of my daughters." Sylvia smiled, and Celeste wondered at the warmth behind it. "I just need you to help me take care of the money."

Early Thursday afternoon, just after Celeste drove off to San Jose, Dr. Roeg called. God, did Sylvia hate Dr. Roeg. On principle. What kind of man goes into a line of work where you watch children die? It was incomprehensible.

"We have the results, Mrs. Levine."

Jesus jesus jesus, was all Sylvia could think as she sat down, bowed her head, and leaned against the wall for support. *Jesus, jesus, jesus.*

He said, "We feel we had a large enough tissue sample to be perfectly comfortable with this diagnosis. At this time we suspect it is an anomalous form of osteomyelitis. There is absolutely no trace of cancer cells." Sylvia was still.

"Does that mean you have to do another biopsy?"

"No, in this case no trace of cancer cells means there is no cancer."

"Thank you," she said. *Thank you jesus thank you jesus thank you jesus.* "Thank you. What does she have?"

"Osteomyelitis. It's a bone infection in a very unusual site. We're prescribing an oral antibiotic." He kept talking, but she had stopped listening. She thought of the mothers she had watched, their damaged children, the centerpieces of these families' lives. She and Becky had escaped!

"These are obviously the kind of phone calls we sincerely enjoy making," he said. "Take care."

Sylvia hung up the phone and began to cry again. The anchor attached to her heart at the bottom of the sea had been hacked off. Now Sylvia had the bends reassimilating. She wouldn't watch her daughter die. She wouldn't watch her daughter die. Sylvia began to laugh, then cry all over again. Sylvia allowed the joy to infuse her being. She wouldn't spoil it, not quite yet, with thoughts of the future, with thoughts of her tasks at hand.

When she was ready, she listened to all of Jack's messages. First cajoling, then weeping, finally badgering, ten different messages. In all of them, the bottom line was that he wanted back in. There were a few particularly nasty calls after he realized she had transferred all their liquid assets out of the joint accounts. With the buzz of joy still in her brain, Sylvia calmly took the mini tape out of the answering machine, placed it in an envelope and addressed it to Celeste. She smiled wryly to herself, realizing that he had not once mentioned Becky.

Sylvia left him a message at work with Faye, his secretary. "Please tell him that Becky is completely fine."

"Mrs. Levine," Faye said. Sylvia knew her. She was a young black woman with short cropped hair who frightened Sylvia with her efficiency and wardrobe. "Your husband is so brave."

"What do you mean?" Sylvia asked.

"His walk down the second tower, of course!" she said. Sylvia caught a whiff of surprise and exasperation.

"Oh," Sylvia said.

"You must be very proud of him," she continued, encouragingly, "for helping all those people."

Sylvia said, "Words fail me."

Then she called her mother and Celeste and Nataly. Upstairs, she peeked in as Becky and Miriam watched TV in her room. Miriam's arm rested on top of Becky's. Becky giggled at something happening on the screen. They could watch it all day, for all she cared. They could stay glued in front of the set for a week. All year! She stepped to glance out of her bedroom window, past the immature landscaping of the tract home yards, across the brittle brand new roofs. Light reflected off of the buildings, the cars, the industry of the San Gabriel valley. A bathtub ring of smog hovered on the horizon. Yet all of this was incredibly beautiful. She called Tamara and the women gushed with relief together.

As she hung up, she thought of those other women, those other mothers she had left behind in that waiting room with their children, with their illnesses.

For dinner she ordered Chinese food for Becky and pizza for Miriam. She had never done anything so absurdly extravagant. It was the best meal she never tasted, sitting there watching her girls and their funny mouths, teasing each other, small teeth chewing while they watched TV. A part of her wished Jack could share this, that he could see what a miracle it was to sit in front of the television with his two healthy children and eat takeout. That he could see their lives, for just a moment, through her eyes.

The Amado women exhaled with relief and joy at Becky's news. At the same time, the destruction that brought down the Twin Towers traveled across the nation, squeezing Celeste and crushing Nataly. As Celeste urged her clients to hold, hold, hold and even buy, clients she had known for years, some nearly a decade, were jettisoning stocks and funds in order to "get off the grid." This recurring theme was a kind of madness. Celeste couldn't find the right words to dissuade them. Her portfolio shrunk and so did her clientele. She would buy as people sold and wait it out. She was here for the long haul. In the meantime, she could cut her expenses. She had alternatives.

Rimsky's shuttered in October. This was Nataly's opportunity to dedicate herself to her dream, to her craft, but that glimmer of hope in New York, Manolito's Gallery, closed the day after the attacks. Yesenia was treading water, just barely holding on.

"That window has closed," Yesenia said solemnly, pissing Nataly off.

Out of work, Peter out of her life, Becky out of danger, Nataly worked on her portfolio, on her art. By November, she had borrowed a few thousand dollars from her mother. Both of them knew the terms of the loan: constant emotional payments in exchange for no monetary return. Nataly thought that the interest was getting a little high, especially when her mother thought she could drop in unannounced.

Nataly had this financial imperative running through her head day and night which she was sure was absolutely undermining any creative thought or deed or plan. The local galleries weren't interested in her work. Her art wasn't selling. She worked on her tapestry. It was not yet ready to be removed from the loom and sculpted into the figure that waited. She worked on other projects, but the loom waited for her.

She stopped at the grocery store on Vermont. She liked it there because it sold ethnic items at half the price of chains. She also liked it for its fresh flowers—not that she was buying any these days. She discovered it blocks from her home when Becky was at Children's Hospital, and she needed a bouquet for Sylvia that wouldn't break the bank. That was the day after Celeste caught her with Peter.

Nataly laughed to herself. She saw the pained and pinched expression on Celeste's face. How long had it been for her dried-up older sister? Old and dead and withered long before Nataly ever would be. Ever, ever, ever.

What was she laughing at? Peter was gone, gone, gone.

Nataly placed a loaf of bread in her cart, stood at the deli counter, pondered between the smoked salmon bits and the salmon roe, then decided on neither. Instead she picked up the much cheaper eggs and some flour tortillas. Thirty-three years old and she couldn't buy salmon roe when she wanted it. Nobody was hiring art instructors at the community colleges.

The first week of January, when the sun slanted across her front window, Peter rapped at her screen door. He looked so vivid, so masculine. *Un hombre es como un oso, los mas feo, lo mas hermoso.* Did she only imagine she could smell his scent?

"What do you want?" Nataly said.

"I want to pay your rent," Peter said.

Nataly raised a skeptical eyebrow, unlocked the screen door and let him in.

He walked through, following her into her kitchen where she poured herself a cup of tea, not offering him anything. He stood there, waiting for her response.

She knew his scent, his taste, his touch. She dipped her tea bag. She had made a private deal. She would no longer see Peter and Becky would live.

"Why would you want to do that?" she finally said.

"Because I need you in my life." He didn't wait for her response. He took the mug of tea out of her hands, set it firmly on the counter and pulled her towards him. She remembered this. This was the way it should be.

And his wife? Who cared? She must know by now what kind of man she married.

And Becky? Who was she that Becky would be whole or sick? No one. Who she chose to sleep with had nothing to do with Becky.

Two weeks later her body had never felt so good. So good. A little fat in the right places, a flat tummy, every nerve ending taut with longing, then slack with satisfaction. Every moment spent waiting for his touch.

How ridiculous, Nataly thought.

They ate chorizo and egg burritos in bed. The orange grease spilled onto her bedspread and now dripped onto the sheets. Peter ate three burritos, then pulled her on top of him.

He had his hand on her naked thigh, stroking it, stroking inwards, distracting her, distracting her from what she wanted to say.

"But Nataly, I can't throw you a party. That would not be discreet."

Nataly had closed her eyes and was moving, then opened her eyes, glared at him, pushed his hands away. "You don't throw the party. Hang one of my pieces up in your home, show it to your friends when they visit, when they seem interested, have a friend invite me to do a showing in their house. You live in Hancock Park, for chrissake. There's disposable income just waiting to be tossed in my direction."

Peter had a familiar glazed look on his face, "I know people who would throw money in your direction. We'd need to install a pole—"

"That's disgusting," she said, falling back into her bed.

"You worry too much about money," he said, kissing the nape of her neck.

"You have too much money to worry," she said, drawing away.

"I've always had this fantasy—" he said.

"Another one?"

"Of having a sex goddess all to myself."

A corner of Nataly's mouth went up. She said, "One day we're going to work on my fantasy."

In March, Sylvia invited Celeste down for a family weekend to celebrate how smoothly the divorce proceedings were going. That night while Sylvia made an elaborate Mexican meal—chicken and pork in a complicated green mole which included sesame and pumpkin seeds toasted and ground, spices, cilantro, epazote, parsely, Swiss chard and more—Celeste trimmed the stems off the vegetables.

While Sylvia fried the nut mixture in lard, in raced Miriam, wailing, trailed by Becky. Becky had ground a lump of chewed gum into her sister's scalp.

"The best way to fix that," Sylvia said, "is to stick your head in the freezer for an hour. But, seeing as how your head's not detachable, we'll have to come up with something else." Sylvia spent the next hour hovering over Miriam's scalp with a plastic tray of ice cubes, freezing bits of the gum and peeling it off of Miriam's roots. In the meantime, Celeste followed Sylvia's directions, sautéed and steamed the rice, refried the beans, finished the green mole.

Mercy stood next to Celeste, peered into the sauce pan, scowled, looked away.

"Why couldn't you two get along?" she said. "Why couldn't you make up with Nataly? Every time, I feel like I'm watching a fatal collision. And it is. Every time we get together and you two are like that, a part of me dies. She should be here." Mercy looked at Celeste. "All I ever wanted was for my daughters to love each other."

"Guilt. You want me to feel guilty," Celeste said. "Don't worry about a thing, Mom, I've already got guilt enough for the three of us."

Mercy scowled. "What are you fighting over?"

Celeste stopped scraping the sauce from the bottom of the pan. "Pain. We're fighting over who hurts the most."

Mercy said, "I don't understand."

Celeste continued to stir.

Sylvia banished Becky to her room before dinner, then after to the kitchen to eat alone.

Mercy said, "That's not right. How is Becky supposed to feel?"

"Bad!" Sylvia said.

Celeste said to Sylvia, "If I had been you, I would have been screaming and cursing and crying." Celeste tilted her wine glass in the direction of Sylvia's glass of soda. "Well done, I am impressed. You make cooking and raising kids look easy. As a single mother."

Sylvia said, "I'm not a single mother. I've got you and Mom and Nataly. And if that looks easy, I'd hate to think what hard is. Trust me, Celly, if Jack were here I'd have been screaming and crying and yelling—and so would my daughters. It is the most wonderful sensation. I feel like I could hike Mount Everest in an afternoon." Sylvia scooped up a last drop of green sauce with a scrap of corn tortilla. "If I can divorce Jack," Sylvia said, "I can do anything."

Celeste hugged her sister. "I'm going to go upstairs and console your daughters."

Sylvia smiled, then noticed the look on her mother's face.

"I can't believe you waited so long to tell me what you were plotting," Mercy wailed. "I can't believe you're going through with this. At least I waited until you girls were grown!"

Sylvia laughed. "You know, Mom, you probably didn't mean it to, but you actually just made me feel good about doing this."

"It's just he was…he was always so nice to me," Mercy said. "I always thought…I always thought he loved you so much." The more Mercy dabbed at her eyes, the lighter Sylvia's heart became. She wouldn't explain it, she couldn't analyze it, but before Jack— before she decided to divorce him—all her energy was taken up with pretending to the girls that this was right, pretending to her sisters that everything was fine, pretending to her mother that hers was the perfect marriage inside the perfect home with the perfect husband.

"What are you smiling about?" her mother demanded.

"I'm sitting here laughing because you're telling me how hard my divorce is going to be on you. Doesn't that strike you as ironic?"

"No!" Mercy said. "It just shows me how much I've screwed up. Only one of my three daughters is married and now even that's gone. How am I supposed to know if any of you are happy? Two of them—spinsters!"

Sylvia nodded her head. She noticed that her mother looked cold and uncomfortable, her hair a strident shade of auburn, her eyes full of hurt. Her mother—her glamorous mother with the highlighted hair, the stylish sunglasses, the perfect nails and the highest heels—suddenly looked old. Sylvia moved to her mother's side and put her arms around her.

Mercy continued, "After the hell I went through, I didn't want any of you getting married, ever. And then, as the three of you floundered around, I realized all of us need someone—"

When Jack had come for his things, Sylvia and the girls had been long gone, up north, staying with Celeste. Sylvia couldn't stand to see him or talk to him any more than she already had to. And now that Jack was out of the house, completely out of the house, down to the last Ralph Lauren sock, Sylvia had music in her heart for the first time since—since ever. Since Celeste's wedding. Since the day she and Nataly had sung for their big sister. The immediate future, like then, was now the entire realm of possibility.

She smiled at her mom again and asked the question that always consoled her daughters. "Want a cookie?"

"No, I don't want a cookie! I want to know how I could have prevented this." Mercy dabbed at her eyes and waved vaguely around. "All of this."

Sylvia said, "Mom, I absolve you of all moral and financial responsibility."

"You're right," Mercy said, "this is completely Edgar's fault. If he had been any kind of a father at all—."

"He had been a kind of father. One of those fathers that's simply not there."

"What about the girls?" Mercy interrupted. "What about Miriam?"

Now that was where all the music disappeared. It was one thing to fantasize about dancing on the grave of your deviant husband, it was another thing completely when Sylvia thought about the impact on her daughters. Sylvia had never lost the weight of responsibility for her children, but when that doctor declared Becky healthy, normal worry seemed as easy and as natural and as insignificant as belly button lint. Looking back on things, Sylvia knew that she could have found something within her to survive a terminal illness. Sylvia knew that the misery of caring for your dying child could be a sacrament, could indeed be something holy. But thoughts of not having to do that filled her with helium lightheadedness.

And the thought that Jack wouldn't be there to second guess her or to belittle Becky made her smile with relief.

But kicking out your daughter's favorite parent? What had Miriam done last night? All brown-eyed, honey-skinned innocence, laying in bed, her hands clasped on her chest—

Sylvia answered her mother. "After her Hebrew prayers last night she said, 'Dear God, please forgive my mother.'" Mercy's eyes flashed in Sylvia's direction. Sixty-one, no makeup, dabbing at her eyes and her nose, and Sylvia could see Mercy was so beautiful, more beautiful than any of her daughters had been. Miriam looked just like her.

"That's because you have too much dignity. You're not at all like your mother. It's a good thing I didn't divorce your father when you were kids. God alone knows who I'd be dragging home with me. And when I did leave Edgar, you all knew exactly why. You, on the other hand, have too much dignity."

"Please stop, Mom, now you're going to make me cry."

"It's true! You're not going to go in there and justify yourself to a nine-year-old! You're not going to go in there and tell her details that would be painful for her to hear and humiliating to you. You're going to let her think her father is an honorable man. And that's probably a very good thing for her. And it's going to be hell for you. But you, my daughter, have the dignity to carry it off." Mercy sighed, sat up, smiled and said, "Nothing at all like your mother. What did Nataly have to say about this?"

Sylvia told her mother, "Nataly said that she knew it and she never liked Jack in the first place." Sylvia sipped her soda. *What a terrible thing to say.* Did Nataly have any idea how big her mouth was? Considering all those horrible men Nataly had dated and brought over to Sylvia's to introduce—tattooed artists, men of questionable means and proclivities. Sometimes she really understood why Celeste wasn't speaking to Nataly. Was she intentionally cruel? Or just thoughtlessly stupid?

"Well," Mercy said, "you're going to have yourself a time with Miriam. I think Nataly still thinks it was my fault her father turned out the way he did. I should have been able to do something about it. I should have been able to prevent all of his shortcomings. And you know, I think she got that all from me. Don't you think Celeste could bring the girls down now?"

The next afternoon Celeste sat on Miriam's bed examining the bedroom. Miriam and Jack had picked everything out of a Pottery Barn catalog. Sylvia had not approved, but Sylvia was overruled. Celeste studied the bedding, the curtains, the furniture. Jack might have had the money once to buy all this, but now he appeared to have nothing.

How convenient when it came time to allocate child support and alimony.

Becky wrapped a roll of toilet paper around and around Celeste's left arm. She had decided she wanted to be a nurse and was playing hospital.

Miriam kept telling her younger sister, "You want to be a doctor. You don't want to be a nurse. Doctors get to come and go, nurses have to stay."

Celeste watched as Becky ignored her big sister and continued to carefully tighten the roll as she wound.

"There," she said.

"But nurse, can I still arm wrestle?" Celeste asked.

Becky's eyes widened, she took a deep breath and said, "With the other hand."

So this was life with two kids, thought Celeste. Except, really, you didn't play hospital all day. But it didn't seem so bad. It didn't seem so overwhelming. "Doctor, I need a nap," Celeste said and lay back onto Miriam's bed. Celeste was thirteen before she had her own room.

Celeste closed her eyes and begun to wonder whether America's elevated standard of living was on the backs of Chinese sweatshop workers when both Becky and Miriam started shrieking. Celeste sat straight up. Miriam and Becky were kicking at each other.

"Stop it!" Celeste yelled, pulling at Miriam who clutched tightly to Becky. "Stop it right now, or I'm bringing Grandma up here to stop it!"

The girls' bodies went limp. Miriam sobbed in a muffled way. It took Celeste ten minutes to discover that they were fighting because of a song. It was Becky's favorite song, and Miriam kept singing it.

"Girls," Celeste said, "the two of you give my flight out an entirely new level of urgency." They just ignored her. "Come on, Becky," Miriam said, "let's go see if we can play on the computer."

By the time the shuttle van honked for her, the shrieks of her nieces and Sylvia's blissed out obliviousness had begun to wear on her. Rattle, rattle. Something knocked around in the emptiness inside her. Ice cubes? A baby's rattle?

On the plane, Celeste ordered a double Bloody Mary. Her mom had asked why wasn't she talking to Nataly. She had neatly skirted the entire issue of Nataly and the doctor. The very handsome doctor. The very married doctor. Nope, she couldn't tell her mother all that. Mercy would swallow it all and blame herself.

"After a certain age, Mom, you're just going to have to let us win or lose on our own." *Their losses would be their losses,* thought Celeste, *her victories her own.* Like that financial advice column she had started with a dot com.

Tuesday morning, Sylvia dropped the girls off at school and headed towards the errands facing a divorcing mother of two young children. She popped in a Pretenders CD. Singing along, she felt young and powerful. The Santa Anas had kicked up the night before: palm fronds and brittle oak, elm leaves, arboreal debris spread over the lawns, jammed against the curb, creating great piles in the streets that

Sylvia swerved around as she headed out. The sky was a brilliant blue, the mountains far away covered with snow. An ordinary beautiful day. There were groceries, of course. And a visit with Tamara this afternoon, to chat about the details of Tamara's upcoming trip to Israel, but before all that, Sylvia had made a promise to herself. She headed towards the pound.

Jack had hated dogs, told her that two kids were enough, was allergic to cats—in short had the same tender feelings for animals that he inflicted on his immediate family. Miriam had always wanted a dog. Early in Miriam's young life, she'd point out photographs of dogs, wave to the dogs being walked down her street, and lobby her father and mother with big eyes and sweet words. This hadn't worked on Jack.

In the meantime, Sylvia researched and read about a variety of breeds of dogs, but there was something about pure breeds that rankled her. What was the word Mexican but a corruption of *mestizo*? What were mestizos if not a blend of bloods, like her children? How many times had the phrase pure bred been used to beat thoughts of inferiority into some mixed blood's brain?

The first time she went to the pound was an idle visit months ago when she fell in love with three dogs. She knew then she couldn't involve her girls in the decision. They'd end up with twenty-five dogs at home. Today there was a parking spot in front of the pound, right on the street. Sylvia swerved in, right behind the sedan with a "Read your Qu'ran" bumper sticker. She ended up spending quite a bit of time at the Humane Society on Raymond Avenue. Her girls didn't know yet what she was planning.

Today was a marvel, thought Sylvia. Today she could do anything. She could take up Russian again. In fact, today reminded her of that story, a story she couldn't shake out of her head, by Zamyatin—"The Most Wonderful Thing." People in the story were dying, but the hope was that something wonderful was being born, something glorious. She'd have to reread it when she got home, then discuss it with Tamara.

Sylvia glared at the pit bulls and pinschers. Maybe not her style. She grinned at a friendly, awkward German Shepherd puppy, still clumsy on its paws. Too big, too much dog poop, too little yard.

It was a mutt that charmed her. About the size of a footstool, a dirty cream color. She needed bathing and grooming. But her eyes were bright, her tail friendly, and a ridiculous sense of connection clicked within Sylvia. "I'll take her," Sylvia said.

There were shots and registration papers and license fees and neutering fees. An hour later Sylvia, with a fat grin on her face, cradled her dog and loaded her into the passenger seat of the car.

"My girls are going to love you," she crooned into its hairy face. But first, she would drop by Tamara's and show her off. As Sylvia buckled herself into the driver's seat, the dog scampered into the back seat. A moment later the dog began to whimper. Sylvia couldn't see her. She unbuckled herself, stepped out of the car, and opened the left passenger door.

The dog sat shivering on the floor directly behind the driver's seat.

Sylvia pulled a serape out of the trunk, plumped it up under and around her dog. Miriam would love her again when she saw this dog.

Sylvia shut the side door firmly. As she reached to open her own door, she caught movement from the corner of her eye. She turned. The pale, white face of the driver was the last thing she ever saw.

Tuesday morning, after her sixth graders had recited the Pledge of Allegiance, Mercy had her students sing, *I'm a Yankee Doodle Dandy!* She loved watching her students sing. With so much wind last night, it had been hard to sleep, but now, watching all thirty-five of her students, she didn't have time to feel tired. From Laureano who arrived from Guatemala, to Emily, whose mother had attended this school. So many experiences to introduce them to, so little time to squeeze it all into. Through her experience with her own daughters, she knew she had no influence whatsoever over adults. But her "Room Eight is Great!" class was its own community.

From Lompoc to Santa Ana, Mercy thought this morning. *From babysitter to teacher. From young stupid mother with young stupid husband to gay divorcée.* She would never, ever retire. They'd have to yank her out with a crow bar.

That afternoon as Mercy's class transitioned from social studies to independent activities, the classroom phone rang.

"Room Eight." Mercy answered. The class was silent. She had trained them to do that. "Hello, what is it?" she said. "What?" not understanding, not wanting to understand, not believing. "What happened?!"

Emily watched Mrs. Amado drop the phone as if it burned her, and begin to sob.

Peter rapped on the screen door.

"What are you doing here?" Nataly said, surprised, happy, but irritated. She was in the middle of working on this tapestry, this tapestry she'd been promising to Yesenia, this piece of art that was supposed to be her ticket to New York one day. She had set the day aside, had entered the realm of her art, and now he was here. Peter walked through, pulled her towards him and kissed the side of her neck. "I came to collect the rent," he murmured in her ear.

"Ugh! I hate it when you put it that way," she said, pushing him aside.

Later, wearing nothing but a silk Japanese print kimono, she was gently moving up and down on top of him, when the phone on her night stand rang. She let it ring, but Peter picked it up and handed it to her.

"Jack," she said. "Of course I'm sitting down," and in that brief instant simultaneously smirked at Peter and thought what a pretentious ass you always are, Jack. Peter moved his hands up her rib cage, higher, higher.

"I missed that, Jack," she said, her voice now hoarse, the lubrication within her drying up, God's judgment on the telephone. She clambered off of Peter, even with him tugging at her, and moved away, anywhere. Now she couldn't see anything, all the light within the apartment was gone, so she stepped outside onto her balcony, still unable to see a thing.

"What kind of sick, fucking joke is this, Jack!" she shrieked into the receiver, "If you think this is gonna help you with the divorce, you are OUT OF YOUR MIND!"

She dropped the phone over the railing. As she ran back into her apartment, she ran into Peter.

"What's wrong?"

"Leave me alone," she said. "Leave me alone!" She felt her way into her work room and began yanking down the first things she came across: the bolts of cloth, the loops of yarn, the rack of threads. She pulled the drawers and drawers of beads out and spilled them onto the floor, where they clattered and spread. She slipped on them, caught herself and felt her way towards the tapestry she had been working on.

She could still see nothing at all. A dark grayness covered everything and in her eyes and ears was just the pounding of her heart and blood. She felt along her work table, found a pair of scissors and started cutting her tapestry into strips. As the yarn and thread gave way, Nataly felt something satisfying in the tension and the shredding, in the destruction of what was supposed to be beautiful.

"Stop it!" she heard Peter. "Stop it!" came his voice and she continued to shred, to feel the threads and fibers give way, end, cease to exist as a tapestry.

She felt him grip her by the shoulders, turn her around, and slap her face. Her head rang with the flashes of light, and then she saw him.

She began to weep, because he looked so masculine, so male. Because of this, she couldn't help herself. And because she couldn't help herself, Sylvia was dead.

"You have to go," she said. "You have to go. It's over. It's no good. Sylvia's dead."

"Sylvia?"

"My sister. The woman with the sick kid who got better. She's dead. She was standing in front of her car, and someone hit her head on. You've got to go. I mean, it's not like you'll be coming to the funeral with me, is it?" Nataly inhaled and picked up one of the new strips to blow her nose on. *Life was shit, life was shit, life was shit.* And everything good—everything good—had such a fucking high miserable price tag. And everything bad stained all that was good indelibly, permanently.

Peter stayed. He steered Nataly into the living room and onto her sofa, where she sat with the kimono draped around her, sighing. How many different ways could she have done everything all over again? She took deep breaths and wiped her nose with her kimono while Peter spoke softly into his cell phone. What about the babies? They would be Jack's, and none of them would ever see those girls again. They would all be punished for hating Jack. They would all be punished for Sylvia daring to divorce him.

"Could I have a glass of water?"

Peter appeared with a glass of cool water.

"Could you get me the phone? I need to make a call."

"You threw it into the courtyard."

From her home Mercy tried calling Nataly, but her apartment phone just rang and rang and rang. Her cell phone picked up on the first ring, which meant it was off. *Ohmygod, she doesn't know yet*, thought Mercy, not leaving a message.

Peter handed Nataly his cell.

"I need you to find my address book. I don't know the number that I need to call. It should be on my nightstand."

Peter handed her the Frida address book.

Right after Jack called Celeste, Mercy called, incoherent. That was okay, because Celeste was incoherent. She had really thought, truly thought, honestly believed, that she would never ever allow herself to again feel the pain she had felt when Skye died. But here it was, engulfing, overwhelming, a tap root into all that grief she had tamped down. As her mother babbled in Orange County, Celeste murmured in San Jose. The pain radiated from the base of her skull, from her throat, from her chest. There was a ringing in her ears, and the faces of Sylvia and her children in front of her eyes. She couldn't hang up on her mother, she wouldn't, it didn't matter if they couldn't understand each other's words. They understood the depth of each other's pain.

When she hung up, the phone rang. Nataly heard Celeste's voice, low, muffled, filled with pain. "Celeste?" Nataly took a deep breath then let it all out in one rush, scrunching her eyes tight, "I'm so sorry. I'm so sorry, Celeste, forgive me. I'm sorry for everything I've ever done. I'm sorry for everything. I'm sorry for any pain I caused you, I'm sorry for being angry. I don't want to be angry anymore, I don't want to feel so bad when I think about you. I can't bear it, I can't bear it another minute. Do you forgive me?"

It was quiet. Nataly knew, in that silence, that it was too late. The silence confirmed that Celeste hated her.

Finally, Celeste said, "Nataly, I love you. I love you." She was quiet again. "I don't understand forgive. I don't understand what you're asking me to forgive you for. But I understand pain." Celeste cleared her throat. "Could we just try not to cause each other pain? Do you think we could start there?"

"I need to hear you say you forgive me. Because I forgive you." There was silence. This was no good, too late, not enough—

Celeste said, "I forgive you. Okay?"

Nataly nodded, then realized Celeste couldn't hear that.

"Yes," she said. "I love you, Cellie."

Celeste later found out that Jack made all the calls, just as he made all the arrangements for Sylvia's funeral. "Lynn will drive me today," Mercy said. "Jack asked me to come. He can't get home right away." Suddenly all that grief turned to rage within Celeste. *The filthy liar.* "He asked me to tell the girls," her mother continued. " He didn't want to do it over the phone."

He didn't want them to hate him. "Don't tell them till I get there, Mom. I don't want you to do that alone."

"Nataly will be there with me."

"We'll all be there."

It was after ten at night by the time Celeste arrived at Sylvia's home. She carried an overnight bag and rapped softly at the door.

"Cellie!"

"Jack!" she said, in surprise. Celeste collided into a reality she hadn't anticipated. His light brown hair was messily swept over to one side. His face look dissolute, but that could be because Celeste knew about Amsterdam and that she hated him. He was alive and her sister was dead. He pulled her and her overnight bag into the house and into his arms, crushing her.

"I'm out of words," he said. Celeste smelled the alcohol on his breath. "Your mom and sister are in there," he said, pointing to the family room. "Do you want a drink?"

"Sure, sure. Thanks, Jack. Thanks for letting us come."

He waved her away and set off with his own drink in one hand.

"Where are the girls?"

"Asleep, upstairs, in our bed."

In the family roo, Celeste had a terrible jolt. There was Sylvia, next to their mother, looking sad and penitent. No, no, it was Nataly, Nataly and their mother cradling each other, unable to move.

Celeste gave her sister a hug and smelled her shampoo, smelled her skin, inhaled the scent of her sister who still lived. With nothing to say, she sat on the other side of her mother.

After a moment, Mercy said, "Nataly and Jack and I told the girls."

Celeste nodded.

Then Mercy glanced around and asked her two daughters, "Did he kill her?"

"No, Mom, he didn't," Celeste said. Jack had been in Phoenix. The police told her they suspected it was a drunk driver. Witnesses said someone driving a dark blue brand new Cadillac Escalade. Perhaps, perhaps they'd even find him. Celeste knew it would have been easier somehow, more intelligible, to put this all on Jack instead of an invisible random driver—a pointless, miserable accident.

Celeste didn't see Jack, but noticed he had set a balloon glass of red on the table and beside it an open bottle of wine. Celeste automatically sipped at it, but it was as if it were finely ground glass in her mouth. She set it aside.

"What about the kids?" Nataly asked.

"They're his kids," Celeste said.

"Will he take them away from us?" Mercy asked, tentatively.

"He can take them anywhere he pleases," Celeste answered.

The three women lay back on the family room's sofa, Mercy in the middle, clutching the hands of her daughters.

Celeste headed up the stairs, tapped lightly on what she had always considered to be Sylvia's door. There was no answer. She walked in.

The door to the master bathroom was open, its light on, illuminating the girls in the bed. Celeste could see Miriam staring up at the ceiling. Becky was curled up, asleep next to her older sister.

"Hi, baby," Celeste said to Miriam.

Miriam deigned to look at her. Her expression was neutral, her voice natural. "Oh, hi Auntie. I've been up all night, thinking. Can I tell you what I think?"

Celeste nodded, noticing Miriam's pajamas. They were cotton with a flower print. Had Sylvia bought those? She held one of Miriam's warm, slender hands between her own.

"I think that it should have been me instead. I wouldn't have minded, not really. I mean, I've had a pretty good life so far. But now it doesn't make sense. I can't take care of Becky. And Dad? He doesn't even like her. I mean, maybe he loves her, but I know he doesn't like her. And it's just kind of icky always knowing your dad likes you but thinks your sister's some kind of dog poop or something." Miriam moved the blankets up to Becky's chin.

"So, I've been thinking that God should have taken me instead. But I can't think of anything in the Torah that says God let somebody travel in time and fix it all."

Celeste kissed Miriam's hand. She looked at Becky, curled in a fetal position, purple veins running across her translucent eyelids.

"You know, right after he told us about Mom, he said we could go out and buy a Nintendo tomorrow. Right. Like I'd want to play on any stupid toy I got because my mom died." Celeste watched for tears. For anything to crack Miriam's neutral face, natural voice. "I'll never be able to see her again, not ever, will I?" Miriam looked at Celeste. "Don't lie to me." But her eyes tried to challenge Celeste to say something else.

"Well, I've been thinking about that," she said. "And you're right. Of course you're right. None of us are going to see her again. But, in a small sense, parts of her are in her sisters and her mom. And between the three of us, maybe we can remind you of what was good in your mom. Lucky for me, she had two kids. And maybe when I need to see your mom, I can see parts of her in you two."

"Aaah," Miriam said, skeptically. She stared up at the ceiling, then turned to Celeste. "Do you think we could live with Auntie Nataly? Or you?"

Celeste pulled Miriam into her arms and rocked her. "Oh, baby.

Auntie Nataly and I would love to have you girls. More than anything. But your daddy loves you. Your daddy wants you. It'll be okay, you'll see."

"Aunt Celeste," Miriam said, her voice muffled by Celeste's hugging and rocking. "Nothing will be okay ever again." Then, in a soft voice Celeste didn't recognize at all, "Will you lay down with me? I asked Grandma to put us to bed cause I thought it might make her feel better. But could you lay down with me? I can't get to sleep."

Miriam moved over and Celeste kicked off her shoes, then got into Sylvia and Jack's bed. She listened to the wind pick up outside. She must have been there twenty minutes before Miriam's breathing became steady and her twitchy body still. Not till then did Celeste get out of the bed and head downstairs. *Nothing will be okay ever again.* How could it be?

S
ylvia's funeral was held graveside at Forest Lawn under a brilliant winter sun. The Santa Anas had swept away the clouds and smog. The gardeners had blown away the scattered debris. That morning at his home Jack had asked each of them—Mercy, Celeste, and Nataly—if they wanted to say a few words, and each of them had declined.

As Jack addressed the gathering of sixty or so people, Becky squirmed around on Nataly's lap, examining the crowd. Miriam sat between Celeste and Mercy and stared up at her father. Jack talked about his courtship of Sylvia in college, the birth of their girls, the struggles within their marriage—how they had recently separated, but were already discussing their future together again. And that, before they were officially reunited, Sylvia had been "called away."

Celeste frowned and wondered why Sylvia hadn't told her about this reunion. Then, she thought, *Damn, you're good, Jack.*

The cantor began a deeply moving song. The rabbi, a young man with a face so friendly it might be declared foolish, began to speak and praise this young Sophia for her contributions to the world at large, for her commitment to raising her children and for her wisdom and skill in the arduous task of being a woman. He mentioned her name incorrectly a few more times until Jack leaned into him and murmured. The rabbi flushed deeply.

Celeste stopped listening. Apparently Protestants hadn't

cornered the vapidity market. The rabbi never seemed to recover from his misstep and continued half-heartedly. *They all are mortal,* thought Celeste. *They all have feet of—mud.* And we just collude with them when we pretend to ourselves that they have some kind of direct pipeline to God. No God, no direct pipeline. Just a vivid fantasy life.

And a dead sister. Celeste looked at her nieces. The girls wore the matching purple velvet dresses their grandmother had bought them for Christmas Eve. Celeste had hung back this morning as Mercy had wakened them, cradled them, explained the day, fed them and later dressed them.

Little seeds of Sylvia. Celeste could remember when her younger sister was six, was eight, then thirteen. Once upon a time. None of that, ever to return.

Miriam clutched her hand as the plaintive singing began again. Sylvia had converted to Judiasm. Did that mean she believed more? Or less? Celeste had never asked her. It had never interested her before.

Celeste watched as a tall, elegant brunette stepped up to the podium, wrangled the microphone off its stand, and stood in front of it. She wore a long purple tailored coat and a lavender scarf wrapped around her shoulders.

"What are we doing here?" she said. "I look at this sunshine, this glorious day, I see Sylvia's friends in the audience, I see her sisters, I see her children, and I wonder, where is Sylvia? What are we doing here?" The brunette looked around at the audience. "When Jack, the man she was divorcing, asked me to speak, I said, no. Absolutely not. I'm going to be sitting in the audience sobbing, bawling my eyes out. But, as you see, I changed my mind." She cleared her throat. "I want to thank, you, Rabbi, for not trying to explain the inexplicable.

"My friend, my beloved friend, my best friend, Sylvia, is gone. And let's not pretend there's some eternal plan to make this all better, because that's bullshit, pardon my Russian. Bullshit which ignores our pain—the pain of her friends, her family, her children."

Nataly glanced at her mother. She was nodding in agreement.

The brunette dipped a pale hand into a deep pocket of her coat and pulled out a slip of paper, glanced at it, then returned the slip to her coat pocket. "But I don't want to talk right now about the pain we are all feeling. I want to talk about the joy that was Sylvia. You may, of course, have known a different Sylvia—Sylvia the room parent, Sylvia the chair of fund raising, Sylvia of the car pool, Sylvia of the UCI comp lit honors, Sylvia the mother, Sylvia the soon-to-be ex-wife, Sylvia the sister, Sylvia the neighbor. Sylvia the fierce, Sylvia the brilliant, Sylvia the passionate, the compassionate. Sylvia the indecisive, the troubled, the confused. Sylvia the joyful. The last one was the one I was just getting to know the best."

The brunette smoothed a stray hair out of her face. "Most of you know of the challenges her family faced this last fall with Becky's health. I remember coming to her house and seeing so much of the food you all had brought to her, the toys and cards you had bought. She shared with me some of those thoughts and times and pleasures. You may already know that after that, she had the heart of a poet. The most ordinary moments to Sylvia were beautiful. Watching her girls. Smelling the morning. Watching the mist of the evening.

"I'm telling you this because this is what she told me."

Mercy saw that small tears were coming down the sides of this woman's face. Was this Tamara? Was that her name?

"So my challenge to you today, this week, this month, is to find something ordinary and see just how beautiful it is. And send a prayer in your heart to my beloved friend Sylvia." The woman turned from the audience, replaced the microphone and wiped at her face with a corner of her lavender shawl.

After the ceremony, Celeste watched as women came up to Jack, their eyes filled with tears and compassion. Long, lingering embraces, wiped eyes, well-meaning women. And Jack shaking his head, as if to say, "I don't know what's to become of us." Celeste was too tired, too sad, to hate him, to think straight.

"Oh. My. God." Nataly said.

Celeste turned and saw their father. Dressed in a deep blue business suit, he struggled up the walkway against the wind. She hadn't seen him in years, and here he was, appearing essentially the same: thick dark hair, unlined face untouched by time, experience, or wisdom. He was clutching at what had to be an infant in his arms. Next to him was a very young, very pale blond woman, wearing a peach straw hat which matched her satin peach dress, too tight at the bodice, too short at the legs. She had one hand at her hat and another at the hem of her dress, keeping it down.

"Oh my god."

"*En todo está, menos misa,*" said Mercy, shaking her head.

He moved with that easy sociable manner bred in the restaurant business. Of course he was late. He always ran late.

Celeste turned and scowled at Nataly.

"Don't look at me," she said. "I didn't call him." *I should have, of course. He should know,* Nataly thought.

Mercy said, "Looks like he's been busy."

The Amado women watched as Edgar made his way straight towards Jack, handing the baby to the young woman. He gave Jack a bear hug.

How unexpected, thought Celeste.

"I've loved you like a son," Celeste heard her father say to Jack, and, "I've known the pain of loss," and, "If you can hang on, God smiles on you." Celeste watched as her father pulled the young woman in, held the baby up to Jack as if he were a supplicant seeking a benediction. He hovered nearby as Jack continued to speak to others.

"They make a perfect couple," Mercy said. Celeste gaped at her. "Jack and your father. They were made for each other."

Nataly held her breath as her father finally headed in their direction. "Do you want to go now?" she murmured to her mother.

"Why?" Mercy said.

Celeste examined the young woman who held Edgar's arm. To other people, her father had always appeared intelligent, charming, entertaining. To her, he was simply the man who watched TV. Who made inane remarks. Who stopped returning the calls of two of his daughters after the divorce.

"Celeste! Nataly! Mercy!" he said, in that flattering public voice of his. "It's been too long. Too long." Celeste stood, endured his embrace, then watched him crush the women on his left. A tear squeaked out and rolled down his cheek.

Nataly said, "I see you have another grandchild. What's this, a souvenir of your secret life?"

Edgar cleared his throat. "This is my wife Allison and my son Edgar Jr."

Allison smiled with an inane obliviousness that never deserts some people. Her lank blond hair turned up at her shoulders. She held out a hand to Nataly, who defended herself against that presumptuousness with a glare.

Allison waved it away and babbled on, "I'm just so happy to meet all of you, you have no idea! Edgar, I swear, talks about you all the time!" She caught herself. "I mean, this is such a terrible tragedy. I think every mother here is thinking, 'There, but for the grace of God.'"

Celeste cut her off. "That's funny. Here all morning I've been thinking if God had any grace he could have picked someone else."

Mercy looked at her ex-husband. "Edgar, Sylvia is dead. Is this—" Mercy held her arm out regally towards Allison, "really necessary?"

"I just thought you'd want to know how I'd been. I just thought you could wish me well," he whined.

Mercy said, "I have always wished you well. Now I am too busy mourning my daughter and mourning my grandchildren's pain to think about you."

Mercy stood, nodded at Allison, and walked towards the parking lot. Celeste and Nataly followed. Nataly waited till they were in her car, the doors and windows shut against eavesdroppers and exploded: "Can you believe it?!"

Mercy, in a low calm voice, said, "Yes."

"No, I mean, can you believe it? He can't even go to his daughter's funeral without trying to be the goddamned center of attention. Goddamn!"

"Goddamn," Celeste echoed. "You know, Mom, in terms of our father, you got it easy. You divorced him. I'm stuck knowing half his genes are in me. Half."

"Half of Jack's genes are in Miriam and Becky, so you better get over it, real soon," Mercy said.

"'I'm so happy to meet you!'" Nataly mocked. "Like, could she have said ANYTHING STUPIDER? It's like saying," Nataly affected a high, breathy voice, "'I'm so glad Sylvia died, giving me this opportunity to meet you in the flesh and display the current objects of your father's affections.'"

In the back seat, Celeste groaned. She tried to control herself but she hated the beauty of the hills that they passed as they drove home. She hated the sun shining so brightly. She hated the people talking casually in their own cars, so completely unaware of her sister's death.

So much like it had been with Skye. But now Nataly was talking to her, in fact couldn't stop talking to her, it seemed, and another sadness was patted down, smoothed away. It was so hard disentangling everything. She felt as if she were confusing Becky with Skye, and Nataly with Sylvia, and her antipathy towards Jack with her father. As if all the same feelings and emotions simply wore different masks of people on top of them. It was getting too hard. This ache within her was too much. She needed a drink.

"So do you think Jack will let us see the kids?" Nataly was saying.

"Of course," Mercy said. "He's always treated me with respect."

That ache within Celeste seemed to spread. The drive back to Sylvia's was taking forever. She was glad Miriam and Becky weren't in the car with them. The pain would be shattering. She watched the debris on the side of the highway, changing shape and composition as they swept by.

"I just don't understand," Mercy said.

"What?" asked Nataly.

Mercy looked out the window towards the traffic as Nataly drove, dancing in and out of lanes. "All these people living, and my Sylvia not." She wouldn't say the word.

They drove north towards Sylvia's house.

Nataly shook her head and said, "She had a son."

Mercy said, "She was so young."

Celeste looked out the window and said, "Sylvia would have said, 'She was white.'"

Nataly changed the subject. "So, Mom, like I was saying, I really loved this guy. But it wasn't going to work out."

"I'm sorry," Mercy said.

"Sometimes I think I'm just like my father." *I am my father. The worst parts of him. And I hate him for it. Peter had been married and I couldn't even give him up after I'd made my deal with God. Self-absorbed, pleasure-driven—*

"You are not!" Celeste said. "He's stupid, arrogant, self-absorbed—"

"And I'm not?" Nataly said, crossing three lanes to make their exit.

"You're just," Celeste stammered, "an artist!"

The women laughed.

Sylvia's and Jack's house was filled with people none of the Amado women recognized. Nataly looked at the bar: gleaming bottles of alcohol, appropriate glassware, and a bartender to combine and serve. Jack had ordered bagels, lox, cream cheese, sliced corned beef, roast beef, pastrami, smoked white fish. *Jewish crap,* Nataly thought. Shouldn't there have been a pot of beans or something? The rest of the area on the dining table was covered with casseroles, desserts, muffins, breads. The platters from so many different households spilled onto the island and onto the kitchen's counter tops. Should she have brought pan dulce? What the hell did other Mexicans, real Mexicans, do at their funerals? Nataly would have to ask Yesenia.

Celeste caught a glimpse of her father in a far room and heard him loudly exclaiming over the beauty of this house.

Celeste stood next to the bar and looked around. She needed something to slake the pain. Vodka martini? A little scotch? She finally settled on a glass of red wine. The bartender poured. She and her balloon glass headed towards the family room. She sat on a sofa and listened to the conversations around her.

The sleek-looking brunette Tamara stood in the corner, talking with a more matronly looking woman. "Yes, that's what he said. But I promise you, if she was getting back together with him, I would have known—"

"But one never knows what goes on between a man and a woman," the matron responded. "And he seemed so certain."

The sleek brunette noticed Celeste and turned towards her. "I'm Tamara. We all loved your sister," she said.

Celeste sipped at her wine. She didn't care who else loved her sister. Didn't care at all. She murmured, "Thank you, I appreciate knowing that." The wine was exactly as she had remembered it, except maybe she wasn't in the mood for wine right now. She set it on the coffee table, then stood and moved away.

Just a few days ago Sylvia had sat here with her. Saturday night. Sunday. Now it was Thursday. They had talked about the divorce. They had talked about her kids. They had talked about Celeste's intermittent love life, Nataly, their mother. They hadn't wasted their breath on their father in years, and now he was pawing through Sylvia's home.

Sylvia had fretted about the new recipe she was trying out that night they were together, the one for the green mole. Her sister had soaked chiles, ground spices, braised the pork, filled the house with a marvelous aroma. Last night Celeste had come across the leftovers in the refrigerator and thrown them out. Ashes. Dust.

Celeste watched an elegant woman direct the caterers and murmur something to the bartender. Celeste watched as two officers came up to Jack and offered their condolences. That was when Jack broke down, and the two officers—a young Asian man and a young Latino— looked profoundly uncomfortable.

Sylvia was dead, and Jack was alive. All of Jack's problems solved: no divorce, no disclosure of the miserable state of his finances, no embarrassment in front of his firm. She should write a book—*When Fabulous Things Happen to Assholes.*

Celeste stood at the bar and ordered a vodka martini. "Very cold, very dry, two olives." She turned around and saw Jack, dry eyed, telling a story to a group of attractive women, their mouths half open. Sylvia's friends, but Celeste couldn't keep track. She caught the phrase. "80th floor, second tower."

"Here you go," the bartender said.

Celeste thanked him, then headed into the home office. She sat at the desk. Now there was only one computer monitor. This had been where Sylvia had figured Jack out. At that moment, Celeste realized that he had wanted Sylvia to figure it out. Why else use an automatically entered password? Why else leave the computer running, even when you were out of town? Celeste sipped her martini and scowled. Her drink was disgusting. She set it aside. Being here, Sylvia being dead, was all disgusting.

On the left were Sylvia's files. Celeste had seen all of the important stuff: the bank statements, the credit card statements, the mutual funds, the money market, the equity line of credit. She had looked at all of it a year ago and more recently as she helped Sylvia organize for the divorce.

But, funny, during these past few months, as the divorce went forward, and Jack wrangled with Sylvia over everything, Sylvia didn't seem worried at all. "I have a little something," she said. "Something embarrassing for Jack. But I won't use it unless he makes me. Don't ask. I call it my 'nightmare fund.' But it's going to have to be really, really bad in order for me to use it."

And, oddly, everything had been relatively smooth. Alimony, school fees, the house, the retirement accounts. Really, surprisingly smooth. Like even Jack welcomed the relief of it all.

What did Sylvia have?

Jack had just gotten back to the house two nights ago. He wouldn't have had the time to go through all of Sylvia's papers. Celeste stood up quickly, left the office to retrieve her bag in a room off of the entry way. It was smothered between a couple of dozen other black handbags. Celeste's was a burnished brown, a bulky briefcase style. Hell, she could probably smuggle an infant in the thing. She made her way back through the women and occasional man.

She glanced at the bar again. He had used Absolut. Why did that martini taste so wretched? Oh God, there was Jack, at the office door. She turned to the bartender and said, "A little Johnny Walker, on the rocks. No water." As the bartender poured, Jack moved away back into the kitchen area. Where was her mother? Celeste took her drink into the office, set it on the desk and started working methodically through the filing cabinets. Had Sylvia stored it here?

There was a rap on the door. Celeste held her breath, picked up her drink and leaned back in the chair, not having to try too hard to appear bereft. "Come in."

It was Mercy, her eyes watery and unsteady. "Jack needs to go out of town tomorrow."

Celeste shook her head.

"He wants me to stay with the girls."

Celeste said nothing.

"—I'm not sure what he was explaining to me. He's their father, he has custody, right?"

Celeste nodded and began to dig through Sylvia's files.

"So what's he talking about?"

"Why, what did he say?"

"He said I would always be able to see my grandchildren. But if someone decided to make his life difficult out here in California, he would relocate to New York."

There it was. There was his weapon. Now he was threatening her mother. Celeste flipped faster through the files, slammed one drawer, flipped through the next, slammed that drawer, opened another. One at a time, she went through each file folder. There were report cards, mother's day cards, photographs. There were school directories, their temple directory. Folders with nothing that seemed relevant to Celeste, nothing in the cards or photographs that threatened Jack.

She opened another drawer. Mortgage payments, insurance records, earthquake, auto, house. These would have been Jack's records. Sylvia wouldn't have stored anything here.

Her mother said, "What are you looking for?"

Celeste shrugged her shoulders.

Mercy said, "I told him I would be here for the girls. Do you think he would take them away?"

Celeste stared at her mother, "In a heartbeat." She sipped at the scotch. It tasted all wrong, and the pain that had started at the base of her skull was now spreading. The small comfort of buzz was far,

far away. She knocked back the entire scotch in one gulp, hoping that something would help. She went back to the file drawer to the left of Sylvia's desk. But this was hopeless. If she had followed Celeste's instructions, Sylvia had put whatever it was in a safe deposit box at her bank. And now Jack, her survivor, would have access to that.

Celeste worked through the drawer anyway, examining each folder, its contents, each envelope, its contents.

There it was.

Fuck.

Fuck.

Fuck.

Goddamn.

Goddamn, goddamn, goddamn.

Celeste stared at the photographs of her sister, of her niece Becky. Becky's chest was a color she'd never seen, deep purple. Sylvia was someone she didn't recognize, a cut mouth, swollen lips, the left half of her face deep blue, green and purple. She looked straight into the camera, daring the viewer to judge her. More and more photographs, showing Becky's back, Sylvia's upper arm, Sylvia's rib cage, Sylvia's thighs. Celeste wished she had never seen them.

"What'd you find?" her mother asked.

Celeste shook her head, placed the glossy photos back in their manila folder. At the bottom of the folder were the negatives. Celeste slid the folder into the zipper portion of her handbag. She looked at her mother.

"Mom, I need to make a call."

"So make the call."

"Could you give me five minutes?"

Affronted, Mercy said, "Are you kidding?"

"Please. Five minutes."

Sighing dramatically, Mercy stepped out of the office.

Celeste pulled out her cell phone and called Victor Resnick.

"Victor? It's Celeste…Thank you, thank you, I really appreciate it…Like hell…Oh yeah, his house, his kids, everything's coming up roses for him. But I've been thinking about something. You've got all of

Sylvia's information, we've got his financial trail. Remember she told us she held something back in case he got nasty?" Celeste listened, then said, "I've got it right here. I want to file for guardianship."

Celeste listened to Victor's arguments. Victor had always been keen on giving the worst-case scenario.

He said, "Courts tend to side with the surviving parent. I know it appears Sylvia's marriage was unfortunate, but he is the father. And he has massive resources to fight this."

"Well, you and I know he does and he doesn't. I have plenty of money, Victor. I didn't realize what I was saving it for until just a minute ago. Will you represent me?"

Victor said, "The truth is Celeste, unless you have evidence of neglect or abuse—"

"He's leaving tomorrow for New York and asking my mother to watch the kids."

"That can be interpreted as a kind and thoughtful action."

"You remember that entire incident in Amsterdam!"

"Alternative lifestyles really don't impact custody in terms of the surviving parent."

Celeste spoke low into the phone, as if her mother were listening at the door.

"I have evidence of abuse," she said.

"Of Sylvia or the kids?"

"Of Sylvia. And Becky. Photographs. Terrible photographs." Celeste cleared her throat.

"In that case, it ceases to be a civil matter. If this is a credible allegation, Child Protective Services will get involved, the children may be placed in foster homes, an attorney will be appointed for them."

"He can't have the children," Celeste said. "He can't have them. Sylvia hinted that Jack really didn't ever like Becky. I didn't have any idea what she really meant." Celeste willed herself to concentrate on her conversation with Victor, to push the images of Sylvia and Becky out of her mind.

"You may possibly just barely have a case," Victor continued. "I cannot promise you you'll win. You may cause a lot of pain as you go about it. You're worked up about it now, Celeste. Your sister died, you think you have proof of abuse. You're upset to begin with. You can't make life-altering decisions in this frame of mind. You need to think about it."

Celeste fingered the manila envelope. "I already have."

"This is going to get very nasty for all parties. This is going to be exceptionally complicated."

"Fortunately, I'm good at complications," Celeste.

Victor said, "You are, Celeste, I already know that. Do you know anything about foster care?"

"No."

"Let me tell you, the operation's a success, but the patient dies."

"I'm suing for custody." She heard Victor exhale. She pictured him behind his desk, his eyes closed, concentrating on what he would tell her.

"I know you are. Listen, again, historically the courts side with the surviving parent. Very simple."

"He's not going to get them. He's not going to get his hands on Becky."

"And how do you know it was him?"

"What? Who else could it have been?"

"How are you going to prove that? You need provenance of the photographs and corroboration."

Celeste hung up. Sylvia's death shredded her heart, the series of photographs of Sylvia, of Becky, pounded at her brain, the scotch was of no use, and Victor had asked the right questions. How could she prove that it was Jack?

"What are you doing?" her mother asked, stepping back into the room.

Celeste shook her head.

Nataly headed upstairs to find Becky and Miriam. They were lying on their mother's bed wearing their dresses, watching TV, watching cartoons Nataly had never heard of. Nataly sat on the bed a moment with them, trying to follow the samurai character, then headed into the master bathroom. She looked in the mirror. This Nataly would never inspire lust in Peter, not with that puffy face, those swollen eyes. She had become her father. And now her father was living his own version of "Happily Ever After."

Was she just as stupid as that Allison?

Nataly looked at the brass sink fixtures. Everything was new and characterless in Sylvia's house. Shiny and shoddy. The brass had rusted green. Nataly sat on the rim of the tub. *God is the loom upon which we weave our lives.* Who said that? Nataly had begun to hear it everywhere. Yesenia must have said it. Yesenia, who said the time was now, come to New York. But now she had to weep gray tears for Peter, gray for lust and lost opportunity, red tears for Sylvia, for sorrow, for pain, for her nieces, and green tears for her father, tears of anger and envy, resentment and embarrassment. Couldn't she just have let Peter go? Couldn't she just have released him, cut the ties, let him loose and be free? Couldn't she just forgive her father and live?

Out loud she hiccoughed, "I forgive my father, I forgive Peter. I forgive my father, oh God, please let me forgive him. Please, please let me forgive myself."

Celeste drove down Colorado Boulevard in Pasadena, checked the directions on her printout, and spotted the office building on the southeast corner. She pulled into the lot behind it. She passed a sign advertising office space. She walked by planters filled with cyclamen.

Sylvia was dead. But, oh, flowers still bloomed.

Celeste scanned the lobby listings, stepped into the elevator and pressed 4. She glanced at herself in the mirrored wall: in her camel-colored Marc Jacobs tailored suit, she looked intelligent and sensible. She had never until this minute stopped to consider how people might feel the first time they came to her office. She had worked so hard on her end to look like a "professional," to come across as competent and qualified. She was so worried about how she would appear to them that she didn't hang art work that would make anyone think she was frivolous or superficial. She never thought about what was in her clients' minds. She stepped out of the elevator and into the corridor.

She wondered, did their mouths get dry, as hers was now? Did they reach the door and want to walk away, afraid of the answers, afraid of the information, which up until this very moment, was what she thought they had always wanted. The right answers, the accurate information. But at this very moment, she knew what they really wanted—to be told that it was going to be all right. She opened the door.

It was a simple office, plain, with cabinet and bookshelves

covering the wall space. The receptionist's desk was empty but piled with paperwork. Through an open office door, she saw Sam Dresner behind his desk. He was on the phone. He waved at her and raised two fingers. She sniffed. Was he trying to convey two minutes? He wasn't even wearing a jacket. She peered at the desk, then sat down in a chair alongside it. She pawed through her bag, verifying for the tenth time that she had brought her checkbook.

"Come on in." He stood at the door and waved her in. Celeste caught a glance of appraisal, one that she had gotten used to as a teenager, the gaze she had ignored in her twenties, the one that she had seen less and less of in her thirties. He held out a hand.

"I'm Sam Dresner and you must be Celeste Amado."

"That's correct." She shook his hand. She realized she had been clutching her bag so tightly she had ridges on her fingertips.

"Please," he pointed to a chair.

For a minute, Celeste felt as if he were parodying her words and movements. Ridiculous. Dresner leaned back into his swivel armchair and Celeste saw the look of male approval briefly flicker in and out of his eyes. He wasn't much to look at—milky white skin, a smattering of freckles, soft pink lips that some men have that always looked too pouty, too emotional. A shadow growing on his gaunt face even though it was noontime. *He must not get out much*, Celeste thought. His eyes were steel gray.

"So you know Victor Resnick," he said. He looked at one of the pages that papered his desk. He nodded, as if he had weighed her and found nothing wanting at all. "You seem to know important people."

Celeste shrugged, "In San Jose, they're important."

"Hey, even in this backwater called Pasadena, I've heard of them. You outlined it a bit over the phone. Now, tell me again what the situation is, what you have and what you want." He tilted his head against his thumb and forefinger and closed his eyes.

"My sister Sylvia was in the process of divorcing her husband when she was killed in a car accident. She was suing for sole custody, although I know she would have accepted supervised custody. Upon her death, I have been told that her husband, Jack Levine, as the surviving parent, is the legal, uncontested guardian."

Sam Dresner remained still. And continued his position of meditation as Celeste told, again, of the Amsterdam affair, the notes she took of Jack's conversations, Sylvia's recorded messages, and lastly, the photographs. Sam Dresner remained immobile, his eyes closed. When he opened them, Celeste felt their intensity.

"What I want is full and complete custody of my nieces," she said.

"Does Victor Resnick hate you?"

Celeste said, "Of course not."

He rubbed his face and said, "Maybe he hates me then. Otherwise why would he send you to me? You haven't given me one thing to work with." He stood up and walked around his armchair, then sat down again.

"Who took the photographs?" he said.

"I don't know."

"You find the friend who took the photographs, and I'll let you know whether or not you have a case. Right now only two words come to mind: snowball and hell."

Celeste pulled her checkbook from her bag.

Sam Dresner said, "No case, no retainer. Save your check for later. Maybe. In the meantime, let me take you to lunch, and we can figure out which of your sister's friends you need to talk to."

He must have noticed a look on her face, because he added, "And if you think I'm using this as an excuse to later bill you for something swank at Bistro 45, you're wrong. It's five minutes away. On foot."

Outside at a taco stand on Colorado Boulevard, Sam Dresner ordered the tacos de lengua combo platter and a medium horchata. Celeste nodded at the cashier and said, "Make that two." They sat down with their rice and cinnamon water at a pine table. Brown men with thick arms and calloused hands sat at the other tables, scooping their food into tortillas. It amused her to see Sam so at ease here, as if he fit right in. Maybe he did.

Sam said, "Even with low rent tastes, you get disappointed. Not here. What's wrong?"

"How much a square foot to lease your office?"

"I don't remember. What are you thinking?"

"I don't know. I suppose I was thinking I could move my business down here." She had been thinking about this a lot. It seemed the best way.

"Good idea. If we get that far, I mean. You want to be close. They overbuilt like crazy. I don't know what it's like up north, but I think you'll like the terms."

The cashier called from the window. Sam stood and brought two heavy plates to their table. He went back for a bottle of hot sauce.

Celeste smelled the minced onions, cilantro and serrano chiles. She was sure the corn tortillas had been seared on a griddle coated with lard, and she knew they'd be good, just as she could tell by the fluff of the rice that it was done just right.

"So tell me about your sister," Sam said, biting into a taco drenched in red sauce with the ferocity of a fanatic. He wiped his mouth with a sand-colored napkin, "And then I'll tell you what I need to know."

That afternoon Celeste unlocked the door to Sylvia's house and found her mother at the kitchen table doing homework with Miriam. Mercy had accumulated a year's worth of sick days. It was a consolation. A small consolation.

Celeste said, "Who was the woman who spoke at the funeral?"

"Tamara Rothenberg," Miriam said, while scrawling the answer to three times three.

Yesenia was on the phone. Nataly pictured her black hair with frosted pink tips framing her eyes and cheeks. Or had she changed it?

"I'm telling you to get out here," she said.

Nataly thought of the work-in-progress she had destroyed. "I have nothing."

"You've got your portfolio and you've got you. Look, I can even swing you a job at this place I know. It's like stepping into a Scorsese movie. And since hardly anybody in New York knows about Mexicans, they'll probably think you're Italian."

"Is that a good thing?"

Yesenia thought about it. "Maybe not for the Italians."

Tamara's house was quite different from Sylvia's. Far from Sylvia's gated community, it was in a neighborhood in Pasadena that had known mansions for over a hundred years. Celeste recognized the style, but couldn't name the architect.

The camphor trees that arched into the street were shedding brittle brown leaves, carpeting the pavement and turning the California spring into a picture of fall. Celeste walked up the cunningly paved pathway, stepped onto the porch, and pressed the doorbell.

She saw a blinking red light within, signaling the security. This was the fourth time Celeste had knocked on their door and rung the bell. Nor were the Rothenbergs answering their phone.

The yard appeared well-maintained, the mailbox was empty of flyers and personal mail, lights flickered on and off at appropriate times, but there was no one home.

That afternoon Celeste stepped into the school office, the final day before spring break. "Hi," she said to the office manager. "I was hoping to get in touch with Tamara Rothenberg."

The woman looked up at her. Her hair was the color of a shiny new penny. "Have you tried the school directory?"

Yes, she had called, emailed and rapped on their door to the point of frustration. The email bounced—there must have been a typo in the directory.

"Yes, I have," Celeste said, trying to keep the edge out of her voice. "The thing is, I'm Celeste Amado, Sylvia Levine's sister."

The woman got up and crossed over to her. Her bust and belly spread the buttons of her shirt. "I'm so sorry, I had no idea. We all miss your sister so much."

"Thank you. Tamara Rothenberg was her good friend, her very best friend, and I would so love to talk to her. Really, it's very important."

The woman made an unhappy face. "I really am not sure how you can get ahold of her."

"What do you mean?"

"Well, it's not exactly something the school officially disapproves of—taking so much time off—and really it's kind of an amazing opportunity, so we don't want to discourage it, either."

"Meaning?"

"I'm sorry. Every year the Rothenbergs celebrate Passover in Israel. Hold on, let me see what I have here."

Celeste mentally calculated the money necessary to send two children to this private school and then pull them out for an extended trip to Israel—annually—while the woman rummaged through a file cabinet, pulled out a manila folder and spread the papers out across her desk.

"When did they leave?"

"I'm not sure, but the boys have been out all week. So, last weekend some time?"

"When will they be back?"

The receptionist found the paper she had been looking for and brought it over to Celeste.

"Here we are. They're taking this week off, we break for Passover starting tomorrow." The receptionist looked at Celeste, "You know about that, right?"

"Of course," Celeste assured her.

She went back to the paperwork. "The kids should be back in school" she mulled a bit over the page, "on April 15."

"Thank you," Celeste said. "Any idea where they're staying in Israel?"

The receptionist pursed her lips and shook her head. "No, no I don't. Sorry!"

Celeste said, "What about family here, do you have their information?"

The receptionist was clearly struggling with how much to share or if she had already said too much. "They might be able to help me out," Celeste said.

"That's who they're visiting," she said. "Their family lives in Israel."

Back in her rental car Celeste sat in the heat of the sun. She would wait. There was no rush, she'd do it right, she'd prepare. This was what she was good at: the long term.

She looked at her car. She'd need something you could drive two kids around in—that and logistics were the things she would tackle now as she waited for Tamara to return.

While she waited, Celeste rented office space a few floors above Sam Dresner. She packed up her office, listed her townhouse for sale, blew kisses at Victor Resnick and reminded all of her clients she was only a phone call or an email away. She researched addresses and neighborhoods and schools until she found a three-bedroom in Pasadena with San Marino schools. The rent was staggering, but the yard was green and fenced. When she got custody, she'd buy something. Not if, but when.

Celeste brought Nataly and their mother to the house, put the key in the lock and opened the front door with a flourish.

"I know," she said walking in, "the floors need refinishing, and the lath and plaster is cracking. But just think—a couple of throw rugs, a few coats of paint and—just maybe—Becky and Miriam."

Mercy's eyes welled.

Nataly waited a beat. "Here I always thought I was the dreamer and you were the practical one."

Nataly scoured garage sales and flea markets to help Celeste furnish her home. She was convinced it needed vintage fabric to make it warm. She found tablecloths and napkins and dish towels. She particularly liked the days-of-the-week hand towels with the cross stitching. At the Rose Bowl, she found Mexican earthenware. At the PCC swap meet, she found a white chenille bedspread.

Nataly could have brought black velvet paintings and Celeste would have deferred—and hung them with love and tenderness.

She watched Nataly unwrap her purchases, spread them on the dining table, artfully arranging the napkins, the dish towels. Celeste cleared her throat. Nataly looked up, alert.

"I know you think I walked out on you when I left home. That's not what I was doing really, not then. I was too embarrassed to face anyone. I was eighteen and I felt so stupid and ignorant getting pregnant, having to get married. And then when the baby died—staying away was penance. It wasn't that I'd forgotten you or left you behind. It wasn't. I'm sorry we never talked about it, but this is about all I will ever say."

Nataly rushed around the table to hold her sister. She spoke softly, "The more I missed you, the angrier I got. We're okay now."

Celeste felt Nataly's warm body against hers. So long ago she had been the one who had carried her everywhere.

"Sylvia never thought I abandoned her."

Nataly stood back. "Sylvia never held grudges. And unlike you and me, she was happy with so little."

It was now a month since Celeste had spoken with the school receptionist. She pulled the used Plymouth Voyager into the parking lot and re-introduced herself to the receptionist.

"Tamara Rothenberg?" Celeste said, more pointedly than she had intended. "I was hoping to have run into her by now. She was supposed to have been back last week. Do you know when the family will be back?"

"We're not sure that they are returning," she said. "More than that, I don't think I can say."

Celeste pressed her, but the receptionist asked her to speak to the head of school who was at a retreat this week.

Celeste navigated the waiting area. She spotted Miriam with a group of equally vibrant girls, and Becky sitting on a bench with the other kindergarteners. She grasped Miriam's hand and swung down to scoop up Becky, who flinched.

"What's wrong?" Celeste asked.

Becky shook her head, ever so slightly, "Nothing."

Celeste shot a look at Miriam whose wide eyes told her she knew nothing.

Mercy waited for them at Sylvia's home and was a rush of arms and kisses and food and questions. Celeste took Becky into the office, closed the door behind her and said, "Becky, what's wrong?"

Becky said nothing.

"Does something hurt?"

Becky said nothing, looked at the ground.

"Look at me, Becky. Did something happen?"

Becky looked up at her, eyes larger than the world, held her lips together and began blinking away the welling up tears. "He said I can't tell you or anyone," she said. "Ever."

"Show me where it hurts."

"It doesn't hurt that much anymore."

"All right. Come here."

Celeste held Becky on her lap until she stopped trembling, until the blinked-away tears disappeared.

The very next day Celeste sued for custody.

Sam Dresner pointed his finger at her and said, "Five percent chance. Five. So many smart moves, Celeste, settling down here, starting up an office, being here. But they're his children."

"Jesus, Sam, tell me something I don't know!"

"I don't want you ruining your life over a lost cause and I don't want you to yell at me later, saying that I gave you false hope."

"How about I yell at you later that you gave me no hope at all?"

"Now, *that* I can live with."

They walked down the street for lunch. Half a head taller than her, solidly built, his stride enthusiastic. This time Celeste had a diet soda and the sopes de carne asada.

By the following Monday, Jack had kicked Mercy out of his home, changed the locks and hired a nanny.

Tuesday morning Celeste started to organize her office. If she just sorted the files, organized the folders, things would turn out all right. If she just put the right amount of energy into making it tidy, neat, professional—the phone rang.

"Celeste Amado."

"You are a fucking piece of work, you know that?" It was Jack. "You. You and your whole family were always pouring poison in Sylvia's ear. All of you were always against me—let me tell you right now, you're not getting my kids."

"Jack, always lovely to hear from you."

"Don't give me that crap. You think you're something, Celeste, but you are thigh high in shit and way out of your league here."

"Your league being the thigh-high shit one?"

"I don't know what you think you're going to get by pissing me off. Your mother didn't seem too keen on this whole thing. I'm sorry you didn't see the look on her face when I told her to leave. But I'm telling you right now, it's for her sake that I'm gonna start by playing nice."

"For my mother's sake?"

"That's right."

"Not for your children's sake."

"You see, there you go again. Antagonizing me as if you are gonna gain something from it. You and Sam Dresner—who, by the way, is a big time loser. I thought someone as intelligent as I used to think you were would have found a world-class talent here. I'm disappointed in you, Celeste. I thought you were savvy enough to come out strong."

"Your compassion and insight have always been two of your strongest qualities."

Jack was silent. Then his voice was low. "I know you think you're being ironic, but the fact is I am calling because of your mother. Drop all proceedings now—and I mean now—and I'll let you, your mother, and even your crazy sister see the kids. I don't know where you get this picture of me, Celeste, but I'm not a fucking animal. The girls miss you all already." He cleared his throat and now his voice was stronger and more forceful.

"That," he said, "was the nice Jack. Now, let's say you don't like the nice Jack or my generous offer. Maybe you think you got the balls to hang tough with me. Let me point out a number of credibility issues, Celeste, just in case you're just as delusional as your surviving sister."

There was a rap on the door, then it swung open. Sam peered over at Celeste, saw her on the phone then waved and stepped out. He didn't see her motion for him to stay.

"The facts as I see them, Celeste, are that you are a bitter, barren alcoholic, unable to hold on to a man. It'll be pretty clear that you're damaged. Your baby died, your only marriage ended in divorce. I have raised and supported a family, been with Sylvia for twelve years. I don't know what you think you've got, but it's nothing compared to that. No judge will ever choose you as a suitable guardian."

Celeste said, "I got you, Jack. And it must have you worried or you wouldn't have bothered to call."

Jack hung up.

That afternoon, Nataly called Celeste.

"Mom's upset. I just wanted to warn you. I mean, I have never seen her this upset."

"Well," Celeste said, "She's going to be here tomorrow. I suppose I should thank you for the warning shot."

"Just who in the hell do you think you are?" Mercy said. "Who in the hell are you to place my grandchildren in jeopardy? I can't even visit them! How in the hell do you think they feel?"

Celeste blinked back calmly. Her mother's hair was streaked gold, auburn and light brown. She wore a purple sweater and her violet-colored contact lenses today. It always jarred Celeste to see these imposter eyes. But the effect was regal and glamorous.

"You're right. I can't visit them either, I have no idea whether they're being well or poorly treated—"

"Their mother is gone, and now we're gone."

"But sooner or later—"

"Sooner or later what, Celeste? I don't know what you want to hide from me, but let's say Jack smacked Sylvia around."

Celeste froze.

"They wouldn't have been the first married couple. And that's not why she was divorcing him."

Her mother was right. That wasn't the reason Sylvia decided to divorce him. She hadn't left him over the beating. She hadn't left him over the money. She kicked him out because of the other man in Amsterdam, months after she had called Celeste for help.

"You're right," Celeste said.

"I never interfere in your decisions," she was saying. "I know, I know, you have a wonderful mind. You're brilliant in everything about money. But listen, Celeste, I never ask you for anything. Not for favors. Never."

"Mom, mom, mom."

"Sweetheart, please drop this. Please, please, please. I've lost so many and now I've lost Sylvia. I absolutely refuse to lose Becky and Miriam. Please, please, do this for me. For me, Celeste, for me."

There was her mother, begging her. *I need to listen to her*, Celeste thought.

"Then he'll let me see them again, Celeste. Then I can hold Sylvia again."

"Mom," Celeste said.

"If you don't drop it, he said I'll never see them again. Never. Not once he gets custody."

Celeste blinked. "Mom, Jack is a bad person, a bad man, on many, many levels."

"And I want to see," Mercy sensed her advantage, "whatever it is you're trying so hard and so long to keep from me. I raised you girls. I lived with your father. I'm an old woman now. What could you possibly think I hadn't seen before? This is just tearing all of us apart. And I don't know how we're going to fix this. I just don't know. I am sorry about Skye," Mercy said. "So sorry, Celeste—"

Now there was her own mother standing across from her, accusing her, accusing her, Celeste, of ruining everyone's life. "This is not about Skye!"

"It is, Celeste, it's all that unfinished business. You never talked to me about it. You never forgave yourself. You have to forgive yourself."

"It's over, it's history, it's passed, Mom."

"You have to forgive yourself."

Celeste collapsed backwards into her office chair. She sank so far, she thought she'd never stand up again. Her mother came around the desk, stood over her, next to her. She felt as if she were dying. She was choking, she couldn't breathe. No, it was just her tears.

"This pain, baby, this pain, you have got to let it go."

"I can't, I can't," Celeste shook her head. "If I let it go, I let her go."

"No, no, baby, she is already gone. How many years do you think you have to pay for that?"

"I don't know," Celeste choked out. "It's just shit."

"That's right. That's life. It's just shit. Let her go. It wasn't even your fault."

Celeste nodded and murmured, "Yes it was."

Mercy wrapped Celeste in her arms. "No, no, no, baby."

Celeste let out a sound from underneath her tears, felt the arms of her mother around her, smelled the scent of the lotion on her mother's hands, closed her eyes. Everything was still. Skye was still. Right now, at this instant, thinking of that name, she did not feel a pang. How could that be? Skye was still. She should laugh at herself. Twenty years later and she's still weeping in her mother's arms. She took a deep breath, hugged her mother, pushed her gently away, found a tissue to wipe her eyes and blew her nose.

Mercy looked at her daughter. Some of Celeste's lightness had returned, she could sense it. Something about her daughter's mouth and eyes. Some of her old Celeste had returned, just a bit.

"Mom," Celeste said quietly, "if he gets custody back, Jack can do anything with those girls and we can't say boo. I will not leave them with him. You're going to have to trust me. You're just going to have to trust me."

"He can see them now. He can! We can't. And if you keep this up, we'll never see them again. Never! What do you have on Jack?"

Celeste gathered herself up. "You do not want to know." Celeste looked into the violet lenses. She was not going to infect her mother's memory with the images of Becky's chest a solid purple bruise, of Sylvia's face purple, yellow and green, of the bruises up and down both their backs. Or with the knowledge that, according to her experts, they had been beaten with bare hands and a club, a pipe or a broom handle, and it was shocking that there had been no broken skin or bones. It was killing Celeste and it would kill her mother.

Mercy looked at her daughter, clear-eyed now even behind the lenses. "Okay, okay. I don't want to know. Are you going to drop the suit?"

"No, Mom. I told you, this is not about Skye."

Mercy felt her mouth tighten. "Will I be getting my grandchildren back?"

"I don't know."

Mercy pawed through her bag again and again, unable to find her keys. When she did, she said, "One thing. I am only asking one thing. Please, please drop it."

"I can't."

Her mother shook her head. "Please, Celeste, please think about it." Then she left.

Celeste went downstairs to talk to Sam. God knew she needed to talk to somebody, and Sam always made her smile. She couldn't understand quite how, but he did. Even when he told her the hearing wouldn't be until June.

June! Her nieces alone with Jack for two more months. June!

Sam wasn't in. His office was locked.

Nataly had said, "Do it. You just do it. Listen to Mom, but do what you want to do. I love you. You know what to do. You can only do what you can live with."

At the end of April, Nataly left LA for Yesenia and New York. At a tiny going away dinner in Celeste's home, Celeste gave her a little blue box with a blue ribbon wrapped around it. Nataly looked at Celeste laughing, "Sometimes I'm glad I have a sister who's so into labels." She picked up the necklace with its delicate lace of a chain and a diamond encased in gold and clasped it around her neck. Celeste adjusted it so the diamond lay just below the hollow of Nataly's throat. It suited her, simultaneously vulnerable and powerful. "They'll think you come from money. It can't hurt. And I want this on the record," Celeste said. "This time it is you who are abandoning us." She gave her sister a fierce hug.

The following week Sam rang Celeste's office.

"Can you come down?" he said

The transition to southern California had been a little more dramatic than Celeste had anticipated. Her income, which she had low-balled, hadn't yet had time to meet her expectations. But it was new. Things took time. Even the hearing, being set in June, gave her plenty of time to find Tamara.

She smiled at Sam. One day she'd have to do something about that warm glow he provoked in her chest. Just a sweet tenderness she wasn't used to feeling. Hope. That's what it was. But she wasn't going to crowd it. She didn't want to scare it away.

Sam wasn't smiling back.

"Sit down," he said. He got up, came around his desk and sat in a spare chair next to her. "Celeste, they summarily dismissed your petition for custody."

"What?"

He took her hands in his. "It's over, and you lost."

"What about the pictures?"

"I told you, there was no provenance. There was no way of connecting them to him."

"Who else could it have been? Did you ask them that? Did you?"

"Child Protective Services were all over Becky. They got nothing. I did everything," he said. "I did everything I could."

"Well, it wasn't good enough!" Celeste gripped Sam's hands and said, "Do you realize that I am never going to see those little girls again?"

S am must have driven her home. Sam must have called her mother because Celeste had no memory of the drive, no memory of calling anyone. Sam had stayed, then disappeared when Mercy drove up. Celeste sat in the living room, staring at the gaps between the strips of raw wood on the floor, those gaps that were desperate for filling and refinishing. The sleek couch she had custom made for her town home in San Jose looked out of place, as if it were disdainful of its slumming. Celeste had laid down on it, then sat up when her mother stepped into the room.

Celeste had done with sobbing. All that remained was the emptiness. "Did Sam tell you it's over? It's over, and we lost. I lost. I lost it for us."

Mercy sat down next to Celeste and put her arms around her shoulders. "Do you hate me?" Celeste whispered.

"How can I hate you? You're fearless, fearless. And you're my daughter."

"I hate me," Celeste said.

Mercy shook her head.

"Those girls, Mom, Sylvia's girls, they're gone. They're gone for good."

Mercy held her daughter close. "Let me tell you something about little girls. This is something I know, and you wouldn't because that was taken away from you twenty years ago. People don't talk about this, but you lose your little girl every day. Every single day she goes away. And the one little girl you thought you knew and loved is replaced by another one. A little older, a little smarter, a little more independent. Finally the one you had fallen completely in love with is all gone. Poof."

"I don't know what you're talking about. I don't know what you're trying to say."

"How could you? I've been trying to figure this out for forty years." Mercy rocked Celeste. "The first day you came back from kindergarten, I didn't recognize you. Just one day. Nataly in third grade was all mine. And then, in fourth grade, she was your father's. And Sylvia—Sylvia was one person one day and another the next. And then, by high school she was hiding bits of herself away."

Mercy held onto Celeste. What was her point? Oh yes, here was Celeste in her arms, again. "Then you, you Celeste, you went so far away. First with Michael, then to Humboldt. That driven little girl I had known was suddenly this woman, this brilliant, complicated, unhappy woman."

"Great."

"I think what I'm trying to say is every day we lose our little girls. All those little girls you have to say goodbye to, every single day. But they come back. Nataly is going to soar in New York. I know she is. Sylvia was really just on the way to being herself again. And here you are. Here you are. My beloved daughter."

Celeste shook her head. "What are you trying to say? What has this got to do with Becky and Miriam?"

"Deep down, they're Amado women. They are a part of us and we are a part of them. Jack won't ever be able to change that."

"No, but he'll be able to keep them away from us."

"Not forever."

Later that night Sam dropped by with a rotisserie chicken and a couple of side dishes. Celeste watched as her mother asked him about his practice, the case, and deftly slipped a few questions regarding his marital status (single) and his paternity track record (none).

Celeste drank her Diet 7Up and asked her mother, "Why don't you look like I feel?"

"Because I never expected you to win. I already decided that if Becky and Miriam are alive and well, I can live with that."

Sam said, "You don't look like you feel either, Celeste. You look amazing."

Celeste stared at Sam. She knew her eyes were raw, her face red and puffy. Later, when her mother asked when she'd be going back to San Jose, Celeste said, "I'm staying, Mom."

"You see," her mother said, "they go away, they disappear, but you wait long enough and they come back."

May was ending. Celeste drove to and from work on streets framed by blooming jacaranda trees. She didn't have a compelling reason to return to San Jose, and she didn't have the energy to pack everything up again. The house she rented was empty and she herself was hollow.

She avoided Sam. At her office she made calls and decisions and then she went home. This afternoon as she turned off her computer, the phone rang.

"Celeste Amado?" The voice was familiar, but she couldn't place it. "This is Tamara Rothenberg."

"Where are you?"

"At home. We've been away. We got back yesterday. I listened to your messages today."

Celeste leaned her head into her hand and sighed. "Tamara, thank you for calling me back, but I don't think there's anything for us to say now."

Tamara said, "Please, please don't think that. Do you have any time right now? My boys are out with my husband, we'd have the place to ourselves."

Parking in front of Tamara's home, Celeste held onto the steering wheel to steady her shaking hands. Anger and dread, anger and relief, anger and hope were running laps through her body.

Tamara greeted her at the door, dressed in sweats, her hair a tangle to her shoulders, her face wan and sad, looking much older than Celeste recalled from the funeral. Tamara crushed Celeste with an unexpected hug, then took her by the arm and pulled her into a room with an armchair and small table.

"Can I get you a glass of wine?" She asked, pointing to her own on the low table.

"How about some tea?" Celeste said, sinking into the armchair.

"Just like your sister," Tamara answered, fussing in the kitchen for a few moments, then bringing a tray with a teapot and matching teacup. Celeste let it sit there. She didn't trust herself to pick anything up at this moment. She wanted to shake Tamara by the shoulders, but she forced herself to wait.

Tamara sat down on the couch across from her and sipped at her wine. "I'm so sorry about Sylvia, about everything."

Could she really just sit there and drink wine and talk about Sylvia this way? So casually?

"You may find this hard to believe, but I can't even remember her funeral." She shook her head, frustrated. "Sylvia. Sylvia my friend. I thought we'd be in each other's lives forever. My husband tells me I spoke at the service. I hope whatever I said lived up to who she was to me, to you." She took another sip, as if steadying herself. Celeste recognized that habit. "Every year we go to Israel for Passover. This year I didn't want to go, it was too close to what had just happened, I didn't want to desert everyone here, coping with that awful, awful loss, but in the end we thought it would be good, for me, for all of us."

Celeste tried to keep her face neutral. She did not care at all. She did not care about their vacation habits, their religious traditions. All she knew was that she had needed Sylvia's best friend, and she was not there.

Tamara continued. She spoke slowly, as if waiting for the words to form in her mind before she could articulate them. Celeste began to notice the weariness around her eyes, the slump of her shoulders, as if she had aged years since the funeral.

"Have you ever heard of what is called a 'fugue state'? Essentially it's a complete melt down. That's what happened to me in Israel. My husband was in charge of trying to get the right care for me there while still having work responsibilities—he tells me it was hard. It was not by my choosing. It was not my choice to make it difficult for everyone around me."

Celeste looked over at Tamara, and saw her eyes dense with pain.

"Now, tell me, how in the hell did Jack get custody?"

Celeste watched Tamara sip and nod and murmur as she told the story, the photos, the lack of a corroborating witness, her inability to contact Tamara. Celeste tried hard not to be accusatory, just accurate and dispassionate.

Tamara poured herself more wine and cleared her throat. "Of course I will swear out an affidavit on taking those photographs. I'll testify from here to the moon, whatever you want, whenever you need."

Celeste said, "I don't even know if we can file again. I'll have to talk with my lawyer." Her hands, however, no longer trembled. She poured herself a cup of tea. It occurred to her she could ask what she had been brooding over for months. "When did it happen, Tamara? When?"

"Over a year ago, February."

Celeste thought back. That's when Sylvia had called her. That's when Celeste had started digging around into the money. She had told Sylvia what she knew when she had flown down for their mother's birthday. Celeste hadn't known the urgency. "I wish I had known," she said.

"I wish to God I hadn't. One of the worst things, you realize, of course, is that there weren't just two of us there swearing to keep a secret."

"Becky," Celeste said. How had she not thought of that?

Tamara pressed her lips together and nodded. "Tomorrow when I take my boys to school, I'm going to talk very, very gently to Becky. If you're right, something's happened again. Then I'm calling Protective Services."

Celeste caught now, for the first time, the determination in Tamara's eyes, a sense of the woman she had seen speak at Sylvia's funeral.

Tamara picked up a legal-sized envelope from the end table. "When I promised Sylvia I wouldn't call Protective Services, that I wouldn't tell anyone anything of what I had seen, I made her promise me something. I've got something else that may help you."

A flush of appreciation, gratitude and concern washed over Celeste. She now had some idea who this friend of Sylvia's had been. And she realized how self-involved, practically rude, she had been. "I'm sorry for your illness in Israel. I should have asked earlier. What happened?"

"Now there you're quite different from your sister. Sylvia would have intuitively divined. Of course you know she worshipped your intelligence, and I would tease her that being smart in one way does not necessarily translate into being smart in all ways."

Celeste felt a flush of self-recognition burn through her.

Tamara said, "But to answer your question, my dear, grief happened." And she handed the envelope to Celeste.

By the end of that week, both children were in Protective Services. Jack was being investigated, but was allowed to visit his children, under supervision. Mercy and Celeste had no visitation rights.

S am sat behind his desk, across from Celeste, his shirt unbuttoned at the top, his gaze intense. What Celeste appreciated about Sam was that he respected her intelligence, that he spoke to her straightforwardly, without a hint of condescension. But when his face took on that look, she feared for the outcome of this case.

"Hearsay evidence rules can be complex. And at times contradictory," he said.

Celeste nodded.

"At times for criminal suits they work in one way, in civil suits another."

Celeste didn't know whether she wanted to slow him down or speed him up. She just wanted it done, resolved, in her favor, with her two nieces filling up the house she had found for them. "But we have Tamara now," she said. "And the statement." The envelope Tamara had handed her contained Sylvia's handwritten account of what had happened, dated a few weeks after the incident. Celeste had glanced at it and stopped, not wanting to know, truly not wanting to know the details. The photographs had been enough. "When the judge sees the picture and the statement…" She stopped. She couldn't say it out loud: with that evidence, the judge would have to rule in her favor, would have to grant her custody.

"We are legally bound to share those photos and that statement with Jack's side."

"What's he going to do with it, deny it?"

"Almost certainly he'll deny it. But what he'll most likely do is try to find the doctor she went to. And that doctor will have to testify that Sylvia did not tell him she was beaten by Jack. Yes," he spoke over her, "Tamara authenticates the photos. But his side can claim lies and subterfuge. They're going to attack Sylvia's trustworthiness."

Celeste shook her head. "Now I really don't know what you're talking about. What do you mean?"

"They could claim Sylvia maintained a pattern of lies. They're going to try to impeach what Tamara says, creating the suspicion that Sylvia lied in her statement and to her."

Celeste shook her head against the absurdity of that logic. Until she remembered. "Oh, God," she said.

"What? What should I know?"

"It was long ago."

"Tell me."

Jack certainly knew—he and Sylvia were engaged soon afterwards. And it wasn't as if she were betraying a confidence, but she felt a twinge as if she were. Yet she had to tell Sam. "Before she got married, Sylvia was a teacher, a long term sub or something. She was terrible at it and was fired. She was so ashamed that she lied to all of us, telling us that she still worked there. I didn't even find out until last year. Over many glasses of wine."

"How long ago?"

"Before she got married. Twelve years?"

Sam nodded. "Ages ago, but still that's not so great for us. Establishes a pattern of behavior. Who knows what they're gonna dig up in between. And like you said, she basically just told you."

Celeste said nothing. She hid the beatings. How long had she been wondering about the money? Could Sylvia have been hiding something else?

Sam continued. "They're going to go for the ambiguity. I would put everything on trustworthiness. While him beating her is a great reason to sue for divorce, they're also going to claim the divorce could be her contemplation of pending litigation, which would give her a bias or motive for fabricating this."

Celeste closed her eyes, "Fabricating the pictures?"

"I'm just telling you how they think, what the strategy is that I'll be preparing for."

She sat up and leaned forward against the cheap desktop. "Couldn't you just fucking lie to me? Let me fall asleep every night from now until the decision thinking that everything's going to be all right? Let me go home, get on the phone and tell my mother the same?"

Sam looked at the papers on his desk. "Lying's good for two things, Celeste. The short term and things you don't care about." He glanced up at her. "Neither of those apply here."

Three in the morning, a still house, an empty street. Even the dogs had gone to bed. Today they would learn whether Celeste was the guardian, whether Mercy would be able to see her grandchildren again. Mercy was skeptical. There would probably be yet another delay.

In April they lost Becky and Miriam to Jack. Mercy had been distracted by Nataly's plans, had bit her lip, written a check and released an untethered Nataly in the direction of New York City. It was Nataly's time. It was what she needed to do. All that was good. Mercy could be proud of all of that. That was fearless. Then the girls were placed in foster care. Since that day she'd been waiting, all of May, and now most of June. Waiting to see if whatever new papers Celeste had waved at her had the necessary heft in the eyes of the judge. Waiting.

Right now Nataly was back in Pasadena, visiting with Celeste. Thank God, Nataly would be with Celeste in court.

During the months that she waited, it was good for Mercy and right for her to lose herself in the classroom. She immersed herself in teaching: exploring the state's missions, discussing why their city was named Santa Ana, assigning research on Spanish street names. Who or what did they represent? Peeling away the surface of the textbooks to find the Spanish, the Native, the Mexican culture overlooked, hiding in plain sight. That was how she made it through her days. Jack sued Celeste. Mercy had a fundraiser for a trip to the

Bowers Museum. Celeste called with another delay. Mercy started a chess club at lunch time.

But now the day had come.

Mercy couldn't even hope that the judge would rule in Celeste's favor. Much too much to hope for, too much disappointment to bear. She wouldn't worry about Celeste. She could only pray that Sylvia heard her every thought and felt the streams of love in her direction and couldn't feel the pain of grief they all bore.

Awake still at four in the morning. She remained in bed. She would not take another sleeping pill, God only knew when she'd wake up again, and she had to meet Celeste.

Nataly was young, beautiful, brilliant and could do any goddamned thing she pleased. Mercy was old, all used up now, tired and bitter.

Mercy got out of bed, stepped into her slippers, and padded into the kitchen. She was tired of the noise in her brain, and she couldn't get it to stop. She rummaged around the shelf where she kept all the liquor bottles. She made a face at them all, then served herself a shot of bourbon. She knocked it back fast, made another face, poured another shot and drank it down like the bitter medicine it was.

She walked back to her bedroom. *Why do we expect so much from our parents?* she thought as she lay back in bed, listening to the now oppressive silence. *They're just as stupid and ignorant of the grand scheme of things as we are.*

Mercy awoke late to a throbbing headache. Before she stepped into the shower, she examined herself in the mirror. She was her mother! After bathing and blow drying, cosmetics helped camouflage those age spots. She smeared that wrinkle-away cream around her eyes and on her throat. Not that it ever did much damned good, but hope springs eternal. *Como semas, sembrara*, as her mother would say. As ye sow, so shall ye reap.

The throbbing in her head wouldn't go away. She stuffed a handful of chocolates in her tapestry bag, *oh God, just in case*, but she couldn't get her hopes too high. Just in case Celeste won. She slipped on a leopard print cloche, grabbed her sunglasses, keys, reading glasses and rushed out the door.

And now she was here at the Union Coffee Shop, waiting. She checked her cellphone for messages. It was dead. She had forgotten to charge it. The waitress swung by, smiled and refilled her cup—her hair was hennaed deep purple. Mercy looked around. She sat at the back row of the rather narrow restaurant. There tables lining the windows to the right of her were empty except for the table of two elderly couples. *Listen to me. Elderly. I'm damn elderly.* The tables lining the wall to her left were empty except a solitary gentleman. Even his manner of reading the paper seemed unfriendly, spread out as it was across the tables that flanked him. Behind him, through the high windows, Mercy watched the movement on the street, and the gray clouds that clustered and hid the sun.

At least my head has stopped aching! Mercy thought, adding half a packet of sweetener into her coffee, thinking about how unhappily snug these jeans she was wearing had become.

Oh God, let today be the day. But she wouldn't get her hopes up.

Unexpectedly the clouds parted and the sun came streaming into her eyes. Up at the front desk she saw—wait—she saw Sylvia and Joey. They were walking into the restaurant. Joey was looking worried. *Don't be worried, sweetheart,* she wanted to say, *I'm right here,* but she couldn't get the words out. She was looking at Sylvia behind Joey.

Time stood still. Nothing moved but Mercy's mind, and it raced.

But how was this possible? What did this mean? The sun was still stinging her eyes. As she looked at the table to her right, she knew the four people there had known each other for years, and had passed from friendship and moved into fixtures in each other's lives. She looked to her left and saw that the solitary man had worked for decades to ensure that he was alone and left well alone. The waitress who was swinging the coffee pot and chewing gum had two teenagers, and they weren't doing their best, but what could she do? She was doing hers, and squeezing some fun out of this ride and if that meant bringing the cook home at night, so be it. Mercy's mother came into her mind. She had really tried her best, had done the best she could under the circumstances. Her best hadn't been good enough for the little girl named Mercy. *I'm sorry, Mother,* Mercy thought. Edgar's face appeared. She thought of the once beautiful man with nothing at all inside. She felt the hell of being trapped within that nothingness. She pitied Edgar.

But what was her Joey doing here? Where did he come from? And how had Sylvia?—there was Sylvia, smiling so broad and so happy and Mercy knew that both Sylvia and Joey were fine. *Thank you God*, they were alive and well and beautiful and whole.

Time moved again. *Estas loca*, Mercy said to herself. It's Becky and Celeste. Celeste was holding hands with that lawyer fellow. And right behind them was Nataly with Miriam. Becky's expression of worry changed to a gleeful smile—her front teeth missing—as she spotted her grandmother. Mercy held her arms wide open and Becky came running into them, crashing into three empty chairs along the way. Mercy closed her eyes as she leaned into her scrawny little neck.

She looked up and saw a smile on Celeste's face that she hadn't seen in more than twenty years.

Acknowledgments

Oh my, what a long ride this has been! And I was sustained throughout it by all of the following people—

A huge hug of love and appreciation to my very first and faithful readers: Elisa Callow, Sheila Laco, Lucia Francis Vigil, Kathe Zamorano and Stefané Zamorano.

A loving shoutout to Bever-leigh Banfield for all of her gushing enthusiasm and encouragement.

A wave of gratitude to the writers in our group who carve out a space each month for our individual hopes and dreams: Janet Aird, Karin Bugge, Petrea Burchard, Linda Dove, Margaret Finnegan and Paula Johnson.

Love and appreciation to Cindie Geddes and our annual retreats at Lake Tahoe—*The Amado Women* was revised there at least twice.

Thank you, Paco Casas, for the captivating cover.

I am grateful for my husband, Barry Rein, and our kids, Leo and Simone, who have endured and shared this journey with me.

And a muchísimas gracias to everyone at Cinco Puntos Press—Bobby, John, and Lee Byrd, as well as Jessica Powers, Mary Fountaine, and Elena Marinaccio—for insisting on bringing the story of these four women to life.